Non-Compliance:
The Transition

Paige Daniels

www.kristell-ink.com

ISBN 978-1-909845-21-3

Cover art and design by Ken Dawson
Book design and typesetting by Book Polishers

Kristell Ink
An Imprint of Grimbold Books
4 Woodhall Drive
Banbury
Oxfordshire
OX16 9TY
United Kingdom

www.kristell-ink.com

Timothy J. Meeker

1958-2013

We lost you too early and we'll always miss you. Our lives
are better because you were in them. There aren't many
people who could dream up making a movie about outer-
space trailer wars or having a joust on a bicycle. You were a
great brother-in-law. I know you're in Heaven now, drinkin'
a scotch and rockin' out to The Barenaked Ladies.

Part of the proceeds of this book will go to establish a scholarship fund for girls to go to engineering school.

ONE

Chapter 1

A Fine Mess

I can barely see the road ahead of me and a chill runs down my spine. The cool air isn't what is giving me chills; it's the cargo in the trunk.

"You okay, Kelly?"

"I'm fine. I just want to get this over with."

"You know, you didn't have to come. Conner, Lindsey and I could've taken care of this."

"What? And let you guys drive my car? I don't think so."

Conner's head peeks up from the backseat. "I'm hurt. Don't you think we're capable of driving your old car?"

"She isn't old. Call her that again and I'll break your arms."

Quinn stifles a laugh and the car turns quiet again. We wind through the cramped streets in the town. It's rainy and the warm summer months are starting to give way to a crisp fall. There are very few people out on the streets tonight.

Good. The fewer potential witnesses, the better.

Our destination is in sight. I park the car as close as possible to the river, and we all get out. Although I'm wearing a rain jacket, the cold rain slices through me. The only light is from the Compliant Sector across the river and the few active displays spewing forth propaganda; the lights on our side have been out for hours due to the energy sanctions. We make our way to the trunk.

Quinn holds a gun out for me. "Here you go, stand watch. If anyone and I mean ANYONE sees us, you shoot them. Got it?"

My heart races. I'm starting to regret my decision to accompany Quinn and Conner on this mission. I give Quinn a blank stare.

Conner answers for me: "I got it, Chief. She can wait in the car."

"No, it was her decision to come. She knew what she was getting into. You need to help me with the cargo in the trunk. We need a lookout."

I grab the gun from Quinn's hands. "I'm fine. I got it."

As Conner and Quinn open the trunk, I grab a glimpse of the two bodies inside. I turn my back and head for my post to avoid seeing too much. I'm not so naïve that I don't know what Quinn and the boys do when they are out, but it's different seeing it firsthand. I agreed to go this time, because I felt it was time to pull my weight.

The streets are quiet, allowing us to carry out our mission. It's imperative that no one catches us. Normally, what goes on amongst us Non-Commers is ignored by Magistrate. He's okay with us killing each other off; the fewer of us he has to deal with the better. However, this is no normal dump. The bodies in the trunk are two of Magistrate's marshals. We found them in front of our compound this morning, no doubt a present from our friend Ramsey. If Magistrate were to find the bodies anywhere near us, then we would all be gathered, chipped, and sent to the other side to be their fucking mind slaves. No trial. No jury of our peers.

I sit hunkered on the park bench hoping that any passersby will take me for a homeless person. I take out a small device and push in a couple of numbers. It should put out a strong enough signal to jam any surveillance devices in the area.

Quinn's words are running through my mind. "Shoot ANYONE that sees us."

Oh God, can I do this? What have I gotten myself into?

Shooting one of Ramsey's men is one thing, but an innocent bystander? I'm not sure I can do that. My stomach tightens into knots. I hop up from the bench and pace back and forth. Still, no sign of anyone. The rain starts to pound and wind whips up my coat. The cold is making the old wounds in my hand ache.

God, what can be taking them so long?

"Kelly! Let's go."

Quinn and Conner are standing by the car. I take one more look around, grab the jamming device, and run for the car. Once inside, my heart feels lighter. I roll on to the main street to head back home.

Conner pokes his head up to the front. "Your first body disposal. I'm so proud."

"Yeah, first and last."

Quinn peers at me. "Who said it was your last?"

"Me. I'm never doing it again. My nerves can't handle that shit. I'm happier being the behind the scenes nerd, thank you very much."

"You're my partner, and that comes with certain responsibilities."

I squirm in my seat knowing Quinn is right. This won't be the last time, especially with Ramsey in town. It's been three months since Ramsey took over Danny's crew. He's been laying low since we took Danny down, but his little gift in front of the compound has made it apparent that he's ready to play now.

The movement of the windshield wipers and the sound of the rain put me in a hypnotic trance, and I start to forget about the events that have just transpired. But bright flashing blue and red lights fill the car, and they bring the stress back with friends.

Everyone in the car lets out a collective "*Fuck!*"

I pull over to the side of the road. Quinn grabs his gun and puts it discreetly under his seat.

"Let me get this, Quinn. Don't go shooting just yet."

"Fine, but you need to get him off our trail. Fast."

"Gee. Really? I thought I would invite him over for tea and cookies."

"I'm serious. Stop being such a smart ass. Don't you realize what's on the line here?"

"No, I don't. Why don't you tell me? Because apparently you think I'm so stupid…"

Our bickering is cut short by a tapping on the window. I roll down the window and I'm greeted by one of Magistrate's marshals, and two of his boys behind him. They're all young punks; the young ones are the worst.

I smile my best cheesy smile. "Can I help you, sir?"

"What are you three doing out here this time of night?"

"Just taking the car around the block for a spin."

"Mmm-hmm. Get out of the car all of you, and put your hands on the hood."

As we get out of the car we are greeted by the snarky grins of the marshals. We put our hands on the hood. The rain is soaking us to the bone. I start to shake from the cold. Each of the marshals chooses one of us to pat down. The one searching me spends a little too much time on my boobs and butt for my comfort.

The lead marshal says, "Shea Kelly, Quinn Knightly, and Conner Dunne, all out on the town to take a little ride. Why am I suspicious?"

I answer back, "I have no idea, sir. We were just in town for a Bible study. We're heading back home to knit scarves for the homeless."

He taps me on the back of my head with his club to shut me up.

"Knightly, you better watch that smart mouth on your woman. It's going to land her in trouble."

Quinn gives me a stern look while I rub my head.

"Turn around all of you. I have something I want you to see."

We all turn around and he makes several taps to the Compliant Active Management System situated on his arm. A 3D holographic image of two marshals projects from his CAMS.

"You guys see these marshals around?"

We all shake our heads no.

"They went missing last night. No one has seen them around. You know, once we find who's responsible for their disappearance, they will be sent to the other side. So if you know anything, you better start talking now."

We all stand silently looking at the cop. Two of the marshals deliver blows to Quinn and Conner with their nightsticks. I lunge to help, but the lead man restrains me.

"Hey boys, looks like we have a lively one here," he says as he looks down at me.

The other two laugh as they deliver more blows to Quinn and Conner.

The lead marshal throws me to the ground and says, "Okay boys, we can come back to them later, we have some real work to do now."

One of the boys grins and unsheathes a knife from his belt. "Time to search the car."

Two of the jackasses go in my car and cut up my seats to 'search' for any contraband. The other one goes around back and opens my trunk and searches.

"You find anything, boys?"

They let out a laugh. As the lead marshal makes his way from the back of the car he makes sure to smash my tails lights and my trunk. This is too much for me to bear; I lunge for him, but I feel arms around me to keep me from getting to the marshals.

Quinn whispers in my ear, "It's not worth it. Just stay back."

I push his arms off of me. We look on in horror, helpless to do anything about what is taking place in front of us. My stomach turns on end as they near the gun Quinn hid. If they find it, we're all as good as chipped. Out of the corner of my eye I see another set of flashing red and blue lights slowly approach and stop. An older marshal with a cigar in his mouth unfolds his massive frame out of the tiny car. Shit. It's Ed Barton. All the marshals are pricks, but he is the king of all pricks. He has a special hatred of Quinn and me. Any time we're out on the town for patrol, he makes it his goal in life to screw with us.

"Is there a problem here, boys?"

The young marshals stand at attention.

The lead marshal replies, "No, sir, we saw these dirty Non-Commers out, and we thought they might know something about Logsdon and Barnes going missing. We were just asking them some questions."

Ed surveys my car and the punks. "Listen, you little pukes. You know you can't detain a Non-commer without a proper zone warrant. Look at you. You don't even have the proper protective gear on. How do you know these maggots aren't infested with the flu?"

All the young marshals get a look of horror on their faces.

"Jesus! You candy-ass losers are going to get yourselves killed one day. Get your shit together, and get your asses out of here. The only reason I'm not going to write you up is because I don't want to deal with all the paper work."

The young marshals give him a blank stare.

The old man bellows, "Move out now!"

They all scramble back to their car, and we're left alone with Ed.

He paces back and forth in front of us and stares us down with his fat face and beady eyes. "You worms make me sick. You do what you please with whom you please. Thank God we have our Morality Codes to keep us honorable. Something that you pukes will never understand. I'm watching you, and when I catch you, I won't screw up."

He gets face to face with Quinn and slugs him. He takes out the remnants of his cigar out and flicks it in my face.

We all stand in the rain waiting for the elder marshal to get back in his car, then file back into the damaged 'Cuda. She doesn't look pretty, but she still drives. We make the remainder of the drive in silence. Once in front of the main house, I let Conner and Quinn out.

Before Quinn closes his door he peeks his head inside. "You need any help in the garage?"

"No, I just want to be alone."

I pull the car into the garage and sit in the car and have a cry for a while. My car is more than just a mass of gears, motors and wires to me. This car is all I have left of my former life and, more importantly, my dad. My life is turning on its end.

My God, I just helped dump two bodies in the river. What the hell am I doing? I'm not this person.

I grab together the courage to get out of the car and inspect the damage. There is a large dent in the trunk and the taillights are out. My heart sinks. My mind jumps to the warm summer days spent in the barn restoring my car, cursing my dad for making me restore her and hating my life. Now the only thing I want is my car, my life, and my family back the way it was. It's amazing the things I took for granted when I was a kid. I close my eyes and a few rogue tears slip out. The scent of soap and cigars fills the air and I feel a hand on my shoulder pulling me close.

Quinn whispers, "Hey, it isn't that bad. We can have her fixed up in no time."

I wipe my eyes. "Yeah, I know. I just . . . "

"I know." He kisses the top of my head and continues, "Come on back to the house. I'll buy you a beer."

There is nothing I can do about it tonight, so I put my arm around his waist and let him lead me to the house. Most of the time Quinn is a monumental prick, but he definitely has his shining moments. Once in the house I sit at the kitchen table and Quinn puts a beer in front of me and sits down next to me.

"You know the last time she got damaged was when I was back in college. I stupidly let Wynne take her out on a date. She came back with a big scratch in the door. I didn't speak to Wynne for two weeks. That's why I don't let anyone drive my car."

"Except for me."

"Yeah, don't let it go to your head."

"What are we going to do about the Vic? So we don't have to drive the 'Cuda around."

"We finally got all the parts in that we need to get her back to normal. I put Gordon on the job of patching her up."

A grumble emerges from Quinn.

"He's a smart kid. We can't have him cooped up in that dungeon all day. If you're that worried about it maybe you should give him a hand."

"I'll think about it."

The wounds on his face are more severe than I thought. I brush his face with my fingers.

"Wow! They really got you good. Do you want me to patch that up for you?"

He smiles and takes my hand from his face. "Nah, I'll fix it when I go up to bed."

He continues holding my hand and starts to rub it. The warmth relieves the pain from the injuries inflicted months earlier. I lay my head on his shoulder and close my eyes. The attraction between us is obvious, but admittedly we both have been too scared or stubborn, or maybe a little bit of both, to take it any further than innocent flirting now and again.

A clacking of heels down the hall causes me to lift my head from Quinn's shoulder and him to let go of my hand. We look up to see Claire's face contorted in worry.

"Robert would like to see you two in his office, immediately."

We go into the office and sit in the chairs at Boss's desk. Boss is sitting there rubbing his head and staring at his monitor. His hands are trembling. He reaches for the bottle of nerve suppressants and takes several. Quinn and I look at each other.

"I just received this message." He makes several clicks on the keyboard and a video plays. The image is grainy; the only thing I can make out is the river and the lights of the compliant side. Then the camera zooms onto a figure holding a large bag and throwing it into the river.

Oh shit!

The image is replaced with one of The Magistrate, who begins to speak.

"Robert, I just saw this image on my security feed. As you can imagine, this is very concerning to me, in light of the two missing marshals. I would like to invite you and Ms. Sweet over for dinner to talk about this. I would hate to have any . . . misunderstandings. I have an opening in my schedule in three days. My assistant will be sending you an appointment."

Quinn bellows, "Damn it! I thought you jammed their recording devices so they couldn't see us."

"I thought I got them all, but if he was using fiber then my EMP device wouldn't work on them. Fiber is almost impossible to detect."

"Fuck! How could you be so careless?"

Here we go again. "Jesus, Quinn, why do you have to be such a mega-prick?" I fold my arms and continue. "I did a sweep and a visual inspection before I went down there. I thought I got everything, but it's impossible to tell."

Boss's voice breaks through our fighting. "It does no good talking about the past. What's done is done. You two will go to Magistrate's to find out what he wants."

Quinn and I look at each other then back to Boss and both say, "What?"

Just then Claire walks in the room as puts a cup of tea on Boss's desk. Boss can barely lift the cup without shaking the contents inside. He closes his eyes in frustration and puts his cup down.

"Yes, you two will go to dinner at The Magistrate's house. You can see that I am in no shape to go. This is no time to be exposing our…weaknesses."

Claire adds, "Since we let the story out three months ago that you two are an item, you haven't made a single appearance together in town, except for keeping the troublemakers at bay. People are starting to wonder. This will be great for convincing the public of your relationship status."

Quinn pounds his fist into the table. "Damn it! I'm tired you playing us like this. It's embarrassing."

Embarrassing?! Who does this jackass think he is? Embarrassing to go out with me?

"What the hell, Quinn? Do you think this is any easier for me?"

Boss's voice rises to a heated level. He slams a fist into his desk – quite a change from his usual calm demeanor. "I'm tired of this constant bickering between you two. You will go. You will act like a real couple. You will not make a laughing-stock of the firm. Fuck each other, or whatever you need to do to make this happen, but it will happen. Do you understand me?"

We both silently nod at Boss. I've never heard him lose his temper like this.

"Fine, you are both dismissed."

Quinn and I both leave Boss's area without another word. Once out in the main hall Quinn turns to me and says, "We should start planning for this OP, now."

"Tomorrow, I've had about enough of you for tonight."

I turn away from him to go talk to Wynne in the computer lab. I need to get away from it all especially, Quinn. The last three months have been a roller coaster with that guy. One minute he's a super sweet the next he's as moody as premenstrual teen. Wynne's always good for a bitch session. Down in the computer lab, Wynne and Nikki are holed away like little trolls in a dark dungeon. We've been training Nikki how to hack into Trade-Net and she has been catching on rather quickly. They both look up from their monitors.

"Hey, how did it go? Or should I ask?" Wynne says.

I sit down in a chair by Wynne. "Punk-ass marshals beat up the 'Cuda."

"Oh, hon, I'm so sorry."

"Yeah, I'm really sick about it."

"Well, you can fix it. You and Quinn are really good at that stuff. But everything else went smoothly. Right?"

"Well…"

Nikki turns around in her chair. "What do you mean by that?"

"I thought I got all the surveillance devices, but I guess not. Boss just called me and Quinn into his office. Magistrate got some footage of Quinn dumping the bodies into the river. It's pretty grainy video so it's hard to tell who it is. Anyway, Magistrate wants Boss and Nikki over for dinner to discuss, but Boss isn't feeling well so he wants me and Quinn to go."

Nikki takes a breath and says, "The good news is that Magistrate wants to talk. If he was intent on sending us over to the other side we would be there by now. You and Quinn need to make a good showing for us."

"Yeah, that's what has me worried. Quinn isn't exactly thrilled about doing this. Actually, he's pretty pissed about having to go and play boyfriend with me. I hope he can put his feelings aside and just be professional about it. Honestly, I'm not terribly thrilled about it either."

Nikki gives me a stern look. "What the hell is your problem? All Boss is asking is for you two to go out for a couple hours and look like a real couple. You two are so selfish sometimes."

I'm taken aback by her comments. "Selfish? I work non-stop for the firm without question. Whatever Boss wants, I'll do it. But I just want one part of my life that isn't on pages for

13

everyone to see. Is that so much to ask?"

"Yes. When you took this job it meant giving your life to the firm. Look at me. I haven't had a real date in years. I'll never get a happily-ever-after. I knew it when I took the position. You two are so busy fighting like kids to see that people like me and Claire envy what you two have. Do you think Claire will ever get to go out in public with Boss? No. So are you selfish? Yes, you are. Play nice with Quinn and get over yourself."

I look at Wynne.

"Hey, don't look at me. I agree with her. You make things way too dramatic and complicated. He likes you. You like him. What's left to think about?"

Nikki adds, "Besides, you are so busy feeling sorry for your-self you have lost sight of the one important thing."

"What's that?"

Nikki looks at Wynne and shakes her head. "Man, your friend is pretty clueless. Shea, you are going to be in Magistrate's house. You, the girl who can make spy gadgets with used cell phones, bubble gum, and paper clips. Think about it."

Wynne and I look at each other and our eyes go wide. As if struck with a bolt of brilliance, Wynne starts feverishly clacking on her keyboards. She looks up and says, "I think if you can link me into any of their systems, I could eventually hack into their important information. Go for something they would never think to protect, like entertainment or sanitation. It will take me a while, but I can worm my way into anything."

I say to Nikki, "You're brilliant."

"This is what I've been trying to tell you people. I'm more than just a pretty face, you know."

"We'll bring this up at our weekly meeting with Boss tomor-row, but I've had enough fun for tonight. It's getting late. I'm going to bed."

They say in unison, "Good idea."

We all make our way upstairs shutting down the lights in the empty main room as we go.

When Wynne and I get into our room she asks: "You said Boss isn't feeling well. How do you think he's doing?"

"Not so good. I have a feeling that he wants us to get into the chip and see if it can possibly reverse the effects of the old chip. I just don't see how. It kills me to see him like this. It scares me too. What are we going to do if he goes? Everyone respects Boss, and without him…"

Wynne takes a deep breath. "I thought the same thing. It's been so crazy around here with Ramsey and trying to get the place back to normal, we haven't even had time to look at the chip. All the while Boss's health is going down the toilet. No excuses, we need to start taking a hard look at that thing."

"Okay after my 'date' with Captain Personality we'll start in on it. I'm sure we won't be out that late."

"You're too hard on him."

I shake my head in disbelief at what I am hearing. "Holy shit! Am I hallucinating? Did you actually say something that might be construed as coming to Quinn's defense?"

"I am a little sleep deprived, but I mean it. You can tell he cares about you, in his own weird way, and all you do is hassle him. When you go out, do something for me."

"What?"

"Be nice to him. No teasing, no bickering, just be nice. You know, act like you're on real date. You do remember what that's like, right?"

"No, not really. You know, he's one of the few people, other than you and dad, I would trust with my life. He's a good friend and I don't want to mess it up with all this romance bullcrap."

Wynne puts her hand on my shoulder. "I know. Just keep an open mind." She smiles. "So, are you saying that guys have never…"

15

"No!"

"Bo-RING! My grandma has a more exciting sex life than you two."

"Well, it's not like we ever have time alone. We're so busy patrolling town or fixing shit up here that we don't have much time to ourselves. The few seconds we do have alone are so freakin' awkward because of that stupid story Claire put out. Besides, once he gets a mere glimpse of the baggage I'm carrying around he'll run screaming. They always do."

"Nah, I think Captain Personality is different. Listen, I know going to Magistrate's compound is a serious OP, but try to have fun with it. Okay?"

"Fine. Let's get some sleep, because I think the next several days are going to be interesting."

Chapter 2

The New Kid in Town

The conference room feels cramped with the whole crew inside it. Boss sits at the head of the table.

"As some of you might know, we have a situation with our Magistrate. It seems he has video footage of Mr. Knightly taking care of the problem Ramsey left at our doorstep."

There is quiet murmuring in the room.

"There is good news. He wants to talk. Mr. Knightly and Ms. Kelly will be meeting with him at the end of the week. There is not much we can do about this until we hear from him. So let us not waste energy worrying about it. Mr. Knightly and Ms. Kelly, I want you to spend time this week planning for the meeting."

Both Quinn and I say in unison, "Yes, sir."

I add, "Sir, Nikki pointed out that we are going to have access to Magistrate's house and it might be worth our time to, um, put some information gathering devices around his place."

He takes off his glasses and cleans them. "Yes, that is a good idea, but make sure you can do it without getting caught. This is not the time to be taking unnecessary risks."

"Yes, sir."

"On to other business. Just when we've calmed the community after the loss of the vaccine, it seems that Ramsey has come out of hiding to stir the community into a frenzy. We've had multiple reports of assaults, robberies, and vandalism. We need to get the situation under control. Suggestions?"

I pipe up. "I think we need to start gathering intel on Ramsey's movements. I have a couple of ideas I've been working on."

Boss nods. "Agreed, Ms. Kelly, please continue with your pursuits."

Quinn adds, "I'm doubling patrols in town until we get this situation under control."

Everyone in the room groans.

Boss says, "Mr. Knightly is right. We need to show more of a presence in town."

Conner says, "Sir, why don't we start training some of the more trusted mercs in town? I'm not saying they should come here to live, but some of the mercs should have a direct line to us, and the community should know that."

Everyone in the room is silent. Conner actually had a good idea.

"Well, Mr. Dunne, that is a good idea. You are in charge of identifying these people and training them."

"Yes, sir."

"Good. Good. Ms. Kelly, have you had any word from your father? Does he have any test results for us on the vaccine?"

"No, sir, he's been pretty quiet lately. It took a while for the vaccine vials to get to him and then it took him a while to get the vaccine to his source for testing. Last communication I had with him he said they think they found something, but he didn't say what. I have a call scheduled with him later this week."

"Keep us apprised of the situation."

"Yes, sir."

"Last item on the agenda: repairs to the compound. Ms. Kelly, you have done a tremendous job overseeing the repairs to our compound from the damage Danny inflicted. Can you give us a status report?"

"Yes, sir. But I can't take all the credit. Ryan has done a great job. There are just a few things I need him to finish up. He should be done in a couple of weeks."

After realizing the damage to the compound was far too much for just us to handle, Boss relented on his rule about outsiders in the compound. Ryan Speer came to us highly recommended by Mr. Ito. In exchange for lessons from Mr. Ito he did minor repair jobs around the dojo. I've found that Ryan is a quick study, professional, punctual, and pretty dang cute. I have to say that I've genuinely enjoyed working with the guy.

As if to highlight my failures, the lights start to flicker. Everyone looks up and groans. These brownouts have become more than just a nuisance lately.

I continue, "But our power systems are starting to show their age. I've repaired them so many times I'm getting to a point where I need new parts. Gordo and Wynne have been trying to get me some, but they're not easy to come by."

"I understand, Ms. Kelly." The lights dim again. "Do the best you can, but you need to make this one of your highest priorities. Does anyone have anything else?"

The crew is silent.

"Well then. We have plenty of work ahead of us."

Boss walks out of the room slowly and we all follow.

Wynne, Nikki, and Gordon all file out of the conference room to the lab. Conner, Lindsey, and Quinn are talking in the hallway. I start up the stairs, but before I'm out of earshot Quinn yells:

"Kelly, where you going?"

I spin on my heel. "Ryan is going to be here in a few minutes. I need to let him in and help him out with our latest project. Then I need to get on with making the snoopers."

Quinn groans. "That fucking guy."

"If it wasn't for that fucking guy we would be at least a month behind schedule on repairs to this place. What's your problem with him?"

"Nothing. You blew me off last night. We need to start planning our meeting with Magistrate. Now."

Conner and Lindsey are smirking behind him.

"Why don't you stop bitching at me for once? Come help me out and we'll plan in parallel. The two bone-heads behind you can help Ryan out while we work on the snoopers."

Conner and Lindsey are laughing at our bicker-fest. Quinn growls and looks at them.

"Fine. Let me finish talking with these two dumbasses and I'll be out there."

I walk outside and a cool crisp autumn day greets me. At the gate a man with a mop of dark brown hair, a boyish grin, and clear blue eyes is waiting.

"Hey, Ryan. Punctual as always." I punch in a code and the gate opens slowly.

He walks through with a tool bag clutched in one hand. He tugs on his ill-fitting flannel shirt and gives me a sheepish smile. "Of course, I can't risk pissing off the most high profile customer I've ever had. If this job goes well I should be able to pick up more work in town. Hopefully, it will be enough to keep Emmi off the streets."

Damn, he's cute.

Ryan's sister is one of the girls who occasionally works the corners for her money. Ryan tries his hardest to shelter her from all the sex and drugs and violence, but she keeps going back for more. I respect him for his dedication to his family, but truthfully I think she's so far gone she'll never get her act together.

"How is Emmi?"

He sighs. "Same old shit. Every time I get her a respectable job and somewhat on the straight and narrow, one of her friends comes around flaunting the newest chemical escape. I don't know, Shea . . . "

And loyal to his family.

"Listen, Ryan, you can't give up on family no matter how fucked up they are. But at some point you're going to have to let her make her own decisions and just be there for her when she wakes the hell up. But I can say you've done a hell of a job here, and when you're done I'm going to make sure the whole town knows about it. So let's stop all this heart to heart bullshit and get to work."

He smiles. "So what do you need me to do?"

Productive, too.

"I think we need to continue working on the self defense system. It hasn't been quite the same since the attack."

"So, uh, will Nikki be helping us out today?"

And totally head over heels for Nikki.

"No, I think Lindsey and Conner will be helping you out today, but I'm sure she'll be around."

"Oh, no, um, that's cool. I was just wondering."

"Uh-huh, just wondering my ass." I point to the two video cameras to each side of the fence. "I think the first thing we need to do is take those puppies down and do a health check on them. We need to align and calibrate them and tweak the laser range finder on them. When you're done with them get the ones in the back of the compound and do the same thing. That should keep you guys busy for awhile. When you're done come get me, I'll be in the garage with Quinn."

"Geez, you're quite the task-mistress."

I punch his arm and laugh. "Yeah, well, get to work before I have to beat you down."

He laughs and then his smile turns down. I look behind me. Quinn.

He glares at Ryan. "What are you doing?"

Ryan swallows hard. "Um, Shea was just telling me what I need to do."

Quinn grunts and stares again. "Then you should probably get on with it, don't you think?"

"Yes, sir." He turns and scurries toward the camera.

"So where's Tweedledee and Tweedledum? I thought they were going to help Ryan out."

"They're coming. Let's go. We have a lot to do."

We walk toward the garage. Great, more alone time with the eternally chipper Captain Personality. Once at the outdoor lab, I open the garage doors to let the light in. Quinn sits at the lab bench while I turn on two soldering irons and set out some of the tools we'll need. My hand doesn't work as well as it used to after my encounter with Burt in Danny's warehouse. I'm actually kind of glad Quinn agreed to come help me.

I turn on the radio. The sound of the newscaster drones in the background:

> *EASTERN REGENTS O'NEAL AND GOMEZ WILL BE IN OUR AREA FOR A CEREMONY CELEBRATING THE MERGER BETWEEN GLOBALTHINK AND NEXGEN, THE WORLD LEADER IN NANOTECHNOLOGY. THOMAS ELDRIDGE, OWNER OF GLOBALTHINK, SAYS HE'S EXCITED ABOUT THIS MERGER AND THE SYNERGY BETWEEN THE COMPANIES.*

Quinn grumbles, "I can't concentrate with that bullshit propaganda."

"Okay, you pick something to listen to." As he hovers over me and the radio, the smell of cigars and soap surround me. God, I love that smell. He smiles and pushes a couple of buttons. The sounds of raw country-blues riffs fill the air. He moves away and sits back in his seat. "Nice. Sounds like that Niko kid who plays on the street corner."

"It is. I bought a couple tracks off of him."

I grin.

"What?"

"You're a sweet guy."

He growls. "You know, that propaganda reminds me . . . what's going on with The Feed? I haven't heard a broadcast in weeks."

"The Feed isn't propaganda, it's all truth. But you're right.

Like I said, Dad's been laying low. Probably because it's harvest time and he gets really busy this time of year. Also, The Feed isn't very reliable. When I talk to him later this week I'll ask him about it. He might have heard some chatter on his end that's making him more cautious. I do worry about him though."

"I'm sure he's fine."

"I know, but he doesn't have anyone looking after him like I do. Anyway, we need to get to work. Can you to take apart those phones over there? My hand isn't working so great."

"Yes, ma'am."

First task, disassemble the old trash cell phones. Generally, everyone in the NCS rejects all forms of technology, but cells phones are the only way we have to communicate. The Compliant never use them, because they use their implanted GovTek and CAMS to make all their calls.

"So, what's the plan for our meeting with Magistrate?"

He pries a phone open and hands it to me and I start to disassemble it. "Well, like Boss said, there isn't a lot we can do until he tells us what he wants. However, I think we should pull up some schematics of his quarters to see where we should plant these devices. We also need to keep our ears open on the street for anything going on at his campus." He struggles with another phone. Once opened, he pushes it over to me. "It's hard to say what he wants."

"So if this is a business meeting, why did he ask Boss and Nikki there?"

"He's a jack-off. He likes to wine and dine people. Shove it up our noses how well off he is and how much power he has. This won't be a quick meeting. We're going to have to make nice and have dinner with him and his wife."

"Aww, our first date."

"Cut the shit. This is a serious OP. It could go south quick. It could be a trap to lure us in, chip us, and make examples of us." My leg starts to shake remembering the trip to Danny's basement. Quinn stops disassembling the phones and puts his hand on my knee. I tense my muscles to stop the shaking. "Hey, I'm sorry. It'll be fine. He's got something on us and I guarantee he wants something in return for keeping his mouth shut. We just need to find out what it is."

Unconvinced, I mutter, "Yeah, right." I turn back to disassembling the phone to take my mind off the impending feeling of doom.

He takes my hand and rubs. I stop working. "I won't let anything happen to you. Understand?"

God, there's that look again. Just when I think everything I do annoys him to the core, he gives me the look. That look melts me. I can't speak; I'm just looking into his eyes like a freakin' fool. Quinn brushes the hair out of my face and draws closer to me.

A shadow is cast on the two of us. "Shea?"

Damn! Just like always, getting interrupted when things start to get good.

"Uh, hey, Ryan. What's up?"

Quinn quickly releases my hand and stops short of yelling. "Aren't you supposed to be working or something?"

"Yeah, I– I just need the manuals for the cameras. Lindsey and Conner said to ask you where they are."

"I think they're in the computer lab in the house. I can go get them for you if you want."

"No, you look pretty busy. We can find our way. Is Nikki in there? I have a couple questions I need to ask her about the defense system."

I smile. "Yeah, Nikki's in the lab."

"Okay, great. If we can't find them we'll come to you. I'm sure we'll be able to find them just fine though." He practically skips out the door.

"I knew he'd find a reason to go see Nikki."

Quinn scrunches up face. "What the hell are you talking about?"

"Duh, Ryan's got it bad for her."

"Well, she better be careful. We can't have her compromising her cover."

"Oh, stop being such a grouch. She hasn't been out with Boss in nearly a month and looks like his fatigue isn't getting any better."

He stares me down. "What do you mean by 'fatigue'?"

Damn, me and my big mouth.

"Um, you know he's been kind of weak and tired lately."

"Uh-huh. You know, don't you?"

"Uh, know what?"

"Cut the shit, Kelly. I remember that report you released via The Feed a couple of months ago about chip fatigue. How do you know Boss has chip fatigue?"

"I sort of figured it out when he asked me to get neuro-stabilizers the first time I came here. Plus, he has all the classic symptoms: loss of muscle control, mood swings, slurred speech. Given his age I'm guessing he was one of the original guinea pigs that had a direct implant put in his brain. Depending on how long he had it implanted he might not have seen the effects for years. Once the effects start to show, it goes downhill pretty quickly."

He gets a smirk on his face like he's excited or something. "How do *you* know about chip fatigue?"

"I learned about it in engineering school."

"You learned about that? I didn't think they taught that stuff in school."

"I wouldn't say it's taught per se, but there were those of us who could put two and two together . . . Hold on. How do you know about chip fatigue?"

He clears his throat and nervously rubs the back of his neck.

"There were a lot of us, especially in the military, that saw the effects of the chip first-hand. The government had no problem using us for their guinea pigs. There's a shitload of former military that are still pretty pissed about the chip."

"Quinn, I'm worried about Boss. I don't think the neuro-stabilizers are working as well as they used to. There's nothing much we can do after they lose their effectiveness."

"We need to stay focused on the task at hand. Let's build these things." He looks at the pile of electronics on the bench. "What the hell am I supposed to do with all this crap?"

"This isn't crap. You have some Grade-A technology here and if you're nice to me I'll show you how put it together to make something good."

He grunts.

I grab one of the open phones and point to the circuitry. "This transceiver is perfect for sending and receiving information. The only thing we need is something we can put in-line that can capture data," –I point to a different part of the circuitry– "which this doo-dad right here is perfect for. With a few modifications, of course. So if you can get that thingy and that doo-hickey out, we'll put them together. Then we can sync them up with our computer and wham bam we have a snooper."

"Your mastery of technical vocabulary is dizzying."

"We're going to have to have to find some point I can access his information systems from. Wynne said if we can get into the low side, like the entertainment system, she can hack into the high side where all the interesting information is, with some work."

"Is this what we're going to do for Ramsey's men? Because going to his headquarters is out of the question. You better think of —"

"Man, don't you think I'm smarter than that? Just take a second to tell me what a brilliant plan I have for Magistrate."

"You have a brilliant plan. So what do you have planned for Ramsey?"

"Like you pointed out, sneaking around Ramsey's warehouse uninvited is probably a bad idea. But there are plenty of his guys who frequent Heads and Tails. I've been working on a way to activate the microphones and video cameras in their phones remotely without them knowing. If my program works the way I intended, the girls won't have to lift a finger. It will keep them out of harm's way. Still, it would be nice to get something on Ramsey personally . . . "

Quinn growls. "Don't even think about it."

"Don't worry; I'm not as stupid as you seem to think I am."

He grunts and we get back to work disassembling phones and assembling snoopers. Just before we get into a rhythm, he says, "Oh, yeah. You and me got patrol tomorrow, bright and early. 0500."

Oh goody, an NCS adventure. I can't wait.

Chapter 3

Teenage Wasteland

The alarm jars me from the few scant hours of sleep I was able to squeeze in. I'm lucky if I can sleep more than few hours at a time. It's been several months since my visit to Danny's warehouse, but I still can't let go. The looming visit to Magistrate hasn't helped much in the sleep department either. I hop up and throw on my trusty cargo pants and a long-sleeved t-shirt. Before I leave the room I grab a thick wool sweater.

Quinn's in the kitchen wearing a suit, finishing up bowl of his crappy twigs and barley cereal, reading the newspaper.

"Running a little late are we? You better make it a quick breakfast. We need to be in town in twenty minutes."

I reach in the fridge and grab a cold stim drink.

"I'm not eating. This will be plenty for me."

As I gulp down the syrupy concoction, the headline on Quinn's paper catches my eye:

> Is player Quinn Knightly still with the frumpy Shea Kelly?

Quinn scans the headline and laughs. My heart sinks a bit. Quinn's never been keen on the façade of our relationship, but his laughing at me like this breaks my heart a little. I swallow down a lump in my throat.

Dumbass. Who needs him anyway?

"So, are you ready or what?"

He stands and rinses his bowl and looks me over. "Damn, you look like shit. Did you sleep at all last night?"

Keep digging, buddy.

"Here's a helpful hint for our date tomorrow: if I'm supposed to be your girlfriend, you might not want to tell me I look like shit."

"Sorry, but if you're not up to going, you can stay here and get some rest."

I trudge toward the main exit and he follows. He opens the door for me. I wrap my sweater tightly around me to keep the cool air at bay.

"No, you need the help. It's not like I'd be able to sleep anyway."

He goes to brush a piece of hair out of my face, but I knock his hand away. He gives me a confused look and turns his back.

"Let's get going. Lindsey and Conner are expecting us."

Since leaving the ranks of patrollee and becoming a patroller, I've come to realize there's a lot more to keeping a presence in town that I thought there was. First, the Sector is a lot larger than we're able to watch with the manpower we have at our disposal, so we have to be very strategic in where we patrol. Those sections that are the most densely populated garner most of our attention. It doesn't hurt if there's a good showing of Tab Reporters catching our heroics of the day. Hey, they're a pain in the ass, but we might as well get some use out of them. The propaganda surrounding us does at least half the work in keeping some of the more unruly folks at bay.

As we walk into town I catch a glimpse of us as we pass by a store window marred by graffiti. He – tall, chiseled, and professionally dressed in his suit. Me – short, dumpy, frizzy hair, in my cargo pants and nasty wool sweater. The Tab reporters are right: I'm frumpy and I look ridiculous next to him. I should really investigate getting a more professional wardrobe if I'm supposed to be the partner and girlfriend of Boss's second-in-command. The quick pace of our walk and the crisp air invigorates me, and almost clears the cobwebs from my brain.

Hopefully, this will be an uneventful patrol into town, but the smell of smoke tells me this will be anything but. Quinn and I both run toward the source of the smell.

"C'mon, Kelly. Let's see what's going on."

Half of the makeshift houses between Frank's and the next permanent building are smoldering. Several families are bundled up poking through smoking remains looking for what few possessions they have. Tab reporters are all around, clicking pictures of the scene. Once they see Quinn and me they turn their attention to grabbing a highly prized shot of us together. Ignoring the flashes and the clamoring, I walk over to one of the residents I know.

"Hey, Erma, what's going on?"

Erma's daughter, Meghan, clings to her leg with one hand and holds a singed doll's head with the other. The girl looks up at me with a dirty face and tears in her eyes. The only thing to keep the cold from her frail little body is a sweatshirt and strip of fabric tied around her head.

Erma looks up from a singed piece of material in her hands. "The Orphans came through and torched the place last night. The only reason I can see they did it was for fun. *Fun!*" She throws down the scrap in disgust and shakes her head.

Unfortunately, we can't keep the town protected twenty-four hours a day, seven days a week. The best we can do is keep our presence known throughout town at random points of the day. We've been pretty successful keeping the Orphans at bay, but lately they've been more organized and dangerous.

Lindsey and Conner come over to us. Conner starts, "Chief, those punks are out of control. This is the second time this month they've struck when we were on the other side of town. I think we're going to have to step-up the organized merc patrol. I've called in some of our more trusted mercs to help. They should be here shortly. "

Lindsey adds, "I was able to catch one of the Orphans and ask him a few questions . . . "

I take a deep breath. "Jesus, Lindsey, they're just kids. Did you have to do it right here in the center of town?"

"Give me a little credit, Shea. There are a lot of ways to get information from people that don't involve torture, especially with kids who are drugged out of their freakin' minds. I can ask them a few questions without them even knowing they gave me what I wanted to know."

Great, now I feel like shit. How someone can inflict so much pain on another person and sleep at night is beyond me. Frankly, it's one of the reasons I distance myself from Lindsey. I know he's on our side, and I know I shouldn't be judgmental since he carries out these acts for our team, but after being through an interrogation of my own I'm a little afraid of him.

"Sorry, Lindsey. What did you find out?"

"It shouldn't come as a surprise that Ramsey's struck a deal with their leader. In return for housing, and all the sKape they can drop, they've been charged with making the town as chaotic as possible. The kid didn't know why Ramsey's so hell bent on causing all this chaos. I'm sure he's not high enough up in his ranks to know what Ramsey's ultimate goals are. We need to be careful, because if the Tab reporters see us doing anything to these kids, even if it's in defense of our town, it will be spun like we're bullying kids. It's probably the reason the marshals aren't doing anything to stop them."

Quinn shakes his head. "These aren't kids. These are dangerous terrorists. I don't care if they're minors. I've dealt with Ramsey before; I guarantee he has plans for us." He continues, and raises his voice so everyone can hear. "I want the word to go out from this day forward that I have *zero* tolerance for this shit. Anyone caught committing crimes against a fellow community member will pay dearly. I will *not* be fucked with."

Meghan whimpers at the harshness of Quinn's voice. The small girl looks like she's going to be blown away by the stiff breeze. Before I'm able to comfort her, Quinn is already crouched down to her level taking his jacket off draping it around her. His jacket probably has enough material to make three outfits for this slip of a girl. He whispers something in her ear and gives her a little squeeze. She laughs and wipes a tear from her eye. He rises and comes over to me. I stare at him slack jawed.

"What? I'm not totally inhumane."

"Quinn, I have a feeling that you are probably one of the most humane people in this NCS."

"Yeah, well, keep it to yourself."

Some of the mercs Conner called in are starting to gather around awaiting orders from Quinn.

Quinn barks out, "Johnson and Markum, I want you two to patrol the Eastside." One massive dark haired man with an olive complexion and a sandy haired man with a smaller frame nod and head off to execute their orders.

"Mullen and Walker, you get the Westside."

A short dark-haired tattooed woman and an average height blonde with her hair pulled back say in unison, "Yes, sir."

"Vaughn and Benton, you're on the Northside."

A small muscular man and dark-skinned muscular woman, nearly as tall as Quinn, are off without a word.

"Graham and Simon, you have the Southside."

A young, thin blonde looks up at an older bald man. "Let's go, Dad."

Man, I miss my dad.

As Quinn and I walk to our destination, I ask him, "Do you think Conner's plan of training some of the mercs has any merit?"

"It has potential. Graham, Mullen and Vaughn have been dependable for years, but they need supervision and training.

We don't have the time for that. We need someone who has time and is trustworthy, and I don't know who that is."

"We'll think of something."

I kick the remains of one of the shacks and shake my head at all the senseless violence. Not only do we have to fight the outside, but we've started attacking ourselves. We won't last long if we continue down this path, and I'm sure this is exactly what *they* want.

I follow Quinn down the street. This is my favorite time of year. Despite living in an absolute shithole, I still enjoy the cool crisp air, the colorful leaves, and, most of all, the open-air market. This time of year, those who own the food plots, and anyone else able to grow as much as an herb, sell their food and handmade wares in the center of town. The proprietors are setting up their tents and tables, barely aware of the smoldering houses across from them. Maybe I can convince Quinn to stop on the way home.

Soon we're at our first stop, Heads and Tails. Judy is behind the bar making preparations for the night. Lexi is fixing some of the lighting on the stage, and several of the ladies are cleaning up. Even in their jeans and t-shirts, every one of them is still stunning.

Lexi calls over to me, "Hey, girl, you came in just in time. I could use a hand over here."

I go over to the stage to help Lexi hang the lighting while Quinn sits at the bar.

Judy takes a long drag off her ever-present cigarette. God, I'm glad I cut way back on my nasty habit.

"Did you guys see what those fucking punks did to the houses out there?"

Quinn answers, "How could we miss it? I've got several mercs patrolling the town and I hope to get more. You let them know if you have problems. They know how to get a hold of us."

An exotic beauty with auburn hair walks behind Quinn and puts her arm around his shoulders. "I already feel safer knowing you're protecting us."

I growl and torque down a nut on the stage lighting hard enough to crack the outer casing of the lighting. I mutter under my breath, "Stupid skank."

Lexi laughs and takes the wrench out of my hands. "I think I'll take this, little miss." His voice drops to a whisper. "If you ask me, you have nothing to worry about. That man clearly only has eyes for you."

"What? I wasn't worried about that. He can look at whoever he wants."

Lexi smiles. "Uh-huh, isn't he supposed to be your boyfriend or something?"

Out of the corner of my eye, I see Vanessa laughing and throwing her beautiful hair around. *I hate her.*

I'm only half paying attention to Lexi at this point. "Uh, yeah, I mean uh . . . "

"Look, honey, Wynne filled me in on the whole fake-but-not-really-fake-because-you-two-are-stupid-and-bullheaded scenario. I can assure you when he comes in here for patrol without you there's no funny business like those Tabs would have you believe. That man is only interested in one woman, and it ain't her," he says, pointing to the vixen by the bar. "I say you go over and show her who's boss. I mean, you can't have her making you, the most powerful woman in the NCS, looks like a chump."

"Most powerful woman in the NCS? Really, Lexi, a little dramatic aren't we?"

"Hey, if the shoe fits . . . "

"You know, you're right. I think I do need to give her a bit of a verbal smack down. Who the hell does she think she's messing with?"

"That's right. Go get 'er."

I saunter over to the bar and the melodious laughter of the super-vixen makes me want to puke. She's putting her hand strategically on his shoulder and back as she talks. Quinn does seem to be ignoring her as he talks to Judy. *Yeah, right. How can anyone ignore such a goddess?*

I'm face to face with the dancer. I growl and narrow my eyes then push her arm off of Quinn.

"Hey Vanessa, I'm sure your own man will keep you plenty safe enough."

She scoffs. "I'm just talking. Is that a crime or something?"

"Do you want to go there? Because I've had a shit week and I'm willing to take my frustrations out on you. Just say the word and we'll go."

She looks at me, then Quinn. Quinn gives her the what-do-you-want-me-to-do-about-it look. She turns away, making sure to flip her luxurious mane my direction.

Judy smiles at me. "That one's a livewire. Oh well, she's a great dancer, and brings in the customers. What're you going to do?" She takes a long drag of her cigarette. "It sure as hell has been crazier in here than usual, but we've been able to keep things relatively in check." She picks up a zap gun from behind the counter. "These babies are worth their weight in gold. Thanks for making them for us. They've helped keep some of the guys at bay."

"No worries, Judy. You let us know if you need something." I grab Quinn's arm. "Come on, Romeo. We've got a lot to do."

As we leave the beauties all say in unison, "Bye, Quinny."

Once outside, Quinn smiles. "Jealous?"

"No, but you were being awfully . . . cordial to them."

"You're always saying I need to work on my interpersonal skills."

"Well, maybe you could work on your interpersonal skills

with Frank or something. If you weren't so nice to them, maybe there wouldn't be so many tawdry Tab stories about you."

He gives me a sly smile, which melts me.

Damn his sexy smile.

"Besides, that's Gordo's girlfriend. She's a skank and I wanted her to know I'm watching her."

"*That's* Gordon's girlfriend?"

"Yeah. What, don't you think a nerd could get a hottie like that?"

"He doesn't look like he'd be her type."

"There are plenty of people that like us nerdy types. Unfortunately, I don't think she's one of them."

"Poor kid."

"Nothing much we can do. But let him figure it out for himself. So, you ready to go to Mr. Ito's?"

"Yeah let's get going. Daylight's burning."

We make our way through the community. As we pass the river I think how the tranquil water hides such a horrible secret beneath. The families of those men are still holding out hope they'll be found. Even though we didn't kill them, I still feel guilty. Now Quinn's life hangs in the balance. How could I have been so stupid? I should've done a better sweep of the area for surveillance. If he has to pay for my mistake I'll never forgive myself.

The brilliant oranges and reds of the trees on the backdrop of the blue sky help cheer me up a bit. The crisp air is a welcome change from the hot, thick air of the summer. We're approaching my favorite part of the NCS: the food plots. Behind Mr. Ito's there are about fifteen acres split up amongst three families who lived in this area before it was deemed an NCS. They grow produce to sell at the local market. It's not enough to sustain the whole NCS, but it's something. Sometimes I'm able to block out the rest of the NCS and pretend I'm back home on the farm.

Of course, the farms at home didn't have shock fences around the gardens to keep out intruders.

We bow and enter the dojo. The familiar smells of blood, sweat and mildew float through the air. The small space echoes with kiai of the students and Mr. Ito barking out orders. The small, muscular Asian man acknowledges us with a head nod. We bow to each to each other.

"Ms. Shea and Mr. Quinn, what brings you here? You aren't dressed for practice."

Quinn answers, "No, sir. We're making rounds today and we want to see how you're doing."

"We are doing well, Mr. Quinn. We are not an establishment that many will harass."

I smile. "That's what we thought, but we wanted check on our favorite instructor."

"I'm doing fine. And how is your newest employee?"

"Ryan's great. He's been a tremendous asset."

Quinn growls. "Yeah. Great."

I smirk. "Don't listen to him, Mr. Ito. Thanks for recommending him. It's really freed up some of our time."

"Ah, speaking of which. It's been several weeks since either of you have been to training. I trust you are keeping current at home?"

Quinn and I look at each other in silence. Neither of us wants to admit we've slacked off.

"That's what I thought. Practice is key. Without it you become weak and out of synch."

We both answer. "Yes, sir."

"I trust now that some of your time is freed up I will see you two back here soon?"

"Yes, sir."

"Until then, you two will be practicing?"

"Yes, sir."

"Good."

We walk out of the dojo. Quinn laughs.

"Leave it to Mr. Ito put us on the spot when we come to check on him."

"No kidding, but he's right. We've been slacking."

"So you're saying you want to get smacked down?"

"Yeah right, old man. I can hold my own against you."

He starts to retort, but he's cut off by screaming coming from the food plots. "Looks like we might get some practice in after all."

Homer Martin, the owner, is surrounded by a horde of Orphans. They're trying to get to his food supply. Homer is a strapping man and he can hold his own in a fight, as I've seen many times working at Frank's, but the amount of kids is just too much for him to hold off.

As we run toward Homer I say, "These Orphans are starting really irritate me."

Quinn responds. "Me too and if Ramsey's behind the surge in activity then this is just the beginning of what we're going to see."

When we get to the melee we see a purple mohawked punk beating Homer with a bat. Not missing a beat, Quinn quickly grabs the punk by his nose ring and throws him to the ground. Mohawk-boy is left writhing on the ground. Two kids climb on Quinn to avenge their friend. I pick up the bat dropped by purple-mohawk boy and beat one of the kids off, and Quinn gets the other.

Before we have time to catch our breath, another wave of angst-ridden teens comes for us. Two emaciated girls with neon dreadlocks attack Homer. He grabs one around the neck with his massive hand and throws her into the other girl. Two of the bigger guys attack Quinn. I run to help him, but a sharp point in my back stops me. An arm wraps tightly around my neck.

The person behind me shouts, "Everyone stop or I'll gut the bitch."

I die a little inside when I realize who the voice belongs to. "Justin!"

"Yeah, Shea, I should do it anyway for what you did to Dad."

He pushes the knife in my back harder. I wince against the pain. He reeks of the acrid smell of sKape. There is no reasoning with him now. Homer is frozen in his tracks. Quinn knocks down the two guys at his side in one quick sweep and moves toward me. Justin pushes the knife in more.

I squeak, "Quinn, I think he might be serious."

Quinn stops in his tracks. "Get your hands off of her, you little shit."

My back burns and blood is soaking my shirt. I can barely breathe with Justin's arm around my neck.

"All you have to do is let us go with all the goods."

"Fuck you, Justin." I stomp on his foot. His grip loosens enough for me to struggle free. I'm not fast enough though. He grabs me around the waist and throws me to the ground, sits on top of me, and puts the knife to my throat. "You're a loser, Justin, and so was your dad."

Quinn, growls. "Shut up, Kelly! It's not worth it."

Homer mumbles. "Speak for yourself."

I close my eyes to collect myself. When I open them I smile big. Justin snarls, "What the hell are you smiling at?"

Before I have time to reply, Mr. Ito has Justin in an arm bar and the knife to his throat. The rest of the students have the punks surrounded.

Mr. Ito says calmly, "Mr. Homer is my neighbor. I ask kindly that you do not harass my neighbors. Understood?" They all nod. "You are free to leave."

All the punks file away from Homer's food plot. Before they get out of earshot, Justin yells, "The Orphans aren't alone anymore. You and me, Shea, we're gonna finish this conversation."

"You can bet on it."

Quinn helps me off the ground as he speaks to Homer. "We can try to have more guys up here, but it's been crazy all over."

Homer growls.

Mr. Ito says, "I think I can be of assistance, Mr. Quinn. I think providing protection for the food plots would be excellent training for my students." The students nod in agreement.

"Thank you, sir."

After exchanging pleasantries with the students, Quinn and I continue on our patrol. He stops. "Are you okay? I should probably check that wound over." The adrenaline of the fight is starting to wear off and I'm becoming acutely aware of the pain. We sit on old park bench. I can see down to the town center from up here on the hill. It looks like the market's in full swing now. Quinn peels the blood-soaked fabric away from my skin and I wince.

"I need to patch you up."

"What, right now?"

Quinn reaches into his pants pocket produces a small zippered bag. "I'm always prepared." The sting of the cool antiseptic wipe makes me jump. "I can tell you this much, Kelly: your shirt's seen better days."

"Great. This was my favorite Maxwell's Equation t-shirt. You know, I was thinking about supervision of some of the mercs in town. Don't you think Mr. Ito would be outstanding in that capacity?"

I feel beads of what I assume to be glue being applied to my cut then pressure being applied. "You know, Kelly, I think I might keep you around."

The pressure lets up and I turn around. "Will you stop calling me that?"

He smiles. "We still have a lot to get done today. We don't have time for your lounging around."

I pop up from my seat. "What are you waiting for? Let's get going, old man."

Chapter 4

How Bazaar

After walking around the neighborhood for hours, my legs and back are aching and my stomach is empty. Just a few more stops to make before I can rest my feet and fill my belly full of cheese sandwiches and beer. The center of town is now at full frenzied pace with the market. It kind of reminds me of the rural area where I grew up, with the exception of the active displays advertising GlobalThink and the Compliant Hotline.

A large capacity transit vehicle passes by with a load of the latest Non-Compliant headed for the Compliant sector. A man next to me growls and grabs a tomato from a vendor and throws it at the vehicle.

"Traitors!"

A small gray-haired tomato vendor yells, "Hey! You gonna pay for that tomato?"

He yells back at her, "Shut up, ya old bat!"

Quinn takes the man by the scruff of the neck. "Pay her."

The man digs into his pocket and tosses a couple of scrip notes on her table. Quinn throws the man to the ground and he scurries away.

Quinn sighs. "You done here? I have shit to get done at home."

"Just give me another minute. I might find something really cool . . . or you can reinforce our relationship ruse by getting me something pretty."

"Unlikely."

"Cheap-ass."

People are dickering at each table, the triumphant walking away with their trophies of tomatoes and zucchinis, the defeated walking to different tables to wage another war for produce. At a tent a few steps down, a dark-haired girl with clear blue eyes is hanging over a marshal. He smiles, kisses her on the forehead, and puts a small shiny pack in the palm of her hand. I rush over to her and Quinn follows behind.

"Hey, Emmi, what 'cha up to?"

She sneers at me. "What do you want Shea?"

"Nothin'. I'm sure Ryan would be happy to know you're here taking shiny packages from marshals."

The marshal responds, "She's an adult, she can do what she wants."

I take the semi-lucid Emmi by the arm and lead her away from the marshal. "Emmi, your brother is working his ass off so you don't have to spend time with the likes of that shit-bag. You need to get yourself clean and get away from all this. I hear Mo is looking for some help in his restaurant."

"Shut up, Shea. I know what I'm doing. I'm just having fun. Ryan's a bore and so are you." She yanks away from me and goes back to the marshal.

"Ugh, there's no hope for her."

Quinn rubs my back. "You can't be the guardian angel for the whole Sector. She has to find her own way. C'mon let's get going."

On the way to our final destination I pass by each tent taking in the colorful array of pumpkins, herbs, flowers, and apples making sure to touch them as I pass. One tent, overflowing with a technicolored quilt of flowers and plants, catches my eye. A beautiful bouquet of yellow roses, with a few purple springs of salvia thrown in for accent, beckons me down to take in the heavenly aroma.

Quinn growls. "Hurry it up, will ya?"

"Leave me alone, I'm finding my inner calm."

I see Quinn smirk out of the corner of my eye. Then a shrill scream pops me out of my flower-induced stupor.

"*Tu! No agarres! Deja mis flores.* No pay, no flowers!"

I sigh. "Hello, Mrs. Contreras, I was just smelling."

"*No hay olores gratis. Si quieres flores, se paga.*"

I look at Quinn and shrug my shoulders. I have no clue what she's saying. He shakes his head and scoffs. "Jesus, Kelly, I thought your mother was Mexican."

"Yes, Quinn, but she passed away when I was three and the Spanish that was encoded on my DNA clearly wore off, so presently I do not speak Spanish. Dumbass."

He shakes his head and turns to Mrs. Contreras. "*Disculpe mi amiga, Sra. Contreras. No quiso maltratar sus flores, solo las estaba viendo.*"

Quinn, my personal translator.

"Hey, hey ask her how much she wants for those," I say, pointing to the roses.

"*Quanto por las rosas?*"

"*Treinta creditos scrip.*"

He turns to me. "Thirty."

I cough. "Holy shit." I do some quick calculations in my head and weigh the options. I better not. Damn my eternal cheapness. My hands fall from the bouquet. "Not today."

Quinn looks at Mrs. Contreras and shakes his head no.

Mrs. Contreras scowls and pulls the bouquet out of my reach. "*Tu amiga si es tacaña. Aunque, es muy hermosa. La tienes que tratar bien. Alomejor comprandole flores?*"

Quinn smirks and nods in agreement.

I narrow my eyes at him. "What the hell did she say?"

He pushes me away from the tent to carry on our patrol. "She said you're a dumbass, and I agreed."

As we walk away Mrs. Contreras's voice rings out. "*Quieres que te guarde las flores?*"

Quinn yells back, "*Si.*"

The smell of pizza from Bobby's reminds me that I'm hungry and I want to get home. No luck at the bazaar, might as well get home.

Quinn says, "Two more stops and we can go home."

"Remind me, I need to look for the 'Cuda's repair manual when we stop at Frank's."

We step inside Bobby's. The warmth of the pizza ovens fights the chill of the autumn air. From behind the counter a tiny brunette whirlwind emerges. "Mr. Quinn, you gotta help me."

"Hey, Mia. What 'cha need?"

"Hi, Auntie Shea. I need help with my robot."

"What am I? Chopped liver?"

Mia already has Quinn by the hand pulling him to the office behind the counter. "I, uh, guess I'll be right back."

Bobby and his wife Jenny are behind the counter making pizzas for the oncoming dinner rush. Bobby laughs. "She's taken quite the liking to him."

"Yeah, I know. I thought the robot would be a project I could help her with, but she always wants Quinn when she comes to the compound."

Jenny says, "We really appreciate you having her over. It really means a lot to her. She isn't too much trouble is she?"

"Not at all, it's good for her to run around even if it is just once a week. Everyone enjoys having her over. She breathes some life into that old place. I think even Captain Personality enjoys it. Actually, I think he enjoys it the most. Weird. So, you guys having any problems?"

Bobby shrugs. "Same old shit. We know you guys are doing the best you can."

"I'm sorry we can't do more."

Just as Bobby and I are finishing our conversation, Quinn materializes from the back room. "I think I got the problem solved. You ready to go?"

"Yup."

Mia climbs up on the counter and waves to us. "See ya later, Mr. Quinn."

As we exit the Bobby's, I give Quinn the look of death.

"What?"

"I got that project for *me* and Mia, not you."

"What can I say? The kid's got good taste."

"Whatever."

We cross the street and are face to face with Frank's bar. I have to admit I miss working here a little. No one ever paid attention to the frumpy barmaid. It's amazing how much I took my privacy for granted back then.

"This shouldn't take long. I think I know where I left the manual. We'll be back home eating cheese sandwiches and drinking beer in no time." We both walk in the bar. "Hey, Frank . . . "

The bar is completely empty except for Frank and two others, a gaunt, pasty teen girl with platinum dreadlocks smashing shit with a bat, and Ramsey sitting at a table calmly sipping a scotch. He's watching the whole ordeal as if it's a sitcom.

"Frank, are you okay?"

He nods and cowers away from the girl with baseball bat.

The girl turns to look at me and gives me a sneer. She's the head of the Orphans, and I know her well. Morgan Anthony used to come around the bar all the time begging for scraps and annoying the hell out of me when she was just a tween. Her mom spent most of the time strung out and who knows who her father is. Morgan was the sole provider for her little sister. I tried to help her as much as I could, but when she started running with the gang and using, I washed my hands of her. I hoped she would get clean for her sister, but she never did.

She drops the bat and sits on Ramsey's knee. He smiles and puts his hand on her ass. She says while smacking her gum,

"Hey, Shea, long time no see."

I peer at Ramsey. "What's the matter, Ramsey, can't find a woman your own age that can stand the sight of you?"

"Actually, Shea, Morgan is very mature for her age," Ramsey replies as he rubs her ass. Morgan smiles and kisses him with plenty of tongue.

Oh, barf.

"You can do so much better than this old man, Morgan. He's using you."

She gets up from his lap and looks me square in the eye. "Says the lady who used to get the shit beat out of her every night by her boyfriend." Her words sting. I want to crawl behind that bar with Frank and die of embarrassment. Quinn looks at me to see if what she's saying is true. She smiles knowing she's got me. She looks at Quinn and continues, "It's true. Ms. Tough Stuff here used to be the personal punching bag of . . . What's his name?" She stops to think for awhile. "Never mind, it's not important anyway. It was funny because she acted all tough with everyone, but not with him. Yeah, he used fuck everything in sight too. Everything but her, that is. But you taught him a lesson or two didn't you, Shea? I guess the competition was getting a little too much for you to handle."

Unable to contain my emotions any longer, I punch her square in the face. She falls to the floor like a ton of bricks. "Shut the fuck up."

Quinn pipes in. "Ramsey, take your bitch and get the fuck out of here."

Ramsey smiles, not the least bit phased that his 'girlfriend' is lying on the floor. "Well, Gunny, it doesn't look like our girl-friends are getting along at all. I'd hoped we could double date or something." He gets within inches of my ear and whispers, "I can see why Gunny likes you so much. He always had a thing for smart girls."

Before I can do anything, Quinn rushes Ramsey and slams him into the wall. "Keep your hands to yourself. If I catch you so much as breathing on her I'll make what I did to Burt look humane."

Ramsey laughs as he's pinned. "You really do like her. Here I thought it was some kind of sham made up for the Tabs. All right, I'll get out of here. I have better things to do today anyway."

Quinn loosens his grip. Ramsey walks away with a grin on his face. As he reaches the door I look down at Morgan lying on the floor. "Uh, Ramsey, would you mind taking your garbage with you?"

"How rude of me." He walks back and grabs Morgan by her hair and drags her out of the bar. "I'll see you two crazy kids later."

That was the single most surreal experience I've ever had. Quinn walks over to the bar. "You, okay, little man?"

"Yeah, those two are pretty fucked up."

Quinn gets on the comms: "Vaughn and Benton, I need you here at Frank's. We've had a disturbance." He looks me over. "Are you okay?"

"I'm ready to go. Hey, Frank, if you find the 'Cuda's repair manual give me a call or text."

"Can do, Shea."

We make the journey back to the compound in silence. I know Quinn's looking at me with pity. They always do. They always say the same thing: "I thought she was such a strong girl. What a shame." Fuck him and his pity. Fuck Morgan for making me remember. Morgan. What wasted potential. I only hope I can keep Mia from turning into that. *Oh God! What if Ramsey and Morgan decided to wait for me at Bobby's instead of Frank's?* I would never forgive myself if anything happened to Bobby's family, especially little Mia. My head and body ache. I need food, my comfy slippers, and beer, not necessarily in that order.

When we walk into the house I'm ready to collapse in a puddle on the couch. Quinn speaks up:

"Come on, let's give Boss our report then we can relax."

Relax? Did he really say, Relax?

Boss is in his office typing away at his computer. He doesn't take his eyes off the screen. "What's your report?"

Quinn answers, "Sir, the Orphans are out of control. Ramsey is using them to drive the town into chaos."

Boss turns to us and takes off his glasses. "Recommendations?"

I say, "Sir, I was thinking about Conner's idea to train some of the mercs, and Mr. Ito would be great oversight. He gives a cohesiveness we don't have time to provide."

"Excellent, Ms. Kelly. Please talk to Mr. Dunne about this. Mr. Knightly?"

"We need to make an example of the Orphans' highest ranking member. We need to send a message to the rest of the kids, and to Ramsey."

My eyes grow wide. "Whoa, wait, are you suggesting we take out Morgan?"

"That's exactly what I'm suggesting. I need to hold true to the promise I made in town. If we don't do something then everyone will see us as pushovers."

"Can't we — ?"

Boss interrupts. "There is no debate here. Mr. Knightly, take care of it."

I know they're right. If I was living on the other side, I'd make some speech about being the bigger person and leading by example, but the rules here are totally different. I take a deep breath and answer back, "If you want it to be memorable, then put Lindsey on it."

I race to the nearest bathroom before either of them can respond and puke my guts out. The extreme sleep deprivation and stress of the last couple of months is starting to wear on me. I stand and look at myself in the mirror. The circles under my eyes are dark. My face is drawn and pale. I take off my glasses and splash water on my face.

When I exit the bathroom I come face to chest with Quinn. "Are you okay?"

"No, I'm not okay. She's just like Justin. I tried to help them, but I lost them. I'm useless."

He brushes a piece of hair out of my face and tucks it behind my ear. "You're not useless. You tried to give them options, but they made the choices that landed them where they are today. Stop taking responsibility for everything."

I pace and rub my head. "No, it's not right, Quinn. I owe her one more shot."

"Shea, what do you want me to do? Boss has already given the order. I can't cross him."

"But what if she's gone? What if she decides to change her ways and become Compliant?"

"Shea . . ."

"I have to try. I can't live with myself knowing I didn't give it one last try. You didn't know her when she was kid. I . . . "

He stops me by rubbing my shoulder. "Fine. If she's not out of my Sector by morning, she's fair game."

I whisper. "Thank you."

"And I'm going with you."

Great, that's all I need.

Chapter 5

Rescue Me

The alley smells of trash and urine. My legs are numb from the cold and standing so long in one spot. I'm starting to lose hope that we'll see her tonight. Maybe, she got smart and decided to stay at the warehouse. Quinn looks at his watch for the tenth time in an hour.

"Listen, if she doesn't show soon we're going to have to get back home."

"Just give it a little longer." I glance at my watch. "This is about the time of night the sKape levels in their bloodstreams are reaching critical mass. They're going to be looking for a way to burn off some of their extra energy and paranoia. You can go if you want."

"Are you insane? I'm not leaving you here by yourself. If she's not here in the next half hour we're leaving, and you're coming with me even if I have to carry you out."

He's right being out here alone; I would be no match for the Orphans. We're already risking it being out here just the two of us.

I let out a long sigh. "Fine."

I lean up against the cold brick wall and slink away into the safety of the shadows. Morgan was a smart kid. It really doesn't surprise me that she took over the Orphans. I tried so many times to show her that there were other ways, but she thought she was smarter than me. I should just write her off, but I can't.

The sound of cackling and yelling stirs me from my day-dreaming. Quinn looks at me and nods, giving me the signal that Morgan is in sight. The sound gets louder as they grow closer. I peek around the corner, being careful not to give away our position. The group is staggering along, laughing and singing. Some of them are shoving and hitting each other. Some are chugging what I assume to be homemade hooch out of glass containers. Morgan is trailing the group looking dazed. The Orphans are just a rag-tag group. They never observe any kind of protocols like protecting the leader or not leaving a team member alone. Good for us. Bad for them.

The group of Orphans passes our alleyway without giving it a second look. Morgan slowly brings up the rear, way behind her friends. Quinn quickly reaches out for her, clapping his hand over her mouth. I look out at the rest of the group and all of them are too drunk or stoned to know anything has gone on. They can't hear her muffled cries above over their own yelling.

Morgan thrashes wildly in Quinn's arms. Her eyes are vacant and she has the acrid smell of sKape surrounding her. Her strength has no doubt been enhanced by the sKape, but her frail malnutritioned body is still no match for Quinn. He responds to her thrashing by squeezing her tighter. She bites his hand. As blood pours down his arm he gives no more than a muffled acknowledgement. He squeezes her tighter and I'm sure he's going to squeeze the life out of her. She stops biting and thrashing.

He whispers in her ear. "Are you ready to listen to my friend?"

She nods, wide eyed.

"Good, because she has something important to tell you. If I were you I'd take her advice."

I whisper, "Morgan, you need to leave this sector now."

She gives a muffled "fuck you" from behind Quinn's hand.

"Listen to me Morgan, you're a marked woman. If you're not gone by morning, Boss is going to make an example of you. Leave, Morgan. You're a smart girl, you can make a life for yourself on the other side away from these stupid wastrels that are bringing you down."

I look out again to see if her group has noticed her absence. They are so far down the street I can barely see or hear them.

"Morgan, they didn't even notice you're gone. What kind of family doesn't notice when one of their own goes missing?"

She gives me a sad look like I'm finally getting through to her.

"Look, I know I wasn't the best role model in the world for you. Maybe if I'd walked away from Logan and all his abuse sooner, then it would've taught you to stand up for yourself. I'm sorry. But learn from my mistakes."

I tuck a wad of scrip in her pocket. Quinn looks at me, shocked.

"Go to Magistrate's compound. They're open 24 hours a day. Tell them that Boss is after you and that you want to convert. Ask to take the 890SE test. You can pass it easy and you'll get dibs on the best jobs that way. They'll put you up for the night and you'll take the test first thing in the morning. They'll convert the money I gave you to credits. It isn't much, but it'll help. Once you go over to the other side, they'll pay for your college and pay for a place to stay. You'll have a career and you won't have worry about this hell hole anymore."

She scowls.

Quinn adds, "If you don't, then you're gone first thing in the morning."

She says a muffled, "Fine."

"No, Morgan, it's not fine. It isn't going to be an easy bullet through your brain. He's going to make an example of you. Lindsey will make it last for hours, hell maybe the whole day. He'll start with your fingers then your toes. You'll be unrecognizable when he's finished with you. Morgan, don't be stupid. Just go."

Quinn adds, "She's right. He won't take it easy on you just because you're a seventeen year old girl. He doesn't give a shit.

You've crossed Boss and he needs to make an example of you. Get out and no one will look for you."

She's sweating, a sign she's coming down from her sKape high. Maybe I have a chance at getting through to her now.

"It's never too late to start again, Morgan. You're young — you have a lot of potential. Come on."

I look out the alley again the teens are beating up some old drunk. We don't have much time before they figure out she's gone.

"Please, just leave."

She slowly nods and whimpers.

I struggle to control my emotions. "Okay then, go straight to Magistrate's. Be quiet, and the other kids will never see you leaving. Go now."

I nod to Quinn to let her go. He slowly releases her from his grip. She smiles at me. Something I haven't seen a long time. Maybe there's hope after all.

"Thank you, Shea. Thank you, for showing me what a spineless bitch you are."

Before Quinn can grab her she runs out of the alley yelling.

"Fuck, we need to get out of here now, Kelly."

The kids are far enough away from us that we're able to get close to the compound where they won't follow us. I trudge up the hill to the house. I'm beyond tired, both physically and emotionally. I need to get to my bed and collapse.

Quinn opens the house door for me. It takes all my strength to cross the threshold. I turn to go up the stairs, but Quinn touches my arm and I stop.

"You tried. None of this is your fault."

I turn to face him. "I know what's going to happen to her and I can't stop thinking about that . . . and what I could've done to prevent it."

He grabs my hand. "Let me get my hand patched up and

then we'll talk about it."

My brain is swirling with all the events of the day. I don't want his pity. I want to be alone. I pull my hand away.

"No, I'm tired. I want to go bed."

I turn and make the trek up to my bedroom.

*

The shadows cast on the basement wall look like demons around me ready to claim my soul. In the dimly lit basement, it's hard to make out the faces on the bodies casting these shadows. It doesn't matter. I know why they're here. It's the same as the night before and the night before that. Their taunting and chanting is the only thing I hear. The first one is on me and his sickening hot breath on my neck makes my stomach turn. Tears involuntarily flow from eyes. I try to find my one friend through the crowd of men. He is bound to a chair and has been beaten to within inches of his life. His head is downcast in shame, avoiding eye contact with me.

"Please, kill me," I croak.

Melon-Head stands over me and sneers. "You had your chance, girly. I'm not about let this end easily for you or your boyfriend."

As he finishes his thought, a man with a glowing red metal stick walks over to Quinn and introduces the stick to Quinn's eye. He screams in agony.

"*Quinn!!*"

I open my eyes and the men are gone, the safety of my bedroom surrounds me. Wynne is sleeping quietly across the room. My dreams have become such a regular occurrence that my night terrors rarely wake her. The clock across the room shows that I've gotten three hours sleep, a new record. I lie back in bed and stare at the ceiling. The full moon behind the old oak tree is casting dancing shadows on the walls of my room, jettisoning me back to my dream. My heart races and I know the war raged against insomnia has been lost, yet again. Like a defeated solider leaving a battlefield, I drag myself from my bed in search of the electronic solace only the entertainment console can provide.

The moonlight provides ample lighting for my journey downstairs to the entertainment room. The only sound in this usually bustling area is from the padding of my bare feet against the cold tile. I sink into the large couch and wrap an enormous tattered afghan around me to keep the chill of the drafty old house at bay. Sticking my hand deep between the couch cushions, I produce a remote.

The broadcast television stations don't offer many options at any time of day. Mostly, the government pipes in bullshit propaganda news, or mindless sitcoms, nothing too controversial that would cause us Non-Commers to actually think. I press several buttons on the remote and a menu of all the movies that Wynne, Gordo, and I uploaded to the entertainment server is displayed. Decisions, decisions. Since my brush with Melon Head and his happy drill, I've probably gone through most of these movies at least twice.

I finally settle on an old-time Kung-Fu movie. The movies from my grandparents' and great-grandparents' era far surpass anything made in the last twenty years, because they are chockfull of violence, sex, and humor at everyone's expense.

I draw my legs into me and put the afghan around my whole body. The yarn fortress that surrounds me gives me a sense of security. I lose myself in the roundhouse kicks, front punches, and bad dubbing. The seat next to me sinks in. I peek my head out from the afghan and see Quinn clad in boxers and a t-shirt sipping a glass of scotch.

Still aggravated from our encounter this evening I grumble,

"Who said you could sit here?"

"Do I need a reservation for this couch?"

"Maybe."

He looks up at the TV. "Way of the Dragon, one of my favorite Kung-Fu movies of all time. It's not often you see a clash of titans like Bruce Lee and Chuck Norris."

I raise my eyebrow. "*You* like Kung-Fu movies?"

"Absolutely. I remember watching this movie with my grandpa when I was a little kid. He said he and his dad used to watch it all the time. I guess he was passing the torch or something. I guess I . . . " He trails off. I wonder how he was going to finish that sentence. "Anyway, you got good taste, Kelly."

I reach out from my yarn fortress and give him a whack on the arm. "Will you stop calling me that? I do have a first name." Quinn's a pain in the ass, but I'm actually glad he's down here with me, not that I'll ever let him know it. "So, what are you doing up?"

He takes a slow drink of his scotch. "I had some stuff on my mind. I couldn't sleep so I thought I'd come down here to get away from the same four walls of my bedroom."

I swipe his glass and take a drink. "I know what you mean. Hey, is this the Laphroaig I got for Boss?"

He grins and swipes the glass back. "Yeah, Boss really doesn't drink much and since it was my idea to have you get the scotch, he gave it to me."

"Well, aren't you a sneaky monkey? Are you the one who came up with idea of testing Wynne and me?"

"Did you think I was going to agree to have a common street urchin come live here?"

"Nice. So you think I'm a common street urchin?"

"No, I *thought* you were just a common street urchin. Now, I think you're an above-par street urchin."

I swipe the glass from his hand again and take another drink.

It warms me from the inside and the tension once stored in my muscles starts to fade. "Thanks a lot." I hand the glass back to him.

"You know how I feel about you."

"Um, you think I'm a pain in the ass?"

"No, I mean yes, you are a pain in the ass. What I mean is that I think you are probably one of the smartest people I've ever met."

"Naw, Wynne has all the brains."

"You don't give yourself enough credit. That's the only reason you stayed in that dive bar so long. You could be running this town if you put your mind to it."

"Pftt . . . Whatever. I think that scotch is going straight to your head."

"Shea, when you were working in that shitty bar, you supplied the residents with goods they needed, kept Danny off their backs, and reported all Magistrate's goings-on. Give yourself some credit."

"I bet you say that to all your fake girlfriends."

He shakes his head. "Seriously, you don't take credit for the shit you should be taking credit for, and shit that's out of your control you want to take the blame for. It isn't your fault that Morgan is the way she is. She knew what was at stake. And I don't know the rest of your history but—"

I swipe the glass from his hand and take a big swig. In an instant, all the alcohol consumed on an empty stomach catches up with me. "No, Quinn you don't know my history." *Oops, that came out a little more slurred than I wanted. Ah, fuck it. Who cares?* I collect myself and continue. "Listen, Morgan used to be normal. She was smart and had a lot of potential, but her mom was a fucked up mess. I used to find Morgan odd jobs to keep her sister afloat, and I would give her whatever cash I could spare." I finish off the rest of the smoky beverage. "Then I started dating Logan. It was okay at first, then I quickly learned he wasn't right in the head."

"That's not your fault."

Crap, I'm feeling dizzy now. "After I threatened him within inches of his life, he stopped messing with me."

"Good. So what's the problem?"

"Jesus, don't you see? He started messing with her. She was just a kid. She just wanted attention and she was getting it from a much older man. She felt loved and important. So I did the only thing I could do to keep her from ending up like me. He won't be bothering anyone now. But she never forgave me for it."

"You can't save the world, hon. The best you can hope for is a person or two at a time." He caresses my face and gives me a peck on the forehead. Seeing that I'm a bit shitfaced, he chuckles. "You need to go to bed. We have a big day tomorrow."

"That reminds me of something else I need to talk to you about."

"Oh, God, what now?"

"I know the last several months of having to hang with me and putting up with Claire's PR campaigns have been hard . . . "

"I never said —"

"Let me finish. You didn't have to say anything. After today, it's clear you have no interest in me. I saw you reading the paper this morning and the reporters are right. I look ridiculous with you. No one believes we're really an item. You hate the bullshit and I feel stupid being with someone who clearly doesn't want to be seen with me. We're stressing ourselves out needlessly."

"What are you saying?"

I sigh. "I'm saying, if you want, after our fun time with Magistrate tomorrow, we can give Claire the show of a lifetime. Break up with me where every Tab reporter and his brother can see. Make a huge production out of it. Be merciless with me. Then you're off the hook, no more me as your partner. In public anyway."

"Claire would blow a gasket."

"Yeah, and don't tell me that doesn't make you smile just a little bit."

Quinn growls. "I don't want to get into this now. We need to get to bed."

I raise my eyebrow. "Was that an invitation, Mr. Knightly?"

His eyes grow wide and he shifts in his seat. "Uh, I meant—"

"I know what you meant. I'm just giving you shit." I stand up and stretch. "You're right though. I'm tired. But think about it." I stagger to my bedroom then I stop in my tracks. "Oh yeah, about our date . . . "

He sighs. "What about it?"

"If this is our first and last date, you better bring your A-game. Just so you know, I prefer yellow roses."

"Well I'd prefer you shut the hell up, but we see how well that's working out."

Chapter 6

Get Ready 'Cause Here We Come

"I think your boyfriend really hates me," Ryan says as I hand him the video camera to mount on the gate.

"He's just skeptical of everyone and everything. He's very protective. I guess it comes with the territory. He hated my guts when he first met me. Now look at us." Ryan gives me a half-hearted smile. He looks like he hasn't slept a wink all night; his eyes are wandering about and he's barely paying attention to me or the job he's doing. The camera he's mounting slips out of his hands. I quickly hold out my hands and catch it. "Dude, are you okay?"

"Uh, yeah, why?"

"Well, you look like shit, you're only half paying attention to your work, and everything I'm saying is going in one ear and out the other. And I'm freakin' entertaining," I say with a smile.

Ryan chuckles bit. "It's nothing, it's just . . . "

"It's Emmi, isn't it?"

Ryan looks shocked. "What do you mean?"

"I saw her yesterday with a marshal. She'll come to her senses eventually. You're a good big brother."

He looks like he's on the verge of crying. *God, what could be wrong with him?*

"No, Shea, I'm not. I was lazy, but not anymore. Your boyfriend has the right idea: don't trust anyone. I need to start taking care of some things."

"What do you mean?"

He rubs his face. "Um, nothing, I just need to start watching over Emmi more, that's all. Come on, let's get to work, these cameras aren't going to hang themselves."

I knit my eyebrows, unsure if that's all he's talking about. "Um, okay. Ryan, if you have something you need to talk to me about, just say it. We can help you out."

"I'm fine, we're fine. Me and Emmi have been watching over each other since I was fifteen. We're . . . "

"Fine. Yeah, I got that." I take a breath and decide not to press my luck with him. Maybe he'll be ready to talk later. I peek over my shoulder and see Lindsey coming down to help us.

Lindsey stops and surveys the work. "Looks good, guys. What do you need me to do?"

I point down to the cart of cameras. "Can you finish hanging these? I feel like our ass is hanging in the wind with a quarter of our cameras down for maintenance. I need to go back in the lab and make um . . . " Remembering that Ryan isn't privy to all our operations, I recalibrate. "Make myself look beautiful for my date with Quinn tonight. I need to start early, there's a lot of work to be done."

Lindsey laughs. "I think Chief likes you the way you are."

"Uh, huh. I'm really starting to like you, Lindsey." I turn to Ryan. "I'll send Nikki out to help here in a bit."

That remark gets little more than a raised eyebrow from Ryan. Dang, something must be wrong.

I make my way to the lab. Nikki, Gordo, and Wynne are busy in the dark cool room, working away on their computers. I plop down in my favorite leather chair and busy myself with various TradeNet transactions. The chair squeaks with every movement I make. Wynne, Gordo, and Nikki stare at me.

"What?"

Wynne scowls. "Can't you get a new chair or something? It's really annoying."

"I like my chair. It's comfy."

"Well at least stop squirming around so much. Everything'll be fine."

Nikki adds, "Like Boss said, it's a good thing Magistrate wants to talk. If he wanted us chipped we'd be gone by now."

"Me, worried? Nah."

Wynne scoffs. "Right, that's why you have bags under your eyes. I bet you didn't sleep more than two hours last night."

"Wrong." *It was three.*

"So what do you and Captain Personality have lined up for your hot date tonight?"

"If I'm not mistaken, Wynne, we're going to Magistrate's house, and if we get back alive I have an exciting night of beer drinking and fixing Quinn's car in store for me. I might just organize my sock drawer too."

"All you guys do is work. Go out and do something afterwards. Go have some fun."

I look at Nikki. "Tell her Quinn doesn't do dates."

"I have to say, I agree with Wynne. Chief needs to get out more, and so do you."

"You're no help."

"Hey, I ain't gettin' any. I have to live vicariously through someone."

"Oh yeah, speaking of getting some – can you go out and help Ryan with the cameras?" I say with a sneaky smile.

Wynne lets out a cat-call. "Go get 'em Nikki. That guy is hot and he likes you."

"Shut up, guys. As far as he knows I'm still attached to Boss. He isn't going to risk his job here, or his life, to hit on me."

Suddenly, I realize what Nikki was talking about last night, about not being able to pursue relationships of her own. "You're right. I'm sorry. But you know it doesn't hurt to look, right?"

Nikki gets up and stretches. "Yeah you're right, and it's a beautiful day. I'm feeling kind of cooped up in this dingy lab anyway. I'll be back in a little bit to give you some pointers on Magistrate and his wife."

"Thanks, Nikki."

Gordon pipes up. "Does anyone care how I'm doing synching up Shea's hardware to our computers?"

Wynne says, "Oh, Gordo, we know we don't have to check on you. You're the workhorse of the group."

"Well, I'm still having some problems. I keep getting bad data packets back."

We both scoot over to Gordon's console and pour over the lines of code. Usually, Wynne or I only have to explain something to him once before he gets it. After another week, he's usually showing us a thing or two. I have no doubt that if he lived on the other side he would have a brilliant career ahead of him. But because he was born over here, being a hacker for Boss was the highest level job he could ever hope to get.

Wynne makes a couple of keystrokes on Gordon's keyboard. "I see your problem. This little booger."

Gordon squints. "Oh yeah, I didn't even catch that. I totally called the wrong routine."

Quinn pokes his head in the door.

"Shea, we need to go over some plans before our meeting with Magistrate tonight. Are you busy?"

Wynne and Gordon are hacking away, unaware of my presence.

"Guys, do you think you'll have these done in time for our meeting?"

Wynne turns away from her computer. "When do you need them?"

"Three hours?"

Without turning from his computer, Gordon says, "No problem."

"You're the best, dude."

In Quinn's room the lights are dimmed and there are several 3D images of floor plans floating in the air. I give the floor plans a twirl with my hands.

"Hey this is pretty cool. Ryan did a good job installing these 3D projectors."

Quinn grunts at the mention of Ryan's name. "You look pretty tired. Maybe you should go rest before we go to Magistrate's."

"Why does everyone keep saying that? I'll be fine."

"You know as well as I do this OP can go south real quick. I need to know that you have my back, and that I don't have to worry about you being too tired or hung over to get the job done."

"Yeah, yeah. Let's look over these plans then I'll think about taking a nap."

"Fine." He situates the floor plan so that the main entrance is facing me. "Off of the foyer there's a library." He makes a couple of more swipes. "Back here on the main level is the sitting room. Both of these might have access to entertainment systems."

"Hmm. Yeah, but both the library and the sitting room are out in the open. They might get a little suspicious if I start rummaging through their entertainment system in front of them." I spin the wireframe drawing looking for answer. A small non-descript room catches my attention. "Right here. This is perfect."

Quinn screws up his face and says, "The bathroom?"

"Yeah the bathroom, everyone has to pee, right? In each of the bathrooms there's a computer that monitors water and energy usage. It reports the data back to a big database. So this means no long hot showers for Mrs. Magistrate, and . . . "

"We have access to their computer systems."

"Yeah. It's not like it will be a simple jump. I'm sure they have all kinds of firewalls around his important stuff, but I'm sure at some point the data from the bathroom and the secret data meet at some kind of crossroads. It's just a matter of finding it and then hacking down the barriers that protect the good information. If anyone can do it, Wynne can."

"Do you think you can get in there and get it done quickly? The longer you're in there, the longer you're going to arouse suspicion."

"No problem, this will be a quick couple of connections. Besides, no one monitors bathroom data for hacking. If takes too long, just tell them the double burrito supreme I ate for lunch isn't sitting too well with me."

Quinn smiles. "Sounds like you got this all figured out. Get some sleep."

"Fine."

I trudge to my bedroom. Quinn's right, but I would never admit it to him. I'm so tired my body aches and my stomach hurts. The warm crisp covers are welcoming. I nestle down and sleep comes fast. For a while there is nothing but darkness. The darkness gives way to a little light, and I find myself in a cold basement. This time Morgan is strapped to a chair. She's crying and pleading for her life. A knife appears in my hand. She cries and thrashes. There is no emotion from me. I lift the knife and let her blood flow. There is a gurgle from her, then she is no more.

"Shea, Shea, you've overslept." Wynne's voice wakes me from my nightmare.

I rub my eyes and sit up. Wynne and Nikki are standing over me. "What the hell were you dreaming about? You were thrashing around quite a bit," Nikki asks.

"Same old shit."

I go to my closet and look through my dresses as she speaks. They are all woefully out of style, but I don't have many options.

Nikki starts, "Okay, this lady is a real space cadet. She'll spend most of the time gossiping with her friends or reading the Tabs through her CAMS. I used to think that she was just playing stupid, but the more I got to know her, the more I'm convinced that she really is that dumb. So the best thing is to just laugh at all her jokes and act like you know what she is talking about."

I take the top three dresses in my wardrobe I hold up the first to get a vote from Wynne and Nikki. They shake their heads no. The second dress warrants the same response. The third dress gets their rousing approval.

Nikki continues, "She's obsessed with the Tabs. She thinks they're gospel or something. Just talk about the latest gossip and you'll be good to go. You and your boyfriend are going to have to keep your tempers in check. Magistrate is a real asshole, you probably know that, but he will make all kinds of digs at you guys. Just swallow your pride and take it. "

I put my hair into a bun and let few tendrils of hair sweep my neck. Next comes the makeup, this event calls for a more understated look than when I used to accompany Boss to Danny's club. A little mascara, blush, and lip gloss do the job very well. I trace the scars left behind by Burt with my finger, it's useless to try and cover them up.

I venture into the bedroom to put my dress on. It's the quintessential sleeveless little black dress. The slit up the side makes me feel extra sexy. I slip on the dress, head to my dresser, and look in a cereal box turned jewelry box. I pull out the only two pieces of jewelry I have: a petite silver locket and a pair of tiny diamond studs. Black heels finish my ensemble; I turn to get the girls' rating.

Wynne says, "Wow, you look all grown up and stuff. Real classy."

"Nikki, unless you have any other words of encouragement for me, I'm going to get out of here."

"Nope. Just smile and look pretty. They'll never suspect a thing."

Wynne says, "Just remember what I said last night. Be nice to Captain Personality."

I grab my purse and shawl. "Bye, ladies. I'll see you in a few hours."

Quinn is waiting for me in the foyer. His suit is a step above those he usually wears into town. It's cut to accentuate his hulking frame. His deep blue silk shirt with a blue silk tie, just a shade darker, brings out his steel-gray eyes. I usually prefer his grungier look, but he's too good to resist tonight. He looks me up and down and smiles. "You ready to go?"

"Actually, I need to get the snoopers from Gordon."

As if on cue, Gordon comes bumbling up the stairs. Out of breath, he says, "Sorry, it took me a little longer than I was anticipating. Wow, you look nice." He eyes grow wide with fear; he looks at Quinn and says, "Sorry, Mr. Quinn."

Quinn smiles.

Gordon puts the snooper in my hand and I place it in a lipstick tube with a false bottom. Quinn takes my shawl and drapes it over my shoulders.

"Let's blow this popsicle stand."

The 'Cuda is waiting for us outside; Quinn rushes ahead of me and opens the car door. A small bouquet of yellow roses with purple salvia accents is waiting for me on the seat. A smile involuntarily comes to my face. I pick up the flowers, close my eyes and take a deep breath.

So that's what he was talking to Mrs. Contreras about.

I manage to get two words out: "Thank you."

Holy crap, if I would've known I was going to get Quince-charming tonight I might've suggested another date or two before he broke up with me.

He grins. "Careful with those. I have a date after this OP."

I elbow him in the ribs and get in the car. As we drive off to Magistrate's, I give the house and extra long look. I hope it isn't the last time I see it.

Chapter 7

Compliants Are Strange

We wind down the streets of town and I stare blankly out the car window. The euphoria of being on a real date is now gone and my stomach starts to knot as I contemplate the reality of our mission. It's a definite possibility that Magistrate could interrogate me and Quinn, then chip and wipe our brains. But then, if we didn't go meet him it would more than a possibility, he would definitely take us all. The memories of being interrogated in Danny's basement flood back; my heart starts to race and my leg starts to involuntarily shake.

Inner calm, Shea.

Quinn puts his hand on my knee and I stop the shaking. "We'll be fine. He's a sneaky son-of-a-bitch, and I guarantee he's going to have something up his sleeve. But we have the upper hand, because he clearly wants something from us."

We arrive at the front of Magistrate's campus and are greeted by two armed marshals. Quinn rolls down his window and one of them approaches.

"Knightly, what are you doing here?"

"We have a meeting with Mr. McReady."

The marshal closes his eyes for a brief second and the gate starts to open. "You know where to go, Knightly. Go anywhere else and you will be shot on sight."

Quinn nods and proceeds through the gates. He's been on the campus numerous times accompanying Boss to various meetings. This is my first time getting an inside glimpse. It's a stark contrast to what lies outside the gate. As a matter of fact, I have to fight hard to remind myself that the NCS lies mere yards away. As we roll along the quaint cobblestone path, we pass the main building on our left, where all the day-to-day bureaucracy takes place. It also houses the community centers for the few families that are stationed here in the NCS. Quinn turns and we find ourselves on a street lined with tall mature oaks. The red and orange leaves stand out against the bleakness of the twilight. Through the trees, are several small limestone bungalows belonging to the Marshals and their families stationed here. Aside from slightly different landscaping, each of the houses is identical. We go further down the road and, as if by magic, a palatial mansion appears. I've seen it many times from the road, but up close it's nothing short of astounding.

"Wow!"

"Yeah, wait until you see the inside."

We park in the cobblestone driveway. Two marshals greet us as we get out of the car. We walk by an elaborate fountain in the middle of the driveway, but I can't take my eyes off of the impressive mansion. Like the bungalows, the mansion also has limestone exterior. The two turrets on either side of the house make it look like a castle. Although this house looks like it was from our country's beginnings, it's nothing more than a new house made to look old. It's if they're telling us it's always been this way.

As Quinn and I step onto the covered porch, I unconsciously squeeze his arm to remind myself that he's there. Quinn pushes the doorbell and a pompous chime to the tune of Vivaldi's *Spring* plays. Quinn looks at me and rolls his eyes. Within seconds the heavy oak door inches open and a tall older gentleman in a suit appears, sporting a head full of silver hair. He regards us with disdain and waits a few seconds before addressing us.

"Mr. Knightly and Ms. Kelly, I presume. Please come in." Once in the foyer the old man says, "Please stand still."

The man taps his CAMS. A panel on the wall next to me opens and two thin black discs no more than half a meter in length appear. One stops in front of me and another in front of Quinn. A blue light emanates from the discs. I assume they are scanning us for weapons and possible contagions. After a few seconds the blue light is gone the discs fly back to their home.

"I will tell Mr. and Mrs. McReady you are here. Please wait." He turns away. The blinking light of the GovTek on his neck sends shivers down my spine.

I look over at Quinn. "Well, he's very friendly."

Quinn gives a halfhearted smile. I take this opportunity to gawk around the house without being judged. This house is several steps above our worn-out, drafty old mansion. Although everything is made to look as though it has old world charm, in reality everything is new and well maintained. The marble floors and white wood paneling throughout give the house a sterile feeling as if no one really lives here. To the left is a staircase leading up to a balcony that wraps around the second floor. To our right is a library stocked with books, which I'm sure have never been cracked open. Not when you could get the latest bestseller downloaded to your chip and viewed through a heads up display. Heck, most people don't even bother reading books anymore. Usually, they just have the audio book read to them through their internal coms. *Such a shame.*

My concentration is broken by the sound of Magistrate's voice. "Quinn, it's good to see you, as always. And Shea, is it?"

"Yes, sir."

He greets us both with a big smile like we're old fraternity brothers he hasn't seen in years.

"Pleased to meet you. Come in. Make yourselves at home."

He leads us to straight back to the living room and motions for us to sit on a couch and he sits in a wing-backed chair across from us.

"I'm sorry to hear that Robert is feeling under the weather. We could've postponed our meeting."

Quinn answers, "Mr. Jennings wants to clear up any mis-understandings as quickly as possible. He has authorized Ms. Kelly and me to make any decisions concerning this matter."

Magistrate smiles. "Excellent, excellent. Robert is nothing if not efficient."

A mellifluous voice breaks in our conversation. "Dennis, I can't believe you didn't tell me our guests have arrived."

Both Quinn and I turn to see a stunning woman wearing a black knee-length dress that is modestly cut, but still accentuates her trim figure. I know from studying up on her and Magistrate that they are both in their early fifties, but she doesn't look any older than forty. The glowing pattern on her dress gradually shifts from infinity to integral symbols. I'm sure she has no idea what these even are. Her hair is a brilliant ice-blue fashioned in an intricate plait. I imagine the pins holding her hairstyle in place are doubling as color modulators. Her CAMS is adorned with designs that change in time with her dress patterns.

"Quinn and Shea, this is my beautiful bride, Martina."

We both stand and shake her hand.

Noticing I'm looking at her fashion she says, "Isn't it simply divine? When I saw the latest designs by Fredrique I simple couldn't live without them. After wearing these I could never go back the dull frocks I used to wear." She gives me the once over then adds, "But what you have on is lovely, dear. It's very, uh, retro."

Suddenly, I don't feel very chic anymore. I shift uncomfortably in my heels. "Um, yeah thanks. That's the exact look I was going for."

Magistrate clears his throat. "Why don't we all go to the dining room? I believe dinner will be served soon."

As we follow Magistrate into a cozy dim-lit room off the living room Martina says, "I'm so glad to have someone else here besides Robert and Nikki. She's not very nice, you know, and Robert is dreadfully boring."

Each of us takes a seat at the table. One of Magistrate's servants comes in from a door that leads into the kitchen and pours us all glass of red wine. I nod my head to acknowledge the Non-Compliant man I see in town occasionally.

Magistrate lifts his glass. "Welcome, Shea and Quinn."

I take a polite sip. *Yuck, I hate wine.* I wish this jackass would just get it over with and tell us what he wants instead of putting us through this torture.

Martina takes another sip of her wine and looks at me and Quinn. "I've been following your story in the NCS Tabs, and it's very intriguing."

I knit my eyebrows. "Our story?"

Claire released a tabloid story about Quinn and I being an item on the NCS tabloids to explain why Quinn and I were spotted making out in the alcove of Danny's club. We were actually making out in an attempt to hide from Danny's thugs. When Claire released that story, that was the point I stopped reading any NCS Tabs.

Magistrate says, "You'll have to forgive my wife, she is obsessed with those rags."

"Dennis, I only subscribe to the reputable ones. Shea, your story is very romantic. You tried to save him from the clutches of those men, but you were captured and tortured. You didn't say one word to incriminate him."

Oh God, this can't possibly get any worse. Quinn eyes are the size of saucers. I just want to find a deep dark hole to climb in for a few years. I take a large drink of wine to take the edge off.

Martina looks at her CAMS and giggles, making several key strokes. She looks up at me. "That was one of my friends. I told her that you and Quinn would be visiting today. She wants to know if the story is true."

"Uh yeah, I guess my plan didn't work so well, 'cause we

got caught anyway." I give a nervous laugh and elbow Quinn in the ribs. "Right, honey? Good times."

I take another large drink. *Please, for the love of all that is good in the world, just make this woman shut up.*

She laughs. "No, silly, not *that* story. Is it true that you two are, you know, expecting?"

As the words leave her mouth, I choke on the wine I was about swallow, spilling it all over my dress. Quinn hands me his napkin and I try my best to clean my frock.

"Martina, that will be all. You're making our guests uncomfortable."

"Oh, I didn't mean to. Don't worry, sweetie, I'll keep it hush-hush. But you really shouldn't be drinking in your state." She looks back down at her CAMS and starts typing away, no doubt about my buffoonery, to all of her friends. "I think it's very sweet. You know, on our side you wouldn't be able to keep the baby without at least a twenty-year marriage contract, two parental licenses, and signed acknowledgement of the Morality Codes. They just passed that legislation last year."

"Really?"

"Yes, it is a lot of work. The marriage contract alone costs ten thousand credits and you need a year's worth of schooling for the parental licenses. Dennis and I never had the chance for children even before all the laws were enacted." She looks sad, as if she's missing something.

Dennis breaks in. "Yes, it is a lot of work, but it's the only way we can ensure that children go only to those who are truly deserving. Surely you've seen some children in some horrific conditions."

Truly deserving? Truly rich, more likely.

I take a breath, seizing this perfect opportunity to make my planned departure. "Um, I hate to break up the conversation, but can I use the restroom? I just need to . . . "

Martina looks up from her CAMS, then at me sympathetically. "Oh yes, how rude of me. Just go down the hall and it's the first door on your right."

I get up from the table, grab my purse and a napkin. "Thanks, I'll be right back."

Oh sweet merciful Jesus, that was the most painful exchange I've ever had to endure. *Me, pregnant?* And now poor Quinn is in there to fend for himself. Once in the powder room, the motion sensor lights come on. I scan the wall for a computer display. *God, I hope it's in here.* I look around, but see nothing useful. Then it hits me: under the picture. I lift the digital display showing various impressionist paintings.

I open my purse, taking out the lipstick along with the multi tool. It looks possible to get behind the computer display pretty quickly. As expected, it pries loose and a mass of wires and glowing LEDs spill out from the casing. Putting the tool in my mouth, and unscrewing the lipstick to reveal the device, I search for the wires needed, clamping our device over them. Done and done. As I put the display back on the wall, a loud knock breaks my concentration.

"Shea, are you all right in there?"

"Uh yeah, Mr. McReady. I had a double-supreme burrito for lunch that's not sitting so well with me."

Hope he bought that one.

Quickly and quietly I put the picture back on the wall then race over to the sink to clean off the wine. I make a couple of quick dabs. *That will have to be good enough.* I open the door and Magistrate is standing there with a stoic look on his face.

"Are you okay?"

"Um, yeah." I pat my stomach. "Not feeling quite right. You know."

"I see."

We walk back to the dining room.

Martina smiles. "I'm so sorry about that. I really need to remember to keep my big mouth shut. Your boyfriend and I were having a riveting conversation."

Quinn is emptying a glass of wine. Mercifully, the servant refills Quinn's glass. As I take my seat, the first course, consisting of a sparse salad, is set in front of us. More meaningless drivel spews forth from Martina's mouth. The second course is a tiny tofu cube, carrot shreds, and melba toast to follow. *Damn these Compliant and their Healthful Living Codes.* The 'dessert', a chocolate flavored gelatin cube, tops off the crappiness of the night.

Quinn dabs his mouth with his napkin and says, "I can truly say I've had nothing like it in the NCS."

Magistrate responds, "I'm glad you enjoyed it. Now, I'm afraid we are going to have to get down to business."

Hallelujah! I don't care if he's going to interrogate us. If I have to hear one more NCS Tab story from that woman's mouth I'm going to shut it for her.

"Quinn, you and I can go in the study and talk business while the ladies continue visiting in the living room."

NOOOOO!!!!

"With all due respect, Mr. McReady, Shea is my partner first and foremost. Whatever I hear, she hears."

Martina coos in the background, "Aww!"

YES! I'm going to have to make sure to thank Quinn properly for getting me out of that one.

"Very well then. Both of you, please follow me."

We follow him down the hall and up the stairs to a set of double doors. We all pass through the door into a nicely appointed office. Magistrate goes behind the wooden desk, and Quinn and I sit in two leather chairs across from him. Magistrate says, "Dim lights." The lights automatically dim. He says, "Show video." A 3D rendition of the video we saw in Boss's office appears out of thin air. Quinn and I watch without uttering a word. The video stops. Magistrate says, "Video off, lights on." Magistrate turns to us. "I'm going to give you one chance to explain."

I smile at Magistrate, "So, Dennis, don't quite have that thought control of the chip down yet, do ya?"

Magistrate gives me an icy stare and Quinn knits his eyebrows at me, and then looks away to stare down Magistrate with his steely eyes. "Sir, I have no idea who's in that video or what they were doing."

"Cut the bullshit, Knightly. We all know who's in the video. I have two families that are still holding out hope that we'll find their husbands and sons. Everyone in this room knows we will never find those men. Will we?"

Quinn says, "So if you know who's in this video why did you ask us here? Why not just take action now?"

I speak up to try and smooth over the situation. "Sir, I believe what Quinn means is how can we help you? You obviously wanted us here, to ask us something. I think we can work together to clear up any misunderstandings."

Quinn grunts.

Magistrate smiles. "Quinn, your girlfriend is quite the diplomat. I can see why you wanted her here. Yes, Shea, there's something that you and your team can help me with. I think we both have a common problem. The same problem who left those bodies at your doorstep. The problem who has left this community in more upheaval than Danny could have ever thought of. He's putting my career in jeopardy. If I ever want to get out of this shithole I need to get rid of Ramsey by any means possible. If we don't get rid of him, I will have no other choice than to prosecute those who I have caught in this video for the murder of two marshals. However, if someone was able to eliminate our mutual problem, then I may be able to straighten out this misunderstanding and make a shipment of the real flu vaccine available for distribution."

Quinn emits a low growl and starts to speak. I put my hand on his to stop him. "Sir, you are correct. We have a common problem and I believe we can work together to achieve our goals. The flu vaccine would be a boon to our community, and to Mr. Jennings' standing. However, my team is going to need some flexibility in order to get our work done. We can't have every marshal in the NCS breathing down our neck, like our little incident earlier this week. Especially Barton, tell him to lay off."

Magistrate lets out a heavy sigh. "Fine. I'll call off the troops and pass the word that no one is to bother you or your team. Anything else?"

Quinn gives me a shocked look. I give him a slight shrug of my shoulders. What was Magistrate going to do, say no?

"No, sir."

Magistrate slouches back in his chair and puts his hand to his forehead. "How about you, Knightly? Do you have any requests you'd like to make?"

"Yes, sir."

"Why am I not surprised? Let's hear it."

"Danny's attack has left the infrastructure at Boss's compound lacking. In order to be at our best, performance-wise, we'll need some supplies. Things we can't find on TradeNet."

"Fine, fine. Provide me with a list and I will see what I can do, but no firearms or weapons of any kind. Are you done?"

We nod our heads.

"Good. This is a limited time offer. If at any time I feel you are not holding up your end of the bargain, I will not hesitate to bring down your whole crew of merry thieves. Got it?"

We both answer, "Yes, sir."

"I'm glad we have an understanding. Now, get out of my sight."

We both get up to leave, but before we head out the door

Magistrate adds one last nugget. "I want a status report in a few days."

I get a slow sinking feeling like we've just sold our souls to the devil. There is no way out of this situation. I answer back, "Yes, sir."

"I trust you know how to make our communications discreet. I can't be seen with miscreants such as yourselves."

We nod and leave the room. Outside, the banged up 'Cuda is waiting for us. Once inside the old girl, I feel at home

At the exit of the compound we wait for the gate to open. Quinn edges out into the street, away from Magistrate.

Chapter 8

Layin' It on the Line

The further we get from Magistrate's, the easier it is for me to breathe. I know our problems are far from over, but being around all those people with blinking lights on their skin, hooked into a hive mind, gives me the creeps. I flip off my impossibly uncomfortable shoes and slip on pair of ballet slippers hiding in the glove compartment. Quinn loosens his tie, looks at me, and smiles.

"What?"

"You did good in there. I had no idea you had those kind of negotiating skills."

"Yeah, I can be a little stubborn at times."

"You? Stubborn?"

"What are you doing? The house is that way."

"I know, dumbass. Aren't you hungry? Or was that tofu and sorry excuse for a dessert enough to fill you up? Last time I looked, there wasn't much more than cheese and moldy bread in our fridge."

"Are you asking me out on a date, Mr. Knightly?"

"I told you I had a date after this OP. You wanna go or not?"

I guess it's break-up time; at least I get a free meal out of it.

"Absolutely. I'm so hungry I think my stomach's going to eat my back. I might as well get as much mileage as I can out of getting all fancy tonight."

He winds past the river and stops at a non-descript double-wide trailer with a simple sign hanging out front reading, Mohammad Chen-Lopez's Famous Shish Kabobs. No one's sure what Mo's shish kabobs consist of, but they're so good no one asks either. We step into the dark trailer, which is decked out in décor a belly dancer would be proud of. It's cramped and smoke-filled, just my kind of place. There's an open table; I grab it while Quinn goes to the counter and orders for us. All the eyes in the cramped trailer are on me. I used to be able to go anywhere in this town relatively unnoticed, but now, ever since those damn NCS Tab stories, I can't go two steps without someone trying to snap my picture. I thought for sure the Tabs would lose interest in me and Quinn after a few weeks, since we are the two most boring people in this Sector. It probably doesn't help that we look like two kids after prom at an all-night pancake house.

As I wait for Quinn I watch the news drivel piped in from the Compliant side. Oh goody, it's time for the Immigration Report. My stomach growls as I zone out to the before-and-after images of Non-Compliant folks who've decided to go to the other side. After getting a mini-makeover, a warm meal, and some credits to start their new lives, the newest Compliants are grinning ear to ear like a bunch of idiots. I sink into my seat, remembering the task I failed at last night. The last image flashes across the screen and my jaw drops in disbelief.

Quinn comes to the table holding a cafeteria tray stacked with several paper plates full of food and two red solo cups brimming with beer. Seeing the expression on my face he asks, "What's wrong with you?"

I shake my head. "Uh, The Immigration Report, I swear I saw Morgan."

A half smile appears on his face. "Hmm, maybe she reconsidered."

I narrow my eyes at him. "Quinn, you saw her last night. There was no way she was ever going to go over."

He doles out the food. "Well, maybe someone talked some sense into her."

"Did you . . . ?"

He scoops a fork-full of meat into his mouth and points at my plate. "You better eat while it's hot, Kelly."

I shake my head and sink my teeth in the steaming tender meat. This is so much better than that gelatinous cube of protein. "You have excellent taste, Mr. Knightly. But don't think you're getting out of this line of questioning so easily. I'll get my answers soon enough."

He grunts. "Wonderful."

For the first time I notice his poorly bandaged hand. I take his hand and inspect it. "You know, you're really shitty at patching yourself up. A bite wound has the potential to get pretty nasty if you don't clean it up properly. You want me to look at it when we get home?"

He smiles. "I might take you up on that one. You do a much better job of patching me up."

"You're damn right I do. I'll take a look at when we get home."

I take a big swig of my beer and the room starts to murmur. Several cameras flash, trying to capture an image of the delinquent mother-to-be.

"Remind me to kill Claire when we get home. She's crossed the line."

Quinn smiles. "She crossed the line along time ago. Whatever happened to 'it's all part of working for the firm'?"

"I draw the line at my womb."

"Good, it's about time you started sticking up for yourself."

"Well, one thing's certain."

"What's that?"

I pat my stomach. "I'm going to have to start holding my planks longer if people think they see a baby bump."

He reaches over and gently caresses my stomach. He puts his mouth painfully close to my ear and whispers, "I like you the way you are."

I sink into his shoulder and forget just for a second where we are. A bright flash from a camera reminds me, once again, that this isn't a real date. I push his hand from my stomach and sit up. "Stop it. You're giving people the wrong idea. Now, they're really going to think I'm pregnant."

He places several kisses down my neck and stops at my collarbone. If I was standing I would be weak in the knees. Strike that, I'd be on the floor in a puddle. Oh. God. Did someone replace Quinn while I wasn't looking? I look up at him breathless, mouth gapping open like a freakin' dork, not knowing what to say. Seeing my expression he gives me a cocky smile, which melts me even further, and returns to eating.

A camera flashes again and sort of brings me back to my senses. "Hey, isn't this the opposite of what we agreed would happen tonight? I thought you would be sending me packing by now."

"I didn't agree to anything."

"But, I thought you were dreading this. You were embarrassed to go out with me. Remember?"

"Where in the hell are you getting that I'm embarrassed to be with you?"

"From you. When Claire said this date would be good for our public image you said it was embarrassing. I thought if you ended it, then you wouldn't have to worry about being associated with me anymore."

"I meant it was embarrassing being exploited like this. It's hard enough getting to know someone even in the best of circumstances. But it's even harder . . . " He turns and rips a camera out of a Tab photographer's hands and crushes it. "When douchebags like this are constantly breathing down our necks."

"Yeah, right, nice save. I saw you laughing at me when you were reading the headline about us being together. I know being associated with me is like having bamboo shoved under your fingernails. It's okay. There's no reason to keep up the sham anymore."

He crosses his arms in front of him and is silent for a while. He speaks in a whisper, "I wasn't laughing at you. I was laughing at that joke of a headline. You deserve better than me."

"Yeah right, why would a guy like you be interested in a girl like me? Everyone's saying it, Quinn. I know better. It's fine if you see me as just a friend."

Quinn reaches over and caresses my face. "That fucker did a real number on you. You constantly sell yourself short. Why wouldn't I like you?"

"I'm not exactly material for a powerful crime lord's girl-friend. I'm short, pudgy, wear glasses and Chucks. I like to work on cars and computers. I read Popular Mechanics and comic books. I'm a dork, Quinn. Seriously, don't worry about being polite with me. It is what it is."

"First, don't call me a crime lord. Second, you are beautiful. You're fun and you don't have any bullshit pretenses. I like hanging out with you, even if you are a pain in the ass. I've been so caught up in day-to-day bullshit that I neglected us. I think we both have. I wish I could be alone with you more." Then he adds with a smile, "Plus, I hate seeing that assbag, Ryan, flirt with you."

"I told you, he's interested in Nikki."

"I still don't like it."

"Quinn, I . . . "

"Still not convinced, huh? Listen, I'm going to tell you this once. So you know I'm not acting for the cameras or Claire or whatever. Since coming here I've done things I'm not so proud of."

"We all have."

He rubs his face and continues, "Will you let me finish? On the other side, I tried hard to be a good man." He stops to collect his thoughts. "But when it was all taken from me I found myself in moral gray area. I'm not a good man now, Shea. I hate this fucking place and what it has made me. But when I'm with you, I forget for a little while that I'm living in this hellhole." I don't know what to say. I look at him in stunned silence. He smiles. "I'll mark this one in the history books. The woman with a smartass comment for everything is at a loss for words."

I can't help but return his smile. He brushes my hair out of my face and puts his hand behind my neck drawing me closer to him. I know everyone is watching us. I don't give a crap either. I'm so nervous I think I'm going sweat through my dress. Geez, I hope he can't tell. Our lips brush together, and then a commotion at the counter makes us look up. We see several Orphans shaking down Mo.

Yup, every time it gets good something interrupts us.

Quinn looks at me. "We'll continue this conversation later." We stand from our table.

"Hey, assholes! What do you think you're doing?" One of the kids turns in the direction of my voice while Quinn sneaks up behind the larger of the two.

The smaller punk smirks at me. "Shea Kelly, you made a big mistake coming here alone. We're going to have some fun with you." He barrels toward me. I stand still at my table waiting for him to reach me. The other thug is still at the counter unaware that Quinn is approaching. The smaller Orphan tackles me and throws me to the floor, but not before I'm able to grab the napkin dispenser from the table. I smash the dispenser into his skull. He falls off of me holding his bloody head.

The larger of the two yells, "You stupid bitch, you're going to pay for that."

Before he can run in my direction Quinn taps him on the shoulder. The thug looks in Quinn's direction and in two heart-beats Quinn jams the shish kabob skewer through the his eye. In two more heartbeats the large Orphan is on his knees screaming in pain.

Quinn kicks the thug in the side. "Tell Ramsey to back off. Tell him there's more where this came from. Now get the hell out of here."

Before the men can make it to their feet, the door to the restaurant bursts open. "Everyone put your hands in the air!"

I look over at Quinn and growl, "Marshals?!? What the crap, I just told that asshole Magistrate to have his boys lay off of us and here they are."

"Shut up, Kelly, and just put your hands in the air."

A familiar voice barks out, "Well, well, I saw you two maggots come in here. It figures there'd be trouble with you two around."

I look behind me to address the marshal. "Howdy, Ed. It's always a joy to see your bright and sunny face."

He grumbles, "We just got a rather interesting message from Magistrate to leave you and your merry band of idiots alone. I wonder why that can be?"

I respond, "Maybe he realizes that we're a bunch of swell people after all."

Ed smacks my face. Quinn starts after Ed, but is restrained by the other marshal. Ed smirks. He runs a finger down from my face to my chest. He lightly runs his finger up and down my cleavage. I'm frozen with fear. Quinn growls and struggles in the massive marshal's grip. "Quinn, you have a fine woman here. She doesn't know her place though. I think you're going to have to take some time tonight to knock her down a peg or two."

Quinn breaks free of the other marshal and starts for Ed. I yell, "Quinn, no! He's trying to get a rise out of you. Just ignore him. He knows if he does anything to us, Magistrate will have his ass."

Ed laughs. "I wouldn't touch a hair on your pretty little girlfriend's head. Magistrate gave an order and I wouldn't dream of ever disobeying it. I heard a commotion in here and thought I would see how I could help you two." He turns to the other marshal and looks down at Ramsey's thugs on the ground. "Gibson, take those two in for a personality reboot via chip."

The two thugs scream in protest. The massive marshal grabs them both by the backs of their shirts like they're nothing more than two sacks of flour.

Ed smiles and pats me on the cheek. "You have a nice day, sweetie." He looks over at Quinn. "Magistrate won't protect you forever, and I'll be there to see you burn for the crimes against our brothers, Knightly. Then I can have some real fun with your girlfriend."

I stare him down. "Whatever, limp dick."

He smacks me in the face again and looks at Quinn. "She just doesn't learn does she? Take her home and teach her where her place is tonight. It might just save her life."

Quinn's face grows red and he takes a deep breath. "Barton, if I ever see you lay a hand on her again I'll hit you so hard your kids will shit blood."

He laughs and follows the other marshal out the door. "As you were."

The occupants of the restaurant slowly get back to their normal activity. Sadly, marshals barging in on everyday activity isn't an unusual occurrence around here. Quinn caresses my face and kisses my forehead.

"You okay, babe?"

Babe? Hmm, I kinda like it.

"I'm fine, aside from the fact that I don't think I'll be able eat a shish kabob again without thinking about what you did to that guy."

"Ed is trouble. We need to watch out."

"Looks like date night is ruined. Let's get out of here. We need to see if our device is working."

Chapter 9

Distractions

We make the drive back to the compound in silence. Too bad, I was actually starting have fun on our date. I should've known it was going too well for something crappy not to happen. We pull into the garage and walk back to the house in the cool night air. I clutch my flowers like a trophy. Quinn has his arm around my waist and a cigar hanging out of his mouth.

My God, he's hot.

This has been the best date I've had in a long time, and once we walk over that threshold it will be back to business as usual. I'm not ready for it to end. Before I'm able to open the front door, Quinn takes my hand and turns me toward him.

"Hey, I had a good time."

I smile. "I'm accused of being pregnant, we made a deal with the devil, you skewered an eyeball and Ed threatened us within inches of our lives. You had a good time?"

"Yup."

He blows a puff of smoke in the air and puts his cigar down in the empty planter to the side of us.

"Yeah, me too. It was the most fun I've had in a long time." I put the flowers to my nose. "Thanks again for the flowers."

"No problem. I knew you were too cheap to get them for yourself."

I start toward the door, but he wraps his arms around my waist and pulls me close. He puts his lips to mine. My stomach turns on end and electricity runs through my body. I run my hand through his hair, bringing him closer. My head is spinning and now my knees are really weak. I thought the kiss in the alcove at Danny's was great, but it turns out Quinn was holding out on me. I'm sure Wynne and Nikki are snooping on us now, but who cares. I lose myself in his perfect kiss. He stops, looks down at me, and smiles.

"We'll do it again sometime, promise. Let's go down and see if the nerd herd can get the snoopers turned on." He places a few kisses behind my ear. "Then maybe you can come to my room and fix my hand?"

I breathe out, "'Kay."

Sigh, back to reality.

All the lights are off and the house is totally quiet. I look at my watch. Around this time the gang's in the entertainment room or the kitchen. This is highly unusual.

I whisper, "Quinn, do you think . . . ?"

He grabs my shoulder and puts a finger to his mouth before I go all the way into the house. Quinn walks over to the planter on the porch, presses the middle, and a tray with two pistols is displayed. We each take one; he signals for me to search the upper level while he takes the main level. I place my flowers on the planter and kick off my shoes, then proceed up the stairs. The first door I come to once upstairs is Nikki's. I hold my breath and listen before opening the door. I count to three then open the door. It's completely dark, but I don't see anyone. I flip on the light. The room is completely empty.

Next stop is mine and Wynne's bedroom. A note is taped to the door. I take another deep breath and read:

Dear Shea,

We all decided to go to Frank's to give you two a little 'alone time'. Boss and Claire are in their annex. Don't do anything I wouldn't do. Don't wait up for us. Be nice to Captain Personality. Have fun.

Wynnie

I'm going to kill her when she gets home.

I go over to the balcony that overlooks the main floor and yell down, "Hey, Quinn, It's cool they all went to Frank's to get a drink."

A growl echoes through the halls in response.

"Give me a minute to get something more comfy on and I'll try getting the snoopers to work."

"I'll meet you in my room in ten minutes."

The comfort of my cruddy clothes awaits me. Dressing in binding, pinching, scratchy clothes is not my thing. First thing off, the evil control-top panty hose. I take off my jewels and put them back in their box. Now to get this dress off; I pull on the zipper and it won't budge. *Damn this old dress.* I make another attempt using a coat hanger to give me more leverage. Nothing. I can't believe the only thing that stands between me and my elastic waistband pants is this stupid zipper. I take a breath and try it again. I will not be bested by a zipper. Nothing. What am I going to do?

I swallow my pride and go across the hall to Quinn's room, and knock on the door.

He greets me wearing a t-shirt and shorts with a cigar in his mouth. "I thought you were getting something more comfortable on."

"Well I was, but I guess my dress had other ideas." I turn my back to him and point to the zipper. "Would you mind?"

He makes several tugs at it. "It's really stuck."

"I know. That's what I was trying to tell you."

He makes one last tug and the zipper comes loose and stops just short of my butt. *Oh God, how embarrassing.* I turn around and Quinn has a smile plastered across his face.

I quickly wrap my arms around my middle to keep my dress from falling down. "Um, thanks. I'll be back in a sec."

I run to my room feeling like a total dork. My trusty long

sweat shorts and t-shirt are waiting for me on my bed. I take my contacts out, and put my glasses on; for tonight I decide to forgo my usual ponytail and just let my hair down. Yup, I'm totally man repellent now. Somehow, this makes me feel safe going back to Quinn. I go over to his room, not bothering to knock this time. He's reclined on his bed sipping a scotch.

"You look much more comfortable now."

Comfortable = man repellant.

I plop myself in front of his computer and start typing away. "You don't mind do you?"

He gets up from his bed and stands behind me. "What are you doing?"

"I know Wynne and Gordon aren't here, but I'm pretty sure I can handle turning on the snooper. If we're lucky, I might be able to see some interesting data packets. Don't hold your breath though." I make several more keystrokes and rub my head. "Okay, I got it turned on, but I'm not seeing anything. Damn it!" I put my head in my hands for a quick breather then pop up and start typing again. "I need to get this done. I have a call with Dad in an hour and a half, and that friggin' wine is giving me the worst headache ever. This is why I never drink wine."

To my surprise, he grabs my hand and pulls me up from my chair. He puts his arms around my waist and draws me close. "I thought you were going to patch up my hand."

I grab his hand and look at the crappy patching job. "You're right. You can't be trusted to do anything like this right. C'mon, I'll get you patched up."

I take his hand and lead him to the bathroom. His bathroom is small and austere, just a shower, toilet, and small sink.

I point to the toilet with my head. "Sit over there."

"Yes, ma'am"

I root through his medicine cabinet and find the items I

need. I take off his old bandage. His wound is already looking red and puffy.

"See, this is what I'm talking about. You need to clean this out properly. Did you know a human bite has more germs in it than a dog bite?"

"You are fount of knowledge."

I proceed to scrub his hand. He winces.

"Sorry, but it's important we get this cleaned out. So, are you going to tell me why Morgan decided to change her mind about becoming Compliant?"

He smiles. "Why would you think I would know anything about that?"

I keep scrubbing his wound. "Gee, I don't know, because you're the only one that knew anything about my plan to get Morgan out of the Sector."

His other hand wanders to my leg and rubs. I nearly let go of the washrag cleaning his wound. "Shea, I could never let you live with the guilt of Morgan being tortured and killed. I went back to town after you went to bed. She was passed out on a sidewalk. I carried her to the compound and told the guard if he didn't take her I'd make sure everyone knew Magistrate was responsible for her death."

I stop scrubbing. I've never been so touched by anyone before. "Oh, Quinn." I don't know what else to say.

He looks down at his hand. Water is getting everywhere. "Hey, you're slacking on your duties. I need my hand patched up, remember."

I blink away the tears forming in my eyes. "Oh yeah, sorry."

I quickly slather his wound in ointment then patch it up way better than his crappy job.

"Here, ya go. Good as new. Well not yet, but it will be."

He continues to rub my leg. "So you wanna come sit on the bed with me?"

I raise one eyebrow. "Sit on bed with you, huh?"

He smiles. "Yeah. We can watch a Kung-Fu movie or something. You said it yourself, Wynne and Gordon can take care of the snooper later. We need a break."

"Or something?"

"If you're lucky."

We go out to his bedroom and sit on the bed. He puts his arm around me and clicks through a couple options. He finally settles on an old zombie movie. I look up at him and say, "Wow, I can't believe *you* of all people have suggested taking a break."

"Hey, even us mega-pricks need to relax at some point. We've had a hell of a week. *You* need to relax. You're running yourself into the ground."

As we watch the movie I sink into his shoulder and he plays with my hair.

"You should wear your hair like this more often. It looks nice."

"What? Frizzy and unruly."

As he kisses the top of my head he says, "Shut up. It looks nice."

The stress of the day is leaving me. Things have taken a turn for the extremely weird. I expected by this time I would've been on an awkward date, 'broken up' with Quinn, and been alone in my room sorting socks. Just to reassure myself that everything is really going as well as I think, I ask, "So, were you being straight with me at Mo's?"

He scoots away from me so I can see his face. "I wouldn't lie about something like that, and you shouldn't tolerate anyone who would lie about something like that. You shouldn't settle for being anyone's fake girlfriend either." He kisses me couple of times on my lips. "As a wise woman once told me, we don't need to figure anything out now. We'll just leave it at I like being with you and you like being with me."

"I know we screw around a lot. But, I'm saying this with absolute sincerity: thank you for getting Morgan out of here. I don't think you will ever know what that means to me."

I get up on my knees and kiss on his cheek. Then sit back down and put my head on his shoulder. He puts his arm back around me.

"It weren't nothing. So, what do you and your dad have on tap for tonight?"

"I'm not sure. It's been a while since we last talked. I'm looking forward to seeing his grouchy face. I'm hoping he has some information on the vaccine for us. Maybe Danny did steal a bad batch of the vaccine and that's all there is to it."

"Is that what your gut tells you?"

"No. I just know there's something more to it. If I was a betting woman I'd say he spiked it with something. But if we can't prove it . . . "

He stares through me with those steely grey eyes. "If you think there's something else going on then there is something else going on. Have more confidence in yourself and trust your instincts."

"Thanks. I just need to find some kind of angle. I haven't been spending enough time on it. There's so much to do. I feel like I'm running at top speed all day long, but I never get anything accomplished. I go back and forth from dealing with Ramsey, trying to get this place back up and running, normal everyday TradeNet stuff, and helping Boss with his condition . . . " I trail off.

Damn my big mouth.

"So how, exactly, are you helping Boss with his condition?"

"I guess you were going to find out one way or another. He asked Wynne and me to investigate the chip. I think he wants us to see if there's a way to reverse the effects of chip fatigue. That's what we've been doing in the lab. Are you pissed?"

"So that's what he did with that chip."

"You know he has a chip?"

"I took him to get it, remember? I just didn't know what he did with it. Do you think it's possible to reverse the effects?"

I feel as if a ten ton weight has been lifted off my shoulders. "Honestly, all the research I've done says it isn't. The chip basically makes your nervous system work too hard controlling all those peripherals. The human brain isn't meant to control heads up displays and communications. That bastard, Thomas Eldridge, lied to the people when he said the outside mounted chips overcame the chip fatigue problem. It just took a little longer for the problems to surface. I predict in another two years we're going to be seeing a lot of people with the same problem as Boss. The sad thing is that it's going to be a lot of kids too. I haven't done research on them. Obviously, there isn't enough data on that subject, but I suspect there are going to be a lot of developmental problems with kids in this generation." The look on Quinn's face makes me stop. I realize I have just laid a lot of information on him at once. I caress his face. "You okay? You look like you've been just hit by lightning."

"Shea, I spent the last part of my Marine Corps career trying to prove exactly what you're saying, but very few people believed me. So now, here's this beautiful woman on my bed telling me everything I looked like an idiot for saying for the past ten years is true. As you can imagine, I might be a little out of sorts. Can you prove any of this?"

"Aww, you think I'm beautiful?"

Quinn shakes his head. "Yes, of course. Now focus. Can you prove everything that you just said?"

I sigh. "No. They took all my research before I was able to prove it. So Wynne and I came over to the NCS to retrace our steps and prove once and for all that Thomas Eldridge is an egomaniacal bastard hell bent on controlling everyone's mind no matter the cost. But we got a little sidetracked. We didn't have enough money to keep up our research. Wynne became a stripper and I became a bartender just to keep our heads above water. Another reason I suck. I can't even complete the task I came over here to do."

His hand wanders to my knee as he speaks. I'm having a hard time concentrating on anything he says with his hands on me. "You do not suck. You're running six ways to Sunday and I think you're doing a good job, considering everything."

I smile.

"Don't let it go your head. Listen, we'll try to figure out how to get you more help so you and Wynne can concentrate on the chip more. I'll take Conner or Lindsey into town with me more or something."

I fake a pout. "So does this mean I'm not your partner anymore?"

"Shut up."

"You know, Boss is a pretty sneaky guy. Teaming us up and not telling us what the other was up to."

His hand slowly slides up from my knee and stops mid thigh. *Concentrate, Shea. Concentrate.* "He's pretty smart. He knew eventually we would figure it out for ourselves. So when we were in Magistrate's office, what did you mean about him not having thought control of the chip yet?"

"Well, some people take to controlling the chip with their brain better than others. When you were in the Marine Corps they pre-screened everyone before they implanted them with the chip to ensure that they were a good candidate, so you probably didn't see these issues much. Since they don't screen normal people before they implant the chip, they had to make some kind of helper, so then the CAMS was introduced. If people can't get answering a call or opening a file with a thought, they can always rely on their CAMS to do the interface for them, either verbally or by touch."

"Ah, here I thought those things were just to see images on."

"Well they are, but they are also helpers. It takes a lot of concentration to correctly get your thoughts relayed to the chip. You can't be thinking about how you want to get lucky with your girlfriend while you're trying to think your apartment door to unlock." He gives me a sly smile at that comment, and his hand slips higher up my leg. I catch my breath and continue the best I can. "The chip can only understand simple commands, and has a hard time filtering residual thoughts. I don't know a lot about CAMS, because I didn't work on it."

"It sounds like your interest in the chip was more than just a hobby. Did you study it in school? Did you work with it formally? How did you get all this data you were talking about? Just a normal engineer wouldn't have expertise with the chip or access to the data you were talking about. What about . . . "

I'm not ready to answer all his questions just yet. He knows far more than I'm normally comfortable letting anyone know about me. Besides, his hands are driving me crazy. I take my only recourse and put my hand gently behind his neck, pull him close to me and put my mouth to his. He pulls me closer and returns the intensity of my kisses. He stops momentarily to say, "I guess this means you didn't want to answer my questions."

"Listen, Knightly, I'll take you into the lab any time you want and show you everything I know. But for now, shut the hell up." I push him down on the bed so he's lying on his back, and I climb onto him, pinning his hands over his head. I kiss his neck and a low growl emerges from him. This only serves to stoke my fire even more.

"Yes, ma'am. Whatever you want."

I give him a wicked smile. In two breaths he is on top of me, pinning my hands over my head. He lets go of my hands and the weight of his body sinks into me. He lightly traces my face with his fingers and smiles down at me. My legs seem to automatically wrap around him. I bury my face in his neck so I'm closer to that hypnotic scent of soap mixed with cigar. I want nothing more at this point in time than to be as close as possible to this man.

He runs a line of kisses from my ear to my jaw, eventually landing his lips on mine. I work my hands up his shirt. The feeling of his warm skin against mine is drawing me deeper into a trance. When I free him from the confines of his shirt, a well-toned body is displayed with an added bonus of several badass tattoos. Hmm, maybe Quinn isn't the stuffy corporate type I pegged him for. He smiles at me while I run my hands over his body inspecting some of his tattoos.

He nuzzles my ear and works his hands up my shirt. "I do believe you're wearing too many clothes."

"Mmm, you should probably do something about that."

He responds by slowly working my shirt off. His smile fades when he sees the scars of my past. His fingers glide across my belly inspecting the raised marks. They healed years ago, but there's still pain. "My God, Shea. What the hell did that guy do to you?"

Damn it! Where's my shirt? I'm such an idiot; no one wants to see this. This was a bad idea.

I frantically look for my shirt, but it's nowhere to be found. My arms fold over my marks. I try to slow my breathing and keep the tears at bay. God, I'm so stupid. "Uh, maybe this was a bad idea. I look horrible. I'm sorry."

He kisses me and brushes the hair from my face. "Calm down, okay? Don't apologize. You didn't do anything. I don't think you look horrible, far from it. We'll do whatever you want, hon. If you ask me, you've given enough of your time to that asshole." For the first time in years, I feel like I might be okay. I'm tired of feeling ashamed and scared. I smile and pounce on the unsuspecting Quinn. Unfortunately, he is so near the edge of the bed that I cause us to tumble to the ground. I laugh until tears stream from my eyes. Quinn laughs. "Smooth move, Ex-Lax."

"Shut up." I lean in to pick up where we left off.

His hands rub my lower back instantly relaxing me. Slowly, they work up to the middle of my back. Simultaneously, my bra comes loose and a chime emanates from my wrist.

Damn it! Damn all these interruptions to hell.

"You got an alarm on that thing or what?"

I look at my watch and let out a long dramatic sigh. "No, it's time to call Dad."

"I suppose you're going to tell me that you never miss a call to your dad."

He's right. I've never missed a call to Dad. Ever. If I missed this call, Dad would be here checking on me. Once he found out I was all right, he'd kick my ass for not making the call, then he'd kick Quinn's ass for making me miss the call. "I can cut the call short, but if I don't show . . . "

He places several soft kisses on my lips and I roll off of him. "I understand. You need to go." He sits up and kisses my ear then whispers, "Don't take too long though."

I hook my bra and find my shirt to keep myself from succumbing to this bad man. "You should come with me. He might have some important news you need to hear."

"That's okay. Your dad hates me. It's probably better if I stay here."

"True, he does hate you."

Quinn looks shocked. "Thanks."

"I don't believe in sugar-coating things. He does hate you. Those NCS Tabs make you look like a womanizing bastard who's banging his daughter and the rest of the female population of the NCS." Then a thought flashes through my mind and my stomach drops. "Oh, crap."

"What?"

"Do you think Dad reads the Tabs?"

"Hell if I know. Why?" I can see the blocks tumbling into place in Quinn's mind too. "Shit."

"Yeah, if he thinks he's going to be grandpa and we haven't even said anything to him, he's going to be pissed. A lot. You need to go in there and explain things with me."

Quinn pauses. "Fine, but you're going to owe me big."

"I'm sure I can think of a way to repay you."

He puts his shirt on and I try my best to straighten my hair. We go into my room and I make the connections to the tablet and wait.

"Hmm. That's weird usually he picks up by now."

"Are you sure the call was today?"

"Yes, I'm sure. I always put reminders in my watch in case I get carried away with something."

Quinn gives me a sneaky smile.

"You know what I mean." I make a couple of keystrokes. Still nothing on the other end. "Quinn, he NEVER misses a call."

"Just give it a bit."

We wait for another ten minutes as I pace.

"Something's wrong."

"Calm down. Let's think about this before you get worked up." Just as I'm about to retort, an image starts to form on the screen. It looks like I was worried for nothing. I see a familiar, grizzled old Marine on the screen. I involuntarily smile at the image of my dad.

"Hey, Da—"

The image starts to speak before I'm able to get the words out of my mouth. "Punkin, if you are receiving this message it means that something has gone wrong. I have hidden all the files. We found something. I need to go. I love you, baby."

The image is gone.

TWO

Chapter 10

A Plan for Dad

The chatter in the conference room buzzes in my ears. I'm barely aware of what is being said. Quinn texted the gang and told them to come home right away. All the bodies in this small area are making the room hot and humid. I'm sitting balled up in one of the chairs resting my aching head between my legs. The walls are closing in on me; I need to get out of here and do something. Sensing my discomfort Quinn comes over, crouches down to my level, and puts his hand on my back. "You okay, hon?"

"No, I'm not. We're in here bumbling around like the fucking Keystone Cops and my dad is God knows where. I need to get out of here. I need to do something."

"I'll take care of this." He stands and bellows, "Everyone shut up and sit down."

The room goes from buzzing to quiet in a matter of seconds. Just as the room quiets, Boss walks through the corridor of the conference room leaning as much on Claire as he is on his cane. His degenerative state takes everyone by surprise. He sits at the head of the table, and everyone turns their attention his way.

Boss clears his throat. "Mr. Knightly, would you please apprise everyone of the situation."

Quinn tells the crew about the deal we made with Magistrate and our encounter with the marshals and Ramsey's crew. He then adds the last detail about my dad. The room is silent.

Everyone's eyes are fixed on Boss as he takes his glasses off and cleans them. He addresses the room, "Thank you, Mr. Knightly. We need to concentrate equally on both of these issues. Mr. Kelly has information that is vital to our team. We need to ensure that it doesn't fall into the wrong hands. Does anyone have any solutions?"

Wynne's voice breaks the silence. "Since Shea's dad had the old style chip, that means that he has a tracker implanted in him. Gordon and I can try tracking him down if you have some basic information about his chip."

I swallow against the hard lump in my throat. "Thanks, Wynnie."

Boss says, "Thank you, Ms. Myers. Does anyone else have any solutions?"

Quinn speaks, "Sir, I think have some ideas for taking Ramsey down. However, we're going to need reinforcements to pull it off."

Boss nods. "I'll see what I can do, Mr. Knightly. Crew, we need to get our compound up and running sooner than we had planned. We can take Mr. McReady up on his offer to get supplies. However, we are going to need supplies that he isn't willing to get for us. Ms. Myers and Mr. Timmons, are you up to the task of getting us these items?"

Wynne answers, "Yes, sir. Nikki will help too."

Boss nods.

Quinn speaks up, "Listen, everyone. Once we formulate the plan it's going to be important that we stick to it. Ramsey is going to be doing his best to prod us into acting before we're ready. We need to wait until we have all our resources together before we act. If we're hasty, we could ruin the whole thing. We have one shot to make this work." Everyone in the room nods their agreement. Quinn turns his attention to me. "Shea, it's clear someone has their sights set on you and your dad. I think it's a safe bet that someone is Ramsey. I want you to minimize your time in town, and I don't want you ever going there by yourself."

Quinn means well, but his words make me feel like a

grounded teenager, and not a woman capable of taking care of herself. I glare at Quinn and cross my arms. He knows I'm not happy with him. I decide to hold my tongue and chew him out later, instead of in front of everyone.

"Mr. Knightly, I couldn't agree with you more. Everyone, you have your assignments. It's getting late. Let's get some sleep so we are fresh tomorrow morning."

Everyone files out of the room except for me, Boss, Claire, and Quinn. Once the doorway is free of people, Boss slowly gets out of his chair and Claire helps him to his cane.

I speak up. "Um, Claire before you leave, can I ask you something?"

"Yes, dear, what is it?"

"Why did you release a story to the Tabs that I'm pregnant?"

Boss looks at Claire wide-eyed. "Claire, tell me you didn't release a story like that?"

"Of course not. One of the locals snapped a picture of Shea and Quinn on the way out of Mr. Ito's. She looked a little . . . frumpy and the story just took off from there."

All the events of the night are making my short fuse even shorter. Claire has always been nice to me, so I try hard to not lose my temper with her. "I can see you haven't done much to counter those stories though."

"Once the story broke, our community started seeing you and Quinn as more likeable entities. The only appearances you two made in town together were to do business. Robert's credibility was threatened by your lack of willingness to show any affection to each other in public. So when that story broke I did nothing to discredit it."

Quinn growls.

"Claire, I think you'll find this evening provided the town with more than enough fodder. Can you please put out a statement that we are not expecting?"

Claire and I engage in a staring match.

Boss speaks up. "Claire will be happy to put out a press release to set the story straight."

"Thank you."

Boss and Claire exit the room and Quinn starts to follow behind them. I grab his hand to keep him from leaving the room. "Not so fast. What's up with telling me, in front of the whole crew, that I can't go into town? I'm not a kid. I can take care of myself."

"Not with Ramsey you can't. You have no idea what he's capable of. He has his sights set on you. He won't stop until he has you."

I put my hands on my hips. "You called me out in front of everyone and made me look like an idiot. Now everyone thinks you don't trust me to take care of myself. We're supposed to be partners. Is it going to be like this between us from now on?"

"What? No. I'm just saying Ramsey is evil. You can't handle him alone. You need to be careful."

I know the events of the last couple of hours are wearing away at my nerves, and I also know I have a tendency to give Quinn and harder time than necessary. Sometimes. I bite my lip and push by him to keep myself from saying anything I'll regret. "Quinn, I'm done with you. I need to be away from you now."

As I head across the hall to the computer lab, Quinn shouts, "Kelly, I know how you are! *Do not* go into town just to spite me."

I wave my hand in acknowledgement as I slam the door of the lab behind me. I close my eyes and lean my head on the back of the door.

"Hey, what's up?"

"Hey, Wynnie!" Gordo and Nikki are also hacking away at their consoles. "I thought you guys were heading off to bed."

"Not when Dad has gone missing. I'll type my fingers into

bloody stumps before I give up on finding him."

"Thanks, guys!"

Without looking away from her display, Nikki asks, "So what was that shouting match about out there?"

"Can you believe the nerve of that guy? Calling me out like a little kid in front of everyone. Telling me what I can and can't do."

Nikki smiles. "He's just looking out for you. You've seen the depths that Ramsey can sink. If he has his sights set on you, I guarantee it will be worse than your encounter with Burt if he gets his hands on you. Burt was an amateur. Ramsey is not. Don't you think Quinn thinks about that? Why don't you?"

I plop myself down on a comfy leather chair. "You're right, but he didn't have to call me out in front of everyone."

"You know as well as I do that Quinn's strong suit isn't diplomacy. You need to stop being so sensitive."

I sigh. "I'm not thinking straight with everything going on. Speaking of which, do you guys have a plan?"

Gordon makes a couple of keystrokes and a map of the United States is displayed on a large wall-mounted screen. "Like Wynne said in the conference room, if you give us some information about your dad's chip we may be able to spike some of the coms between it and the global satellites. Then we will be able to get a location on him."

"Okay. Dad didn't tell much about his career in the Marine Corps, but we can try to piece together what we can. Dad first joined the Marine Corps about forty years ago. I think that wasn't long after they made the tracking chips mandatory for service members."

Sounds of keys clacking fill the air then several pictures of chips are displayed on the other mounted display. Then Wynne asks, "So where did he go to boot camp? East or West Coast?"

"Um, East, I think."

More clacking sounds. "Okay, we can eliminate these three chips because they were exclusively handed out on the West Coast. That leaves us with three candidates. Do you know the time of year he joined? If you could give a season and year that would help a lot."

"Geez, I don't know. Dad didn't talk about that stuff a lot."

"Hon, I know. Just try to think of some story he told you about joining that might help."

I close my eyes and slump in my seat. I brush away a tear. Then one of Dad's stories comes to me out of the recesses of my brain. "Dad said that he didn't join the Marine Corps right out of high school like a lot of other kids. He actually worked the farm with his dad for a while, but times were getting tight and the war was escalating. Dad decided to join up with the service while his dad got the farm back in financial order. He said it was right when he turned twenty-one. His birthday is in December so that would mean he joined forty years ago this December."

"Great, that actually helps a lot. That leaves this model right here." A picture of one chip is left on the display. "Gordo, you're going to need to hack into the chip registry."

Gordon's eyes grow wide. "Are you sure about that? The National Chip Registry isn't like hacking into TradeNet."

Wynne answers back, "I know. But the only way we're going to be able to ping his chip is to get into the registry. Dad Kelly is smart enough to keep a low profile, so I doubt we'll find a trace of him on the Internet. The Registry is the only way. If anyone can do it, you can. I'll be right with you every step of the way."

Gordon shakes his head and turns to the keyboard. "If you say so, Wynne."

Wynne turns to me and Nikki. "There's something else that has been bothering me. Quinn mentioned something about your dad hiding some files. I bet you a million dollars he wasn't talking about hiding pieces of paper in a physical location. I know he hid something out in cyberspace for us to find. I think you need to work on finding these files before someone else does."

I smile at her and turn to the workstation closest to me. "I'm on it!"

"I think this would be a great opportunity for you to learn more about Magistrate. Shea, did you turn on the snoopers yet?"

"I did manage to turn them on, but I couldn't see any packets yet."

"That's fine. Sometimes it takes a bit. Nikki, see if you can see any information coming through, then we'll go from there."

"Roger!"

I'm so proud of Wynne. In the span of a few short months she has gone from being a stripper in shitty bar to a confident leader.

As our work progresses, the cans of stim drinks and snacks pile up exponentially over the work area. The poorly ventilated room is starting to fill with the stench of body odor and junk food. There are no windows in our lab so it's hard to tell how much time has passed. Gordon's head is slumped over on his keyboard, Nikki is empting her fifth stim drink, and Wynne is putting eye-drops in her eyes. Yet, we aren't any closer to our goals.

"Hey, guys!" Gordon wakes from his nap, and Nikki and Wynne turn to face me. "We need to get some sleep. We aren't doing Dad any favors by not being at our best. Plus, we all need showers."

They laugh.

Wynne responds, "You're right. Everyone take a break, we'll meet back here in a few hours."

Nikki and Gordon stretch, get up from their seats and file out of the room. I stay back to help Wynne shut down the lab.

"How ya doin'?"

The extreme sleep deprivation and all the emotions of the

night finally catch up with me. I crumple in my chair and the tears spill down my face. "Oh, Wynne I have a really bad feeling about this. I don't think I'll ever see Dad again. I feel so guilty. Here I was making out with Quinn when Dad needed me. I'm just . . . *sick* about this."

Wynne stares at me with her mouth wide open, and then attacks me with a big hug. "You were making out with Quinn? I'm so proud."

I struggle away from her. "You're missing my point. I got lazy and look what happened. No more. I need focus more on business, and work harder."

"That's the stupidest thing I've ever heard. First, I seriously doubt your dad was being abducted at the same exact moment that you and Quinn were making out. Even if he was, there wasn't anything you could've done about it. Would you feel better if, instead of making out, you were scrubbing the bathroom with a toothbrush? It's fine that you were doing something that made you happy. We'll find your dad. Hey, you have me on the case. What could go wrong?"

"I told Quinn about me and the chip."

Her eyes grow wide. "How'd he take it?"

"He was actually pretty excited. It turns out he knows about chip fatigue too. He spent years trying to expose the truth about the chips when he was in the Marine Corps. I think he might have gotten blackballed or something. He kept asking me a bunch of technical questions about the chip. I didn't want to get into answering everything, so I jumped him."

"That's my girl." She puts her hand on my shoulder. "I'll shut down the lab. You need to get to bed. "

"Thanks again, Wynne, for everything."

I trudge my way up the stairs. A light from the kitchen catches my eye. Quinn is sitting at the kitchen table with his head in his hands. I walk over; the table is scattered with drawings of

Ramsey's compound, notes, and Quinn seems to be sleeping. I put my hand on his shoulder and whisper in his ear, "You should really go to bed."

He jumps up and looks as if he has no clue where he is. He takes off his reading glasses and glares at me. "Don't sneak up on me like that."

"I wasn't trying to sneak up on you. I just thought you might be more comfortable in your bed."

He grunts. "I have too much to do here. I need to come up with a plan so we can start getting the supplies we need. It's going to be hard. Traditional weapons are going to take too long to procure."

I sit next to him. "Well, maybe you need to think about things that would slip in past the radar."

Quinn rubs his face and puts his hands in his head. "I know, I can't really think straight now."

"Duh. Maybe, because you're tired?"

"What are *you* doing up so late?"

"We were trying to see if we could find dad and maybe some of the files he hid. We didn't get very far."

I look out the window. The sky is starting to turn a light shade of pink. "I think we need a little break. You wanna go out and watch the sunrise with me?"

"Aren't you still pissed at me?"

"Yeah, but I'm too tired to bitch at you right now. Are you coming outside with me or what?"

"Let's go."

The crisp air is invigorating. The sky is starting to turn shades of pink and blue, but it's still dark enough to see some stars. I take his hand and lead him to an oversized outdoor couch. We sit and I put my head on his shoulder and he puts his arm around me. "You know, I never get tired of watching the stars. I always wanted to be an astronomer or something like that, but that didn't really work out."

"Why didn't it work out? You're smart enough. You could've done it."

"Things like that are for people who come from money. My dad was a poor farmer and the government was good enough to pay my way through college. But I had to major in a job field that had a big growth prediction, low numbers of potential hires, and something I got high aptitude scores on. Electrical or biomedical engineering were my only choices. Not that I'm not complaining, that's just the way it was."

"So what did you choose?"

"Both for a couple of years, but then I found my true love was electrical. Also, the money was better. The only goal I had was to make enough money to buy the farm so Dad didn't have worry about that bullshit anymore. I still send what money I can back to him, or I did anyway. I had this stupid idea I would come here for a couple years, make some money on the black market, and in my spare time bring down GlobalThink. Then I'd go back home, marry a cute farm-boy, have a couple kids, and run the farm with Dad. Pretty stupid, huh?"

He kisses my head and pulls me closer. "Actually, it sounds pretty great."

I nestle in closer and my eyelids start to feel like they're made of lead. Quinn's breathing is getting slower, which relaxes me even further. My eyes blink and I don't try to keep them open.

Chapter 11

Sabotage

"So you gonna sleep all day?"

I slowly open my eyes and shiver against the cold morning air. It takes me a second to remember why I'm sleeping out on the patio furniture.

"Geez, how long have we been out here?"

"Not too long." Quinn squirms a bit. "Um, would you mind moving up. My arm fell asleep. I need to move it around."

We both writhe awkwardly until we come to a mutually agreeable sitting position. His arm around my shoulders pulls me close. Everything that happened last night feels like a dream. Did Quinn and I really make out? Is my dad really gone? My stomach growls with absolute dread at the thought of losing him forever.

As if sensing my thoughts Quinn kisses the top of my head. "Your dad is smart. The fact he had that he had a message ready to go in an emergency situation says so. Don't worry about stuff you can't change. You'll find him if he wants you to find him."

I scoot away from Quinn. "What do you mean don't worry? He's my dad! He's my only family. I put him in that situation, damn it! Why the crap did I think it was a good idea to send him a vial of vaccines or scans? I'm selfish and I should've never involved him."

He takes my hand and rubs. "You're right, he's your dad and you're going to worry no matter what. My dad was a drunk and I worried about him until the day he died. Your dad wanted to help you. He knew the risks of helping you. The point is you can't let your worrying diminish your focus for finding him." He pulls in closer and kisses me slowly on my lips. "Understand?"

Now I'm starting to remember all the making out. "Yeah, I guess, but—"

"But nothing. You can't be constantly thinking about what's happening with your dad on the other side. Focus on your piece of the puzzle and do the best you can. Otherwise, you'll drive yourself crazy."

"I'll try." I scoot onto his lap and put my arms around his shoulders. "Thanks for talking me off the ledge."

"I'm used to it."

I lean in to kiss him, but I'm stopped by a loud bang.

"What the hell was that?"

Another loud bang.

I hop off of Quinn's lap and he stands.

Another loud bang.

"Let's go see what the hell's going on."

We run through the house, stopping in the entertainment room to grab a few guns out of the trunk-turned-coffee table. The crew is running down the staircase heading for the weapons in the trunk.

Quinn barks out, "Conner and Lindsey, come with me and Shea outside. Nikki, go down with Wynne and Gordon and protect the intel. We can't risk that falling into anyone's hands."

They all let out a collective, "Yes, sir."

As I follow the boys toward the front of the house, Wynne passes me and says, "Still wearing the same clothes as last night, huh?"

I wrinkle my nose at her and head outside. There are flaming bottles being lobbed over our fence. Boss is out of his annex and takes aim at one of the punks trying to make his way over the barbed wire. The emaciated youth with purple spiky hair falls off the fence. As soon as he falls, the rest of the kids flee from the scene, but not before a girl with buzzed hair and tattoo scrolled across her face lobs another flaming bottle our way. Quinn tries to get off a shot, but she's gone too quickly.

Conner runs toward the lab as he calls, "I'm going to go get a fire extinguisher, be right back."

Boss, Quinn, Lindsey, and I walk around the small fires to the fence. They didn't do any real damage. Ramsey is clearly trying to send us a message.

I look up at the cameras. "I don't get it. The compound defense system should've warned us."

Boss nods. "Yes, Ms. Kelly, it looks like you may have some troubleshooting ahead of you."

Then something catches my eye on the camera. I look over at Quinn. "Hey, babe, you think you can give me a boost up to the camera." Lindsey and Boss scrunch their eyebrows at me. "What? Boss, you said we need to start getting along better."

"That I did."

Quinn smiles and lifts me up to his shoulder, which is just enough height that I can see the culprit of our camera issues.

Damn.

I look down on the men. Conner puts out the fires and walks over to the group. "You can put me down. I think I see what the problem is." Quinn puts me back on the ground. "Conner and Lindsey, did Ryan say anything to you about having trouble with the cameras, or not being able to get everything hooked up?"

Conner says, "No, he said he was able to get everything calibrated and hooked up no problem."

Double damn.

I take a long breath. "It looks like the cameras weren't even hooked up. I think—"

Quinn shouts, "Fuck! I knew it! I'm going to get that ass-clown."

"I knew something was off with him. I should've pressed him harder."

114

Lindsey shakes his head. "Shea's right. Something's up with him. My gut tells me there's something deeper going on here."

Boss rubs his chin and is silent for a brief moment. "Lindsey, I trust your instincts. I believe it would benefit us to find out what the root cause of our problem is, rather than just eliminating one of the symptoms."

"Umm, hey, guys."

We all turn to the voice coming from outside the gate. Ryan is smiling at us as if nothing has happened.

"What's up?"

I push the code on the gate. "C'mon in. We've got some work for you."

He slips through gate, smiling. "Great, just point me in the direction and . . . " Noticing we're all glaring at him, he stops looks around the compound and takes in the damage just inflicted. "Shit!"

He turns back for the gate, but before he's able to get away Quinn grabs him by his arm. "Not so quick. You're coming with us."

"I didn't have a choice, I swear!"

Quinn practically drags Ryan to the house. "There's always a choice." We follow as Quinn knocks open the front door with his foot. He walks over to the stairs and throws Ryan down them.

"Jesus, Quinn . . . "

"Don't start with me, Kelly."

We all go down the stairs; Nikki, Wynne, and Gordon are staring at us.

Quinn growls, "Nikki, take the traitor into the conference room. He has one shot to tell us what the fuck is going on."

Without even questioning, Nikki nods, puts Ryan in an arm bar, and guides him into the conference room. She plops Ryan into a seat and we all sit and stare at him.

Boss takes a deep breath. "Do you care to explain yourself?"

Ryan is sweating and fidgeting in his seat. He scans our faces and looks at the table. "I . . . I can't . . . "

Quinn pounds his fists on the table and Ryan jumps. "That's it then. Lindsey, make a good show of this one."

Lindsey starts to get up. Ryan's eyes grow wide and he starts to shake. "No, no, you don't understand."

Boss says coolly, as if ordering a latte, "Then make us understand."

"It's my sister, Emmi . . . "

Shit.

Boss says, "Go on."

"She isn't stable. She's hooked on sKape, or anything else that anyone passes across her face. She's tried to get clean loads of times, but . . . Anyway, it got out that I was working with you and she started running her mouth to the Orphans. The other night she didn't come home, but I got something from Ramsey." He reaches for his back pocket.

Conner says, "Not so fast, put your hands on the table and we'll get whatever you need."

"Fine, it's my phone, in my back pocket."

Nikki walks around him and glares at him as she puts the phone on the table.

"Can I show you something?"

Quinn and Boss nod.

Ryan makes a few swipes to his phone and holds his breath then throws the phone onto the table. He struggles to get the next few words out. "He has her. I had to . . . "

We look at the picture of a beaten half-conscious girl with one of her fingers missing. Wynne gasps and turns away, Gordon runs out of the room, and I let out a deep breath.

I say quietly, "You should've told us. I told you we could help."

"I know, but he said he'd kill her. I thought I would do one thing and be done with it."

Quinn growls, "It's never one thing. You owe us, Ryan."

Boss adds, "Yes, I do believe you'll have to make amends."

Ryan looks to me as if pleading for me to take his side. I can't, he's betrayed my trust. Ryan looks away then, and says, "What do I have to do?"

Quinn takes a deep breath. "You need to get us some intel, and it better be good too."

"How, am I supposed to do that? It's not like Ramsey lets me run around his warehouse unattended."

"You better be thinking of something really quick."

Ryan yells, "I don't know what to do!"

"Lindsey, get this fuckin' guy out of here."

Wynne clears her throat. "If I may interrupt this testosterone fest, I think I might have a solution. How about I put some useless and false nuggets of information on a memory device? I can also infect it with a worm that will send information back here, kind of like we did with Danny. Just tell Ramsey that you were able to get into our lab and copy a bunch of our shit, but you weren't sure what you got."

Ryan is sweating. "He's pretty smart. I don't know if he'll go for it."

I pipe up. "I don't think you have much of a choice, Ryan. This is your sister's last hope. And yours. Do it and help us take Ramsey down, and we can get your sister back."

He looks at us and pauses. "Fine. I'll do it."

Wynne says, "It'll just take me a few minutes and I'll get you something." Then she's gone from the room.

Ryan looks down at the table and mumbles, "I'm sorry, I had no choice. I had to protect my family."

Wynne comes back in and places a thin piece of transparent plastic in front of Ryan.

Quinn whispers, "You have a choice now. Make the right one."

Chapter 12

The Other Bosses

I squirm in my high-backed leather office chair in an effort to make myself more comfortable. We're back in the lab. I'm trying to sift through the files Dad left me to find some kind of clue of where he has gone, or maybe a hint of what he found that was so dangerous. Nikki is going through the intel from the snooper planted at Magistrate's house, Gordo is hacking his way through the chip registry, and Wynne is overseeing it all. Hours of staring at the computer display hasn't purged Ryan's treachery from my mind. How could I have misjudged someone so much? He was so charming and sweet. I think everyone feels the same way: betrayed and shitty. We all kind of liked having a different face around the compound. Now, I'm not sure if we'll ever trust anyone ever again. My flowers sitting in a vase on the desk catch my eye and make me smile. They look a little wilted, but they're still the best thing anyone has ever given me. I'm never throwing them out.

Wynne breaks the silence. "So where *did* you sleep last night?"

Wynne, always trying to diffuse touchy situations with raunchy humor. I love her.

"We fell asleep on the outdoor couch. The sunrise looked pretty and we just fell asleep looking at it."

Nikki looks away from her monitor. "Uh-huh. So have you broken your dry spell yet?"

I blush. "No. Seriously, nothing happened. We were just sleeping."

Wynne looks at my flowers. "Damn, it looks like Quinn brought his A game last night and he still didn't get lucky. You're a tough one."

"Shut up. Dad getting kidnapped tends to put a damper on the whole romantic vibe."

Wynne laughs. "Well when you two finally do get around to doing anything, Quinn better carb up, because — "

Gordon swings away from his computer. "Do you girls talk about anything but sex? God! I'm trying to work here. If she said they were just sleeping then they were just sleeping."

Wynne's eyes grow wide. "Geez, who pissed in your cereal this morning? So have you made any headway, Gordo?"

"Actually, I've been able to get through one of their firewalls, but every time I hack through one, five more pop up. I've never seen anything like this before."

"Have you thought of trying to find a session that wasn't closed properly then doing an old fashioned telnet?"

"I think I've almost got their encryption algorithm on the firewalls figured out."

"Like you said, Gordo, this isn't TradeNet you're hacking into. Make sure they don't spike your line and catch you. They'll string you up by your balls if they catch you. No one wins awards for fancy. Just get it done."

"Don't worry." He makes a couple of keystrokes and a large map of the world is displayed with several green glowing dots at various countries. "See, I'm not going directly from our computer. I've hijacked a couple of other sites to do my bidding. I'll be offline before they even track it to our hemisphere."

Wynne rubs his mop of a head. "You learn quickly, Padiwan, but don't get cocky."

"Okay, okay."

Wynne turns to Nikki and me. "So, ladies, have you had any breakthroughs?"

The lights dim and the images on the screens flicker. We all hold our breaths waiting for all our work to be wiped out. Fortunately, the power rebounds quickly and we all turn to our stations and quickly save. Everyone shoots me a dirty look.

"What? I'm doing the best I can. I'll get it fixed as soon as you get me shit to fix it with."

Gordon responds, "I've been trying, but they've been guarding it like it's gold."

Wynne sighs. "We'll keep trying, but for now make sure your battery backups are always charged. Nikki, have you found anything from Shea's snooper?"

"It looks like the device is working fine. I'm getting data packets, but I haven't been able to get into anything very interesting yet. It looks like Mrs. Magistrate has been using more than her share of water rations on her showers. So far that's all I've been able to get."

"Good job, guys. Keep at it. You'll find something eventually. It'll take a while before we're able to get anything substantial. I just wanted to make sure it was working." Wynne turns to me. "What about you, lady? Any luck?"

"Not really. I've gone back to our old transmissions to see if I could find anything and nada. I've hacked into Dad's computer to see if I could find the files he was talking about. So far nothing's standing out."

"Don't worry. We'll find something."

We all go back to our tasks, with Wynne popping in and out at each of our terminals offering help when needed. The clacking of keys and humming of the computers is actually comforting. Dad's computer is an archive of old memories. I scan each image looking for any residual data that might be hiding within it. It's hard for me not to stop and look at the pictures as I go. My first pony, the day I learned to ride my bike, and, my personal favorite, me and Dad working on the 'Cuda. It's hard not to get a little emotional looking at these. The sound of the door opening breaks my concentration.

A loud baritone rings out, "Shea, Boss wants to see us."

"Why, what's up?"

Quinn comes up behind me and looks over my shoulder. "Is that you in a prom dress?"

Nikki and Wynne come over to my terminal. Nikki laughs. "Holy shit, look at that hair!"

Wynne snickers. "Hey, that Milliken kid cleans up pretty good. I never saw him wear anything but jeans and a t-shirt when he'd visit you in the dorm."

I close the images on my display. "Yeah, whatever, assholes."

They all laugh and go back to their terminals. Wynne looks up at the big display on the wall. "Gordo, you need to log off now!"

I look up and see one of the dots on the map has turned from green to red. Gordon looks at Wynne. "I've almost got it. I'm through four of their firewalls. Give me a couple of seconds and I'll get through the last one."

Another dot turns red. Wynne yells, "You don't have a couple of seconds get off now!"

Quinn looks at me. "What's going on?"

"Gordon is trying to hack into the National Chip Repository to find Dad. The dots up there represent terminals he's going through to cover his tracks. It looks like they've spiked our line. They're trying to find out who's making this hack. He needs to close his session now so they don't find us."

"Damn it, you guys! I almost have it."

Another dot turns red.

Quinn bellows, "Turn it off now, kid."

Wynne runs over and rips the keyboard out of Gordon's hands. She makes a several keystrokes, and all of the dots stop glowing, signifying the session has ended.

"What the fuck? I had it. I fucking had it. Now I have to start all over again."

Wynne's eyes grow wide. "No you will *not* do this over again. It's too dangerous. If we're lucky, some grandma in Singapore is getting the blame for this and they won't track it to us. You got too cocky and we can't afford that. We need to regroup and figure out a different way. I'm sorry, Shea, but this is far too risky. We'll find your dad."

"I know, Wynnie."

Gordon gets up and slams his seat into the desk. "You treat me like a kid. I could've been in and out of there before they tracked it to us."

"I'm treating you like a kid because you're acting like a kid. It wasn't just you who was in jeopardy of getting caught, it was the whole crew. Grow up, Gordon."

"You know, there are times I wish you never showed up here. You're too old and cautious."

Wynne's eyes narrow. "I may be old and cautious, but I know more about computers and hacking than you will ever hope to know, *kid*."

Gordon's face grows red. He leaves the room and slams the door behind him.

Wynne rubs her head and slumps her shoulders. "Man, I guess now I know what it's like having a teenager."

I pat her shoulder. "Just let him calm down. I'll talk to him later."

"Thanks. You two better go. Me and Nikki will take care of things down here."

We walk up the stairs. "So what's wrong with the kid? I've never seen him act like that before."

"That skank finally broke up with him. Between you and me, she was only seeing Gordo because of his affiliation with Boss. She moved on to greener grass when she saw that Gordo wasn't drawing too many Tab articles. It's really the best for him, but he doesn't see that right now."

"Ohh, rough."

"Yeah, she's a pretty young thing, and more than likely

Gordon's first screw. So I think he's heartbroken."

We continue on to the main floor of the house. Quinn stops just short of Boss's office. "I've been meaning to thank you for what you've been doing for Nikki. There's nothing worse than feeling useless."

Ever since Boss's condition started deteriorating, he's made fewer appearances in town. This meant there wasn't as much of a need for Nikki's services as Boss's girlfriend/bodyguard; she couldn't go into town on normal security details, because she'd blow her cover.

"Well, don't just thank me. Thank Wynne too. Nikki's a smart lady. Have you considered it might be time to put her on normal security detail? Boss hasn't been out in over a month, and it doesn't look like he's getting any better. Nikki's good at the computer stuff, but I think she gets antsy being behind a computer all day long."

"I'm not willing to burn that bridge just yet."

This is a touchy subject. Putting Nikki onto normal security detail would be admitting Boss didn't have any chance at getting better. Quinn isn't ready to go there just yet. It's probably best to let this subject drop.

"You didn't answer me before. What's this all about?"

"Boss has a video conference every quarter with some of the other NCS bosses and he wants you to sit in on this meeting."

"Why?"

He holds open the door to Boss's suite for me and says, "You're just going to have to find out for yourself, aren't you?"

We walk into the reception area. Claire greets us with a smile. "He's ready for you two."

Boss is sitting behind his desk. His face is drawn and his usual neat appearance has given way to crumpled clothes and a five o'clock shadow. I suspect he's been up all night formulating plans of his own. He looks up at Quinn and me and gives us a tired smile. "Please sit. I'm about to have a meeting and it's important that you two are present."

Boss makes several clicks on his keyboard. The large display on his wall shows three faces. They all say in unison, "Good afternoon, Robert."

Boss turns to Quinn and me. "Good afternoon everyone." He points to me and Quinn. "You all have met Quinn Knightly before. This is Shea Kelly, Mr. Knightly's partner."

"Shea, I would like you to meet Mr. Richard Wyatt. He runs Non-Compliance Sector 981, East Coast Section."

A blond man in the upper right-hand portion of the display gives us a nod.

Boss continues on, "Ms. Liz Roman runs Non-Compliance Sector 3108, Mountain Section."

An olive-skinned brunette gives us a smile. "Nice to finally meet you, Shea. I've heard a lot about you."

"Mr. Nathan Ferguson is the head of Non-Compliance Sector 314, West Coast Section."

A dark skinned man smiles and gives us nod of acknowledgement. "Welcome to our quarterly meeting."

"Shea, those who run the various NCSs throughout the country started having these calls several years ago so we could keep abreast of what was really happening in other parts of the country."

Liz Roman smiles. "It helps knowing what tricks the government is playing on our sister NCSs. What do you have for us today, Robert?"

"Midwest Section has had some rather interesting incidents over the course of the last several months. We have a local that is causing quite a bit of upheaval, and our magistrate has offered access to the flu vaccine in return for ridding our community of this man."

The faces on the display show concern. The East Coast boss

speaks up. "That's bullshit! We've had far more flu casualties than you have. Why are they offering it to you?"

The dark-skinned man speaks. "We haven't been offered anything either. I wouldn't take a damn thing from our magistrate. There has to be strings attached somewhere."

Boss speaks up, "I believe our proximity to GlobalThink has made us a prime target for rolling out their vaccine, but I fear this vaccine is more than meets the eye."

The East Coast man speaks up again. "If we were offered a vaccine, I'd take it in a heartbeat. The locals would stage a coup if they knew I had access to a vaccine and didn't give it to them."

Liz bursts out, "Nice, Rich, you would rather stay in power than keep your people safe."

"It's not about power, Liz!"

"The hell it isn't!"

Boss voice rises above the conflict. "Everyone, let's remember that we are on the same side. Mr. Wyatt does have valid points. His section was hit the hardest with the flu and it isn't an easy decision to make. Ms. Kelly has obtained a sample of the vaccine and we are having it analyzed. Our magistrate, as far as I know, isn't aware that we have these samples. It's imperative that we keep Magistrate off our trail. I would appreciate any intel that you may encounter. We must work together during this time."

They all nod. Liz says, "Robert, you can count on us."

Nathan adds, "Yes, anything we find we will make sure you are informed."

Boss says, "Thank you all."

They respond, "Thank you, Robert."

The screen goes blank. Boss turns to us. "Ms. Kelly and Mr. Knightly have you made any progress since last night?"

"Not really, sir. Gordon tried getting into the National Chip Registry to find Dad, but that didn't end so well. We're going to have to think of a different strategy. I've been looking at

Dad's computer to see if there are any files he left behind that would give us clues as to where he's gone or what he found. He knows how to wipe things and not leave a trace. I doubt I'll be able to find anything."

"Has anything come through on the worm Ryan planted at Ramsey's?"

"No, sir. I'm sorry about Ryan, I totally misjudged him."

"Ms. Kelly, you've been working less than twenty-four hours on this. Ryan might not have had a chance to give Ramsey the memory device yet. You will make progress. As for Ryan, I believe he is a good man, and he had his family's interests at heart. Hopefully he will make the right decision. If he doesn't, I fear I will have no other choice than to make an example of him.

"I understand, sir."

"Mr. Knightly, do you have a plan in place for the removal of Ramsey?"

"Working on it, sir. I have Nikki working on procuring goods. Shea and I will sort out the finer details, then we'll brief the team."

"Very good. If there is nothing else . . . "

I bite my lip and gather the courage to ask Boss a question that has been plaguing me: "Sir . . . this has nothing to do with our present situation, but what were your intentions when you gave me and Wynne the chip to investigate? We've had it for months now and I'm not sure we're accomplishing what you want." I pause to gather the courage for what I'm going to say next. "Sir, I don't think there is a way we can counter your chip fatigue with another chip. It doesn't mean I'm going to stop trying, but I thought you should know that I'm not really hopeful."

Boss gives me a weak half-smile. "The fact that you are discussing this in front of Mr. Knightly does my heart some good. I'm glad you two are communicating. I have to say, when I first paired you two together I wondered if I was doing the right thing. When I'm gone, the two of you will be a force to be reckoned with."

My stomach drops. I look over to Quinn; his eyes have grown wide. "Sir, I'm sure that will be quite a while from now —"

Boss interrupts me, "Now is not the time for platitudes. You and Mr. Knightly have enough experience with the chip to know I don't have long. I never intended for you to find a cure for me. The effects of the chip must be exposed. I fear there are other secrets hiding in it. Shea, you need to do what you came over here to do, expose the truth about the chip. I believe Mr. Knightly will be a great boon to your research. There are others who are confident that you two are just the pair to get the job done."

Others?

Quinn looks unfazed by Boss's last comment. "Shea's smart, sir. I'm sure she can —"

"Quinn. Shea. In your experience, how long has someone in my stage of chip fatigue lasted?"

I feel a lump form in my throat. In all the cases I've read, someone in his stage usually has less than a year before their body gives out. I fight hard to keep the tears back. In the short time I've known Boss, he's been like a surrogate father to me. I can't bear the thought of losing someone else. "Sir, there has to be some way."

"I have come to terms with my mortality. Now that I know you two are up to the task of taking over, I am more at ease. Both of you need to come to terms with your role within the firm. That is why I asked you here to meet with the other NCS leaders. That is why you met with Magistrate and not me. Claire is preparing a story to be released exposing the truth behind my relationship with Nikki. It's the right thing to do."

I reach over for Quinn's hand and he squeezes mine and takes a breath. "Sir, we're ready to do whatever it is you need us to do."

"I know. Now, if you two would excuse me, I have some other work to attend to." Quinn and I start out of the office, but Boss starts talking again. "Oh, Mr. Knightly and Ms. Kelly?"

We turn back and look at him.

"If I give an order to take care of someone in my Sector, next time I expect my orders to be followed without question. I can't have those who are second-in-command second guessing my orders."

My stomach sinks realizing he's talking about Morgan. I nod my head.

Quinn answers, "Yes, sir, it won't happen again. Shea had nothing to do with it. It was my decision."

"I understand, Mr. Knightly. You are both excused."

We walk out to the foyer in silence. Outside, the sun is starting to set, and I'm starting to feel warn down from the excitement of the day and the lack of sleep of last night. I heave a deep sigh.

"So now what?"

"We need to start making our plans for taking down Ramsey. I also think Mr. Ito is right. We've been getting pretty lax with sparring practice lately and I think a workout will go miles in helping me clear my mind."

"What do you say we kill two birds with one stone? We'll work out, then we'll go over some plans. I'm going to check on Gordo, and then I'll slip into something more comfortable. I'll meet you in the gym in a half hour."

"Roger that. I'll see you in the gym."

Chapter 13

Do Not Disturb

Outside the sky is overcast making the brilliant orange and reds of the changing trees stand out even more. The chill of the air causes me to pull my thin jacket around me even closer. I walk around the grounds looking for Gordon, hoping he's still here. If he's spotted around town by himself, Ramsey's men will club him like a baby seal just to make a point to Boss. Out of the corner of my eye I see Quinn's garage door open. Inside, a portly curly-headed kid is bent over the Crown Vic with a beer in his hand.

"Hey, Gordo, you okay?"

He tightens the connections on the air filter cover as he speaks. "No, not really. Why does she have to treat me this way?"

I grab a wire brush and start scrubbing the corrosion from the battery leads. "She's hard on you because she knows you're smart and are capable of great things. You need to listen to her, she knows what she's talking about."

"She doesn't take me seriously. I ran the whole show before she came here. Now I feel stupid and useless."

I put my hand on his back. "No one thinks you're stupid and useless. Shit, everyone here can't believe you've done as much as you have without formal schooling. Heck, it took me and Wynne a couple years in college to get as far as you have."

He grins. "Really?"

"Yeah. Look, I know it's hard to fit in when you're the youngest one here. Me, Nikki, and Wynne probably aren't helping matters by henpecking you so much. I'll talk to the girls about cooling it on the sex talk. You're one of the nicest, smartest guys I know."

"Great. Nice and smart, that's what girls go for."

I smile and rub his back. "The right girl will. That chick in town was no good for you anyway. She's a skank. You deserve better."

"Thanks, Shea."

"Have you made much headway on the Vic?"

He smiles and walks around to the driver's seat. He turns the key and the Vic purrs.

"I'm impressed. Quinn'll be happy."

"Yeah, right. He's never happy."

"Good point. Come on, let's get back to the house. Wynne needs your help."

He turns off the car and we walk back to the main house together. Gordon looks at me. "So if it's true, what you said about the right girl wanting a nice smart guy, why are you with Quinn?"

"Whoever said I was right in the head?"

Gordo smiles and opens the door for me. He starts to go down the stairs, but I yell for him. "Gordo! Quinn is damn smart and actually pretty nice when he wants to be."

He shakes his head. "Whatever you say." And he's off like a shot down the stairs.

Ah to be young and moody and again. Okay, to be young again.

I go up to my room and change into shorts and a t-shirt for my workout and brainstorming session, then barrel down to the gym. A good workout is just what I need to purge my system of all the emotional turmoil of the last couple of days. Quinn is in the gym doing push-ups, unaware of my presence. I take several seconds to watch him do his exercises.

Damn, he's hot.

He looks up at me and smiles. "How long have you been standing there?"

I smile with arms folded in front of me. "Not too long."

He gently puts his hand on my shoulder and rubs. I close my eyes and allow my arms to fall to my side. Without warning

130

he grabs me and puts me in an arm bar. He presses me against one of the walls.

I wrench my neck around to look at him. "Oh, you fucking dick."

He laughs and growls in my ear. "I told you we were going to spar. You got sloppy."

It's on now. No mercy. I stomp my heel into the top of Quinn's foot and he steps back. I turn and give him a swift upper cut to his jaw, then follow up with a roundhouse kick to his ribs. Unfortunately, he is quicker than I am, and he catches my foot mid-strike and throws me to the floor. I respond by sweeping his feet out from under him. We're both out of breath and look at each other for two heartbeats. He nips behind me and puts me in a chokehold. "Nice, but you're going to have to do better than that with Ramsey's men. You telegraph your moves too much. You spend too much time thinking. You need to know how to counter moves right away, and not think so much about it."

I gasp. "You spend too much time talking." I deliver an elbow to his ribs and knock the wind out of him. His arm grows slack enough for me to escape. I scramble to my feet and hold my hands up to block my face. We smile at each other, each knowing the other is starting to grow tired. He throws several punches, and as I block them, a searing pain goes through my arm. I smile knowing it's killing him that he missed me. "Maybe, you should look into getting some Geritol, old man, you look a little tired."

We dance around for a few seconds in an attempt to catch our breath. I give him a glare, then I smile right before landing a flying front kick in his solar plexus putting him on the ground. I smile then my eyes grow wide when he doesn't move. *Shit, I hope I didn't actually hurt him.*

"Quinn, you okay, buddy?" He coughs then lets out a laugh. Before I know it he cuts my legs out from under me and I land flat on my face. He climbs on top of me and puts my arm in a bar behind me. It's still tender from blocking his hits, so it doesn't take me long to tap out. He rolls off of me and I roll onto my back. We both look at the ceiling for several seconds to gather ourselves. Quinn turns over on his side next and looks down at me and smiles. Quickly his smile turns down, and he wipes my nose; a spot of crimson appears on his fingers. "Shit, I'm sorry. Are you okay?"

"Yeah, I'm fine." I rub my arm and wince. "Just remind me next time that you have a lot more force behind your punches than my arm can take."

"You did good. Not good enough to go out on the town by yourself, but good." We help each other up.

"You ready to finalize our Ramsey plans?"

"Yeah, let's go to my office. I'll pull up the plans of the warehouse."

As we walk across the hall I say, "Thanks for the workout. It really helped take my mind off Dad for a bit."

He opens the office door for me. "How ya doing with all that?"

I take a seat. "Not good. I keep thinking about how I wasn't there for him. I have no idea where he is and it's driving me crazy. And Ryan – I can't help thinking about him and his sister."

He leans over and gives me lingering kiss. *Oh. God.* Then he sits in a chair across from me and takes my hand. "Ryan made his choices and now he has to live with them. He could've come to us sooner."

"I know."

"And your dad taught you everything you know. Doesn't it make you feel a little better that even you can't find him?"

"No, not really. I shouldn't have given him any of that information. It was stupid. Now I've made him a target. Someone has him and there's not a damn thing I can do about it."

"You know as a well I do that he would've badgered the

hell out of you until you let him help. Don't take everything on yourself."

"I know, but—"

"But nothing, your dad's a tough old guy. Try your hardest to find him, but also trust that he knows what he's doing." He lifts my hand to his mouth and gives it a kiss. "Okay?"

I nod. Somehow he's actually managed to make me feel better.

He swings around to his computer and makes a couple of keystrokes. A 3D rendition of the warehouse floats in the air. "Good, then let's get to work."

"So what do you have in mind?"

"We're going to have to take him by surprise. The guerilla warfare on the streets isn't doing anything but causing a lot of collateral damage. He's hoping to wear us down one by one. We need do one big surge and just go biblical on his ass. The problem is getting enough supplies and people to do it."

"I think if we're creative enough we won't have to rely on conventional weapons. I'm pretty sure Magistrate won't have a problem getting us fertilizer and diesel fuel, if you know what I'm saying. I'm sure Nikki, Conner, and Lindsey can come up with something good."

"I like the way you think."

He spins the wireframe drawing of the warehouse around. He points to the back area on the drawing. "We know Danny used this area as his headquarters. This is probably the part we should hit first. We need to get some intel on his movements so we know the best time to strike. Hopefully that plant from Ryan will give us something soon."

"I have the snooper program working, I just need to install it at Judy's. That, in conjunction with Ryan's plant, should give us something."

"Good. We need to take out as many people as possible then go and take out Ramsey. Once we take out that fucker and as many of his followers as possible, things will simmer down. We need to show the NCS we're serious, make everyone else think twice about challenging us."

"This has the potential to work. We're going to need more people to pull it off though. I think maybe a talk with Mr. Ito is in order. Let's go tomorrow during our normal patrol and we can stop at Judy's and install the program too."

"Good thinking. We'll brief the team tomorrow. I don't see why we shouldn't be ready to execute in less than a week." He looks at the clock, stands, and stretches. "We've made pretty good headway. It's time we went to bed."

Never missing an opportunity to recycle an old gag, I say, "Another invitation, Mr. Knightly?"

He looks me square in the eye. "I'm game if you are." He kisses me behind the ear.

It takes a few seconds before I'm able to compose myself. "Um, I . . . "

He chuckles and opens the office door for me. "C'mon, let's get out of here."

As we walk down the corridor I notice glowing coming from under the lab door. Nikki, Wynne, and Gordo are, no doubt, working their little hacker butts off in there. I look at my watch. It isn't late, but with the night we had last night they need some rest. I look at Quinn and, as if reading my thoughts, he gives a nod. I open the door and stick my head in. "Hey, take a break, you guys. You didn't get any sleep last night. You need to be fresh. Take a shower, get something to eat, and I'll meet you here in the morning."

Wynne looks at the crew. "You heard the lady. We'll hit it hard tomorrow."

I close the door behind me and look at Quinn. "So where are Lindsey and Conner?"

"Out on patrol, but I'm going to call them back. They haven't had enough sleep either. We need to regroup. If someone has an emergency, they can always give us a call."

We go up the stairs to our bedrooms. With each step I take the adrenaline from the sparring match is wearing off and the pain goes through my body. I need the help of the banister to get me up the last few stairs. Once at the landing Quinn looks me over, wipes my nose again, and wipes it on his shirt. "You just don't know when to give up, do you?"

"Dad always said I was a little bullheaded."

"Take your own advice and get some sleep. Although, I know you won't. You'll stay up all night looking for your dad and his files."

"At least you're smart enough to know better than to talk me out of it."

"If you need a distraction, you know where I am."

I go into my room and jump in the shower before Wynne or Nikki get up to the bathroom. The hot water relaxes my tight muscles and I stand awhile. I move my arm gingerly. It's going to hurt for a while, but I'm pretty sure I just bruised it good and didn't do any significant damage. I take a deep breath and turn off the shower. I dry myself off and put on my comfy jammy shirt and slippers. When I open the door, the cool air of the bedroom hits my skin, and leaves me chilly. Wynne is on her bed reading a magazine.

"Hey lady, you might want to look at your tablet. It's been acting weird."

"What do you mean by weird?"

"I just got up here, but it's been blinking on and off for a while now. It's kind of freaking me out."

The tablet looks to be off. I jiggle a couple of wires and nothing happens. Then the screen comes on and stays on for several second then off again. The screen comes on again, this time for a shorter period, and goes off again. I sit in a seat in front of the tablet to watch for a while.

"What do you think it is? It's kind of creepy."

"I've seen this before."

Off-on, off-off-on-on, off, on-on-off-off, off-on-on-off.

"Holy shit! Wynne get me a pen and paper."

She runs over with a pen. "What is it?"

"Just hold on." I write down the sequences until they start to repeat. Then I run over to Wynne's computer and type in the sequences. I stand and give her a hug. "He's alive!"

"What? Who?"

"Dad! He's sending me a message via the tablet. That was Morse code. He said that he's safe. He said to stop looking for him and that he would talk to us soon."

The tablet has stopped blinking. My heart feels ten times lighter and all the pain of my sparring session is forgotten. "Hey, I need to tell Quinn. I'll be back in a few minutes."

Before the door shuts all the way I hear Wynne say, "Uh huh, I'll see you in the morning."

"I heard that."

I knock on Quinn's door. He shouts, "What?!"

Not waiting for an invitation, I burst through the door, eager to tell him my news. He's lounging on his bed, watching the display on the wall. There's a cigar in his mouth a glass of scotch is perched on his nightstand. I take a running jump on his bed and land right next to him. "He's okay!" I give him a big hug.

Quinn takes the cigar out of his mouth and puts it in the ashtray on his nightstand. He pushes himself up to a sitting position. "Whoa, now. Who do I have to thank for this sudden attack?"

Suddenly, aware that I'm wearing only my nearly see-through t-shirt and panties, and he's just clad in his boxers, I blush. "Uh, sorry. Um, it's Dad. He's alive. He just sent me a message on my tablet via Morse code. He didn't say much, just that he wants us to stop looking for him and he'll talk to us soon."

He takes me in his arms and kisses my head. "That's great!"

I sit up and look at his display. There's an old-time western playing. "Ooh, Clint Eastwood. Sorry for barging in, I don't want to interrupt. I'll get out of here and let you have the rest of the evening in peace. I just thought you should know."

I start to get up and he gently grabs my arm. I wince. The pain is definitely starting to set in now. "I told you I was up for being distracted. Stay here for a while."

The chill of the old drafty house makes me shake. "Aren't you freezing? All you're wearing are those little boxer shorts."

Yeah, that's all he's wearing. Yum.

"Nah, I think it's refreshing." He pulls back the covers. "Join me under here, I'll keep you warm."

Oh, what the hell.

I nestle in and lie on my side intertwining my legs with one of his. The warmth of the covers coupled with his body heat makes me instantly relax. He rubs my arm and kisses my cheek. "Sorry about your arm." He brushes my face with his hand. "And your nose."

"Eh, I've had worse."

"Yeah well, not by me. For now on, if you want your ass kicked you're going to have to go to Mr. Ito. I won't be doing it anymore." I bite my lip and brush a tear from my eye. He pulls me closer and I run my hand through his chest hair. "So, you like westerns?"

I let out a nervous laugh. "Yeah, especially the ones with space cowboys, but Clint Eastwood is pretty cool too." I continue to play with his chest hair. "So, what did Boss mean by there are others who think we're just the pair to do the job? What others?"

"Let's give it a rest for the night, okay? I want to be with you, not talk work bullshit."

I should push him more, but the only thought I can clearly

get through my brain is how to get those boxers off him. We're so close together that I ache. God, it's been so long I think I've forgotten what to do. I wish he would just touch me. As if reading my thoughts, he turns on his side and starts to run his hand along the curve of my hip, then around to the small of my back and slowly rubs. His hand wanders slowly up my stomach to my breast and lightly caresses. A whimper of anticipation escapes me. I'm barely able to catch my breath. It's just my little t-shirt and his boxers that separate us. He smiles, then draws closer and nuzzles my neck. A loud knock at the door makes us both pop up.

"Chief! Me and Lindsey are back. You want us to come in and give you a report?"

Quinn growls. "If you even touch that door knob I'll stuff your balls down your throat. Leave me alone. I'm sleeping. I'll talk to you in the morning."

"Uh, yes, sir."

I hear padding down the hallway and muttering about Quinn being in rare form.

Quinn gets up from the bed and heads toward the door.

I give him a little pout. "What's wrong?"

He smiles and locks his door. "I don't want any distractions." As he walks by the display and computer he turns them both off. "We've been getting a lot of those lately."

"Good thinking."

He crawls back into bed, hovers over me, and smirks. "Whatever will we do without any distractions?"

I push the covers back, gently pull him closer to me and kiss him. He sinks into me and runs his hands through my hair. "I'm sure we can think of a couple things to do."

Chapter 14

Afterglow

What a beautiful morning. I open up the kitchen windows to let some fresh air in. The crisp fall air tickles my nose. The house is quiet since I'm the only one awake right now. I open up the fridge and see our weekly delivery of groceries has arrived. Feeling inspired and well rested, I decide to try my hand at some morning baking. I crack a couple of eggs in the bowl, followed by the sugar and oil. Next comes the milk and flour, and last but not least I add the applesauce made by one of our locals. Baking is one of the many pastimes I don't get to do much. There's usually so much to do, the most I have time to do is eat a quick sandwich or grab a stim drink. Even with Boss's resources we usually don't have enough stuff to make baked goods. Wynne or Gordon must've done some excellent trading for this stuff.

I sit at the table and read my tablet while my creations bake. It's rare that I get the house to myself. The only sound comes from the wind rustling through the dry leaves. The smell of the cinnamon in the muffins is wafting to my nose, making my mouth water. I look down at my tablet:

SHEA KELLY DENIES RUMORS OF PREGNANCY

Thank you, Claire.

The sound of footsteps makes me look up from my tablet. I guess the smell is starting to wake up the troops. Nikki sits beside me. "You're up early, and baking too. Aren't you a regular Holly Housewife."

I put my tablet on the table and get up to check the muffins.

"Yeah, I actually woke up with some extra energy this morning. I thought you guys might enjoy something other than dry cereal." I take the muffins out of the oven and put them on the counter. They are the perfect shade of golden brown.

Gordon, Conner, Lindsey, and Wynne shuffle into the kitchen like zombies and sit at the table. Wynne says, "Baking and up early."

I put the muffins on a plate and place it on the table in front of the crew. I sit down and they all grab one and take a bite.

Nikki offers between mouthfuls, "Yeah, whatever you did to get that extra energy, keep doing it. These are awesome!"

Everyone nods in agreement. Wynne smiles. "Extra energy, huh? I have an insider report that says she didn't sleep in her bed last night. And if I'm not mistaken, Quinn's room hasn't been soundproofed."

I say with a mouthful of muffin, "Shut up, Wynne."

Nikki grins from ear to ear. "Oh, I get it now. Congratulations, girlfriend."

Gordon snorts and looks down at his muffin. "Good. Maybe Quinn will be nicer to us now."

Lindsey gives us a blank stare. "What? I don't get it. Hey, where *is* Chief? He said he was going to fill us in on the plans this morning. He's never late."

I shake my head. "He had a late night last night. He's still sleeping." Wynne and Nikki snicker. Ignoring their juvenile reaction, I continue, "I have some good news. I made contact with Dad last night. He's okay. He said not to try to find him that he would make contact with me shortly."

They all cheer.

"We can relax about finding him for now. But if I haven't heard anything in a day, I don't care what he says, I'm going to try to find him. For now, here's what we need to do: we're going to pull an all-out surprise assault on Ramsey. The guerilla warfare on the streets isn't getting us anywhere."

Conner nods his head. "Amen to that. We need to take care of this asshole as quickly as possible. I'm tired of dicking around."

"Exactly. We need to have a well thought-out plan. There won't be any second chances with this one. Conner, Lindsey, and Nikki, I need some ideas from you: devices that can inflict maximum pain that we'll be able to get from Magistrate or have readily available. We don't have to time to go through TradeNet. I also want you to look at blueprints of Ramsey's compound and see what we can do. Figure out some CONOPS and estimate the manpower we'll need to pull them off."

Lindsey nods. "Can do, boss lady."

"Wynne and Gordo, we still need to figure out what the crap is up with that vaccine. I bet you a zillion dollars Magistrate isn't offering us the vaccine because he wants us to live long and prosper. We need to know what's going on with it before we have it in hand. We'll have to wait until Dad contacts us to get to his files, but for now see if you can get a read on the spike I put in Magistrate's line, and see if Ramsey's spike is up and running."

Wynne gives me a fake salute. "Aye-aye, captain."

"I'm going to wake up Quinn. We're going on patrol. While we're out we're going to talk to Mr. Ito about training some of the mercs to take up the slack for us in town. I also need to install the snooper program at Judy's place. We'll meet in the conference room at 1400 to discuss next steps."

Lindsey says, "Um, Shea, I don't think waking up Quinn is a good idea. He was little cranky last night."

I grab the last lonely muffin sitting on the table. "I'll take my chances, Lindsey."

As I climb the stairs the surreal nature of last night hits me. Just a few short months ago, I was sure Quinn didn't even know how to spell fun, now here I am delivering a bedside muffin to one of the most patient and caring guys I've ever been with – not that my experience in this arena is very comprehensive. I reach for the door knob and stop momentarily.

What if he has regrets? Well, he's going to have to face me sooner or later.

The room is still dark and the only sound is his soft snoring. The blankets on the bed are rising and falling with each breath. I put the muffin on the nightstand and sit next to him.

I whisper in his ear, "Daylight's busted. Time to get up, babe."

He startles. For a split second he looks stunned at my appearance on his bed. He rubs his face then gives me a peck on the forehead. With his raspy morning voice he says, "Morning, beautiful. How long have you been up?"

"A while." I reach over and grab the muffin off the nightstand and awkwardly thrust it into his hands. "Um, I made you breakfast."

He smiles and starts to eat. "Thanks."

"I hope you don't mind, but I gave everyone an assignment to work on. I told them we would meet in the conference room at 1400 to discuss next steps. I thought we could go on patrol, talk to Mr. Ito about training some of the mercs, and install that program at Judy's."

His eyes grow wide.

"What's wrong?"

"Nothing, this muffin is great."

"You sound surprised."

"You never struck me as the domestic type."

"I have all kinds of skills."

He smiles and puts down the muffin. "I know." He cups my jaw with his hand and kisses me gently at first, but then each kiss grows more intense. As he leans into me, I ease myself down on to the bed.

"You're an evil man. We really have a lot of work to do."

He falls to the side of me and props himself up on one elbow. As he plays with my hair he asks, "Are you having regrets about last night?"

"No! Are you?"

"No. So what's with leaving before I get up and acting antsy to get out of here?"

"I'm not antsy . . . "

He gives me a sideways look.

"Okay, maybe a little awkward, but not antsy. It's been a while for me. I'm not really sure how to act."

He rubs my tummy and kisses my cheek. "Me too, but I'm sure we can figure it out together."

Oh, hell I can't resist him. I turn into him. In between kisses I say, "You know, we really need to get into town and talk to Mr. Ito."

He replies, "You're absolutely right."

"And I really need to install that program at Judy's."

"I couldn't agree more."

He slides his hands up my shirt and lightly teases the soft flesh waiting underneath. The warmth of his hands keeps the chill of the air at bay. A soft moan escapes me and I relax in his arms.

"You know, you aren't making things any easier."

"Good."

"Well, it's not like we have a set appointment. It can wait a bit."

"You make an excellent point."

We sink into each other. For the first time in months we're not worried about schedules or the chaos in town, we just have each other.

Chapter 15

Not a Normal Patrol

"Why are you walking so fast?"

"Well, Quinn, someone kept me at home longer than I was planning. We still have a lot to get done before we meet with the team later this afternoon." I turn and smile at him.

"Okay, next time I'll skip that first step to hurry things along a bit. And maybe that last step too. Then there were a couple steps in between we could've hurried along. "

"It works both ways, buddy."

He smiles. "So first stop, Franks?"

"Yeah, I guess we should check on the little weeble-wobble. Seems Ramsey's got his sights on him."

The crisp fall air breathes life into me. It feels more like a delightful stroll into town than a patrol. Maybe today will be an incident-free day and I can just enjoy a nice walk around town. The sound of a woman hurling insults my way rips me back to reality.

I shoulda known better.

"Shea Kelly, you're killin' my boy!"

As I turn to address her, a rotten vegetable of some sort lands squarely in my face. A pale gaunt woman with clothes hanging in tatters about her runs toward me and Quinn. She doesn't look strong enough to harm a kitten; I stay frozen in place waiting for her next move.

"Ya hear me? You're killin' my boy!"

"Ma'am I don't know —"

"That's right. Y'all don't know me or my kin, but y'all kept the vaccine from us just the same. Now my boy is payin' the price."

"I-I'm sorry it's just —"

Quinn breaks in, "With all due respect, that vaccine could've caused major damage. Shea didn't do anything wrong."

The woman's eyes fill with tears. "He woulda had a chance. Now he has nothin'. And it's all because of y'all."

There's nothing I can say or do to make things better. I remember last year, when Mia was on the brink, how her parents would've done anything to make her better. It's understandable why she's yelling at me, I'm the closest thing she has to a reason for her son being sick. As I start to speak again, a man comes from behind the woman and grabs her gently by the shoulders.

"Althea, what'cha doing?"

"They're the reason our boy is sick. They need to know what they're doing to us." He tries to guide her away from us, but she resists. Tears are streaming down her face. "Don't try to pull me away. They sit up all comfortable-like in that mansion up yonder not caring about what goes on with us regular folk."

"Ma'am, I—" Quinn squeezes my shoulder and I stop short.

The man whispers, "Althea, we have to go. Billy still needs his momma."

Althea wipes the tears from her face and composes herself. "S'pose you're right." She looks me squarely in the face. "I gotta tend to my boy. He needs me. 'Course *you're* not a momma. You'll never understand." She walks away from us in the arms of her man.

Her words are a dagger aimed straight for my heart. I let out deep breath. Quinn puts his hand on my shoulder.

"You okay?"

Althea's jeers are still ringing in my ears, and I barely register Quinn's question. I walk faster, as if I can outrun the pain. Her comments, along with my new-found relationship with Quinn, have opened up an old wound that has never properly healed.

"Slow down. What's your problem?"

"We have a lot to do. Keep up, old man."

I pick up my pace, but the memories stay with me.

With Quinn being more than a foot taller than me, it isn't much of a challenge for him to keep pace. He grabs my shoulder.

"Will you stop? What's your problem?"

Losing steam, I meander over to an old park bench and sit. He follows. It's only right he knows.

"That woman . . . "

"Don't get too worked up over her. She needs someone to blame. She's facing losing the most important thing in her life. Don't take it too personally."

"I know there's no way we could ever know what she's going through. If it makes her feel better to yell at me, then that's fine. It just that . . . "

"What?"

"She's right. I'll never know what it's like."

"To have someone close to you have the flu?"

"No, dumbass." I take a deep breath and let it out. "To be a mom."

"Oh." He tries to lighten the mood by putting his arm around me. "Don't worry about that. There's still time to find that cute farm boy and have a couple of kids."

I squirm in my seat a bit. "No . . . there isn't. Wynne's the only one who knows this. I want you to know, since we're — "

"What?"

My leg starts to shake. "*He* took care of any chances of that ever happening. The exact words from the doctor were 'highly unlikely to ever conceive'. When it first happened I tried to push it out of my mind, because I never thought I would be with anyone else. Now, with us, those stupid Tab rumors, and that woman saying that stuff, it just kinda dug up old memories, I guess."

He's just staring at me, making me feel stupid.

Damn, here come the tears. Just stop it, Shea. You're making a fool of yourself.

I take off my glasses and wipe my eyes then give a fake laugh. "I guess it's for the best anyway. Can you imagine me as a mom? What a disaster. We should get going."

I get up to continue our walk, but he pulls me by my wrist back down to the bench with him and takes me into his arms. "I fucking hate this place." He squeezes me tight and whispers in my ear, "It wouldn't be a disaster at all."

After a few seconds of crying on his shoulder, the bright flash of a Tab camera reminds me of our outstanding duties. Quinn growls at the photographer. The photographer whimpers and runs away from us before Quinn can reach him.

I force a chuckle. "Nothing's sacred, I guess."

"Little shit, he better run. If catch him in town I'm going to shove that camera so far up his ass he'll be taking pictures of what he ate last night."

"Come on, enough dramatics for today. Let's go see Frank."

It's just a short walk to Frank's place. There are several patrons already gathered for their early afternoon pick-me-up. It's amazing how quickly the smell of cigarette smoke and stale beer can fill your nose. Frank perks up from behind the bar.

"Hey guys. How are ya?"

"Finer than a frog hair, Frank. Has Ramsey or any of the Orphans been in lately?"

"Not since that last incident. Since Morgan went to the other side they've been kind of quiet."

"Good, I'm sure they'll regroup soon, but hopefully they'll lay low for a while. Did you find the 'Cuda's manual yet?"

He rubs the back of his neck and shuffles a bit. "Uh, I've been pretty busy and haven't had time to go through your stuff. I promise, I'll get to it tonight."

"Uh-huh, I'm sure. Just get it to me, okay? I need it."

"Sure thing."

Quinn and I head for the door, but before we get outside, Franks says, "Hey! I did forget something. One of Ramsey's guys was here lookin' for Shea."

Quinn growls, "One of the Orphans?"

"Nah, figure this is one of his higher-ups. Some old dude. Gave me the creeps."

Quinn says, "Thanks, we'll keep an eye out."

The wind has picked up and has quite a bite to it. I pull my wool sweater closed and fish around in my knapsack for gloves and a hat.

"I guess it's time for my self-esteem to take a nose-dive. Let's go to Judy's and install that program."

He chuckles. "No need to be self-conscious."

He's lying, but I love that he's making the effort to lie to me.

Inside Heads and Tails some of the girls are on the stage practicing their sets for later tonight. Others are cleaning the bar. Judy pops up from the bar.

"Hey you two, I didn't expect to see you."

I lean on the bar. "I was wondering if you could help us with something."

She lights up her cigarette and takes a long drag. "Shoot, darlin'."

I look around to make sure no one but Quinn and Judy are in earshot. "I just finished a program that will get me access to Ramsey's guys' phones. Hopefully, I'll be able to get some intel on their movements that way. The girls won't have to do a thing this time. I just need access to your computer to install the program. All you have to do is push a couple of buttons behind the bar here and it will install itself on their phones. Of course, I have a patch for you guys so it won't install on your phones."

"Sure, what the hell." She pours herself a whiskey and tasks a swig. "Danny was a pain in the ass, but Ramsey . . . he's batshit crazy. The other day he had some older guy in here looking for ya. Sexy as hell, but he was fucked in the head too. Anything we can do to get that fucker outta here, I'm on board for."

"Thanks, Judy."

I sit at the bar and rifle around in my knapsack to look for the storage device holding my programs. Judy hands me her computer.

"This shouldn't take too long, and then we'll be out of your hair."

I put the memory device in the computer. Judy takes another long drag of her cigarette. "Take your time, darlin'. You know, you look different. You're kind of glowing; you got some color in your cheeks. You look real pretty. What'cha doing different?"

I blush.

Quinn responds. "Yes, Shea. What *are* you doing?"

"Shut up. Why don't you make yourself useful and take my tablet out of my knapsack and log on to one of the computers at home while I'm working here."

She looks at me, then him, and smiles.

As I continue typing, the thick smell of perfume surrounds me.

"Hi, Quinny. Helping us out?"

He clears his throat. "Uh, hey, Vanessa. It's more Shea than me." He turns slightly away from her to continue his work, but she doesn't get the message.

She drapes her arms around him. "Smart *and* handsome."

I grit my teeth to keep from punching her out. "Quinn, I'm going to send you a data stream from Judy's computer just to make sure her computer isn't sending you corrupt data packets."

"You know, it turns me on when you speak geek like that."

Vanessa looks shocked and backs away from Quinn slightly. I decide to add a nugget to turn the knife a bit. "Well, tonight, I'll make sure to whisper sweet nothings in your ear about 14 inch-pound 5/16 inch torque wrenches."

"You know what I like, baby."

Vanessa crinkles up her nose. "Well, I have to get ready for tonight. You two have fun." She stomps off.

I keep typing at my computer as I say, "That's right, skank, just keep on walkin'."

Judy laughs. "She needed to be knocked down a peg or two."

"Okay, I think we should be about done. Judy, can we borrow your phone?" She puts the thin clear rectangle on the bar. I make a few clicks to my keyboard. "Quinn, see that icon to your right? Click that a couple of times."

Judy's phone lights up and the camera snaps a picture.

"Do you see the picture on the tablet?"

"Yup."

"I think it works. Let me take the app off your phone." I make a couple of clicks on my keyboard. "Okay, this is all you have to do. Hit this key and click this icon and the software will install wirelessly to anyone's phone in the bar. I've installed an app on all your phones that will block the snooper app. Let me know if you have any problems."

"Thanks, doll." Before we're out the door she adds, "Quinn, you keep the color in my girl's cheeks. You hear?"

"Yes, ma'am."

Once we're outside Quinn's face grows serious.

"What?"

"I don't like the sound of one Ramsey's higher-ups looking for you. I shouldn't have brought you into town."

"Oh, Quinn, I'll be fine. Frank and Judy tend to be a little over dramatic."

"Still, we need to be careful. Ramsey is far more dangerous than Danny could ever think to be."

"So when are you going to tell me about your history with him?"

His expression goes cold. "I told you enough."

"Oh, really? I don't think you've told me anything. Don't you think I can handle it? Don't you trust me?"

"Can we not do this here?"

Noticing that people are starting to stare at our bickering, I concede. "Fine, but don't think you're getting off the hook that easily. We're going to continue this conversation when we get home."

"Lovely."

We continue on to Mr. Ito's without another word. Same old shit from Quinn; it doesn't really surprise me. Our regular argument about Ramsey has almost become comforting. I still wonder what's so horrible he feels he needs to keep it from me.

The dojo is empty except for Mr. Ito practicing a kata. His moves are breathtaking; he's more fluid and flexible than a man half his age. He turns in our direction and we bow to him.

"Good afternoon, Mr. Quinn and Ms. Shea. What brings you here today?"

"Good afternoon, sir. Quinn and I would like to talk to you about a problem you might be able to help us with."

He gives a half smile as if knowing what we are going to ask him. "I'm always willing to help, Mr. Quinn. Please come back to my office and tell me how I can help."

As we walk back to the office, Mr. Ito asks, "How is Mr. Ryan working out for you?"

Quinn grunts.

"Well, turns out Ramsey got to his sister. We caught him trying to sabotage some of our equipment."

"I'm so sorry, Ms. Shea. Ryan has never given me cause for concern. Trust me, that I would've never recommended him if —"

Quinn stops him. "We know, he took us all for a surprise. He has one chance to prove himself."

Mr. Ito nods. "You've been more than fair with him."

We continue our walk past the worn mats that line the dojo to a cramped office. There's barely enough room for us all. We relay the details of Magistrate's offer and our problem with Ramsey. Mr. Ito listens in rapt attention.

"Basically, we need you act as overseer to some of the mercs we hire, and train them. I know you train most of them anyway, but we need you to teach them to work together as a team. We also want you to act as our point man in town."

Quinn adds, "We know this will take away from your normal classes, but we're prepared to offer you compensation for this work."

Mr. Ito nods and leans back in his seat. There is a long silence as he considers our words carefully. He starts slowly, "Mr. Quinn and Ms. Shea, I'm humbled by this offer. Our community has fallen on hard times. I would be proud to lend my services to you."

I smile. "Thank you, sir. This will be a great help to us."

We all walk out of the tight quarters. Before we leave the dojo, Quinn adds, "Conner or Lindsey will be here to discuss details with you soon."

"I look forward to working with them."

We walk toward the food plots. I turn to Quinn.

"Mr. Ito's a good guy. I'm glad he decided to help us. He's probably one of most hard-ass sensei I've ever dealt with."

"How long have you been taking lessons?"

"On and off since I was ten. I wanted to take dance classes, but Dad wouldn't hear about it. It was karate classes for his little girl, or nothing. Mr. Ito was actually one of my first customers here. Somehow he knew I knew how to work with TradeNet and he asked me to get him a couple of items he had trouble purchasing. We kind of formed a friendship after that. But when Logan, um, attacked me, that's when he took me under his wing. He made sure that I would always be able to protect myself. I'd probably be better at it if I wasn't so damn clumsy and awkward."

He chuckles; I notice he doesn't retort my claim. We continue walking down the street making quick stops at the food plots and several other businesses. All of them have similar stories to tell: the Orphans and Ramsey's men are growing more oppressive by the day. Some of them are understanding and know we're trying the best we can. Others are not so generous. I look at my watch: it's getting close to our meeting time with the crew.

"We have time for one more stop, then we have to head back. Let's check on Bobby."

"You just want to play with the robot."

"Maybe."

We walk into the eatery. Mia is on the floor with the robot in her lap and a screwdriver in her hand. Bobby and his wife are struggling with moving the large table they use as a counter. Quinn scurries over and takes Jenny's side of the table while I plop down next to Mia.

"Auntie Shea, can you help me with this? This damn screw won't turn."

Jenny yells, "Mia!"

"Sorry, Mama."

She tries unsuccessfully to stifle her laugh. "Just mind your manners, Miss Mia. Shea, there was a guy in here lookin' for ya. An older man. Must be one of Ramsey's fellas. He was a strange sort."

Quinn grunts as he wrestles with mammoth table. "That's it. When we're done, we're going back home. It isn't safe for you here."

"Quinn, you can't keep me locked up in the compound forever." I turn my attention to Mia's robot. "I think I've found your problem. You're turning the screw the wrong way, ding-dong. Remember, righty tighty, lefty loosey?"

"Oh, yeah."

Sitting here makes me feel sort of normal. I'm playing with my friends' kid. My boyfriend is helping move large pieces of furniture. Maybe later we can drink beer, eat pizza, and play cards like normal couples do. The outside door opens and the quiet of the store is filled with screams.

Or maybe I can kick some punk Orphans' asses. Sigh – so much for normal coupledom.

"Nobody move. Give us all your scrip and no one gets hurt."

I look over my shoulder. Justin is standing there gaunt and pale. His tattoos and piercings make him look miles different from the boy I used to know just a few months ago. He sneers at me and Mia. "Shan, get Shea and the girl. Jax, get the woman."

I hold Mia tight in my arms. Shan rushes over to me and Mia and puts a knife to my throat. The other boy goes over to Jenny and punches her right in the face. She crumples to floor.

"Mommy!!"

Quinn and Bobby drop the table and start toward me and Mia. The punk pushes the knife to my throat, and a trickle of blood runs down my neck. Quinn and Bobby stop in their tracks. Jax rips Mia out of my hands and puts a gun to her head. I squirm in Shan's sKape-enhanced stronghold. The knife scrapes away flesh as I struggle in his grip.

"Daddy! Help me!"

Justin laughs. "Now, Dad, get me all the rich-stuff or you'll have to spend the evening cleaning baby's brains off the floor."

Bobby goes to the small office area behind the main room of the restaurant.

Quinn growls at Justin.

"There's going to be a reckoning between you me one day, son."

"I'm not your son. You and Shea took my father. Maybe we

should take out your little whore now."

Shan squeals with delight and pushes the knife harder. A cool breeze from the door brushes my skin. There is a sound of bones cracking and in seconds Jax and his gun are on the floor and Mia runs toward Quinn, who scoops her up. My attacker loosens his grip and I throw him over my shoulder and slam my foot into his windpipe. Justin and I race for the gun. Justin gets to the gun seconds before me; he cocks the hammer and grins. Time slows as his finger feels for the trigger. I close my eyes waiting for the inevitable outcome, but it never happens. I open my eyes and Justin is quivering on the floor with one of Bobby's knives pinning his hand to the floor. I look over to the door to thank our savior, but I'm barely able to get the words out of my mouth.

"Daddy!?"

Chapter 16

Father Knows Best

The gray-haired man wearing a baseball cap surveys the aftermath of the melee. He takes the rolled cigarette out of his mouth, throws it down, and grinds it into the floor. He glares at Justin, who is sweating and trying with all his might not to scream in pain. Dad strolls over to Justin, wrenches the knife out of his hand and places it to his throat.

"Don't you ever think of laying a hand on my daughter ever again, got it?" Justin glares at dad. Dad pushes the knife harder against Justin's throat. "Got it?"

"Yeah."

Dad lifts the knife. "Good. Now, go on, get outta here and tell all your little friends what I told you."

Justin runs out of the restaurant. Bobby dashes from the office with a lock-box in his hands. Seeing the carnage he comes to a dead stop. He looks up and sees my dad.

"Shea, that's the guy that was looking for you. Get out of here, I'll take care of him."

As I sit with Jenny's head in my lap I say. "It's okay, Bobby. This's my dad."

Bobby lets out a breath and sets down the lock box, then takes Mia from Quinn's arms. "Thank you, Mr. Kelly."

"Weren't nothin'." Dad looks over at me. "You okay, girl?"

Quinn squats down to inspect my wound and wipes the blood from my neck.

"Yeah, Dad. I'm– uh– what the hell are you doing here?"

He smiles. "I told you I'd find ya. Your old man still has a few tricks up his sleeve. We need to get rid of these guys before anyone sees them here."

Bobby replies, "I don't think anyone will be missing them much. I'll take care of it."

Jenny starts to regain consciousness. "Mia, where's Mia?"

I help her to a sitting position. "She's fine. We're all fine." Jenny surveys the pizzeria and jumps when she sees Dad. "It's okay. That's my dad."

Mia climbs out of Bobby's arms and runs to Jenny's.

"Love you, Mommy."

Jenny gives Mia a hug. "This is bullshit, Bobby. You've put our family in danger long enough. Me and Mia are leaving."

"Mama, no."

Bobby slumps. "Jenny, I . . . "

Feeling weird about sitting in on a family dispute, I interrupt. "Bobby, are you sure you got it? If so, we're going to —"

"We're fine. Go ahead."

Dad slings his seabag over his shoulder and heads out the door. Quinn and I follow and walk toward the compound. Then it suddenly dawns on me: my daddy is here. I hug him so hard he drops his sea bag. It's so different seeing him in person. Even though my dad is average height and build, he still exudes a strong presence. His hair is cut in the military style that I've always known him to wear; the only difference is that his hair has more gray than not now. His face looks worn and weathered like the last five years have taken a particularly harsh toll on him. I wipe the tears from my eyes.

"I missed you too, Saoirse."

Quinn holds out his hand. "It's good to meet you, Mr. Kelly. I'm —"

Dad swings his bag over his shoulder and turns away without shaking Quinn's hand. "I know who you are."

I shrug my shoulders at Quinn. "Well, Dad, let's get you to the compound. I'm sure you need some rest and a warm meal."

"Sounds like a hell of a plan. Let's get out of here."

"Sir, you're welcome to stay with us for as long as you like."
Dad grunts in response.

That's Dad: busting my boyfriend's balls. Quinn's my boyfriend. My life really has taken a turn for the weird.

Quinn and I walk in front of Dad a bit. Quinn looks at me and says softly, "Now that we know your dad was the mystery man looking for you, you know what this means?"

"Ramsey isn't after me?"

"No, Judy thinks your dad is sexy."

I push him and laugh. "Oh, gross!"

The silence amongst us is growing more awkward with each step. "So Dad, what the hell's going on? Why are you here?"

"It wasn't safe for me there anymore. I'm sure you noticed I haven't sent out any of your Feed messages. I kept finding spikes in our line. It wasn't safe for me to receive any of your messages. I hope to God the last emergency message I sent you didn't get us into any trouble. The more information I found out about the vaccine, the closer they got to us." He points to a wound on the back of his neck. "I had to go off the grid. Put my chip into an old nag. Then I built a decoy chip with fake information to carry with me while I was on the other side. That bought me some time to get over here. What I have to show you is too important to send over the ether. I had to personally deliver it to you."

We go through the iron gates that surround the compound.

"I told you, Quinn, he taught me everything I know."

"I can see where you get it from."

Quinn smiles at Dad. Dad growls. We walk up the driveway to the house.

"Sir, is there something I did?"

Oh God, Quinn, don't go there.

Dad gets inches from Quinn. "Is there something you did? I can't believe you have the nerve to ask me that. You may think it's okay to treat my daughter the way you do, because of your standing in this community. I don't give a fuck who you think you are; you're a maggot to me. I can't believe you would willingly take the mother of your child into a dangerous situation like that. Damn, son, look at her. You pert near lost them both. You aren't even worthy to lick dog shit off her boots. You will get your head out of your ass and you will do right by my daughter and my grandchild. Roger that?"

I guess Dad does read the Tabs.

Quinn is standing wide-eyed and stunned.

"Uh, Dad."

"Saoirse, don't defend him. You shouldn't be with this assbag, but it is what it is. He will do right by you."

"Dad!"

"What?"

"I'm not pregnant. That was just bullshit propaganda. Most of the shit they report isn't true. Quinn is about the only person more boring than I am."

Dad looks at me then at Quinn and is silent awhile. He slaps Quinn on the back.

"Glad to hear it. So, you with my daughter?"

"Um, yes, sir."

Dad grunts. "Treat her right or I'll break every bone in your body." He looks over at the house. "Hey, nice place. I've been sleeping on the street for the last week. It'll be nice to get some shelter."

He walks over to the house leaving me and Quinn behind.

"Your dad scares me."

"He's . . . colorful."

We all walk into an empty foyer. I check my watch again; even with the brawl we still have time for a little snack before our team meeting.

"Come on, Dad. I'll make you a snack and you can tell us

what's so important. We have a meeting with the team in a bit, so it'll be good to know so we can brief them."

Quinn and Dad sit at the table. I go to the fridge and find some cheese. In the cabinet below the kitchen island is some stale bread. Good enough. As I make several stale cheese sandwiches, Dad fiddles with his belt buckles and produces a tiny chip. He reaches for my tablet and makes several swipes then finds an open port and sticks the chip in. He continues making pushes and swipes. I walk over and place the plate of suboptimal sandwiches on the table. He doesn't miss a beat as grabs a sandwich and takes a bite. A high pitched squeal from the entrance of the kitchen causes him to stop.

"Holy. Shit. Dad-Kelly!!!"

A rambunctious redhead barrels into the room and hugs Dad with all her might.

"Hey, Wynnie. Good to see you."

"Jesus, Shea. When were you going to tell us your dad was here?"

"We just walked in. He's hungry. I thought I'd feed him first."

"I'm so happy to see you." She looks down at the tablet. "So, what'cha got there?"

He makes several more swipes and taps.

"Once I received the vaccine I sent it off to some of my friends who work in an analytical chemistry lab. As you know, we had a hard time finding anything. Then they put it through a mass spectrometer and we found something very interesting." A graph pops up with several peaks of different sizes. "We found traces of Cadmium, Zinc, Silicon, and Selenium."

I say, "Interesting, those aren't elements I would expect to find in a vaccine."

"Exactly, little one, so we took another sample of the vaccine and put it under an electron microscope to see what could be giving us these readings." He makes several keystrokes and another image of colorful disks pop up.

"Oh, Dad, is that what I think it is?"

"Yup."

Quinn growls. "So is this a language only the Kellys speak?"

Wynne says, "You'll get used to it."

I say, "Guys, those are quantum dots."

Wynne responds, "Shit. This could be bad."

Quinn asks, "What in the hell is a quantum dot?"

I respond, "Quantum dots are nanoparticles. This is what they make qubits out of, the things that make those super quantum computers work. Quantum dots have other uses, like medical imaging. They can attach themselves to cells and when excited by light or electricity they emit light at various frequencies that can be seen with certain scans."

Quinn growls. "So, are you telling me they can inject this stuff in with the vaccine and it will attach itself to our cells, and when they 'turn-on' these dots they can track us? Or do God knows what else to us?"

"That's exactly what I'm saying."

Chapter 17

Everyone is gathered in the conference room looking at the display decorated with colorful disks.

"I still don't get it. How are those tiny things going to do anything to us?" Conner asks.

I can see why Conner is confused. These quantum dots look more like Halloween candy than elements of a supercomputer.

I answer back, "They're still experimental. I bet you a plate full of cheese sandwiches they want use us as their lab rats. These dots are like computers. They can be programmed to do very simple tasks. They can join together to do more complex tasks. It's impossible to tell from this picture what these qubits are programmed to do. Generally, the qubits are dormant until they're activated with some kind of electromagnetic pulse. If I could just get my hands on what they're activating the vaccine with, that would tell us so much."

Quinn's eyes narrow. "Don't even think about it. It's too dangerous. We'll think of some other way, but there is no way in hell you're going to try and sneak into Magistrate's compound and look for something that may or may not be there."

"I did it at Danny's."

"Yeah, and we all know what happened to you there. I'm telling you, Shea, sneaking in that little shit's hideout is a whole different thing than trying to get into an ultra secure compound."

Quinn and I stare each other down.

Dad breaks the silence. "Quinn's right, little one. We need to exhaust all options before we do something like that. Before I left home, the expert I was collaborating with gave me a huge file of all their findings. Problem is, it's locked down tighter than Fort Knox. I'm gonna need help crackin' the code then figurin' out what the hell all this technical mumbo jumbo is."

Boss nods. "Mr. Kelly, I appreciate everything you risked to come over to this side and share this information with us. Your services to this NCS have been invaluable. Ms. Kelly and Ms. Myers will be useful to our pursuits."

We both nod.

Lindsey speaks up, "Sir, I know Shea and Wynne are smart, but this is far beyond hacking into TradeNet or making home-made snooping devices. What makes you think they're going to be able to crack the code of the some of the most technically sophisticated items on the planet? No offense, ladies."

Boss looks at Wynne and me. "Ladies, would you like to field this one?"

Wynne and I look at each other. Wynne gives a deep sigh and a nod signaling me to go ahead. I take a deep breath, searching my thoughts for what to say and how to say it.

"When we were over on the other side, we worked with the chip. We found out it has some pretty nasty side effects. Our goal was to come over here and prove it."

Conner growls. "Hold on. You two used to work with the chip? The chip that we all came here to get away from? Jesus, first Ryan now you two?"

Lindsey interrupts, "Conner, take a breath. Hear them out. What kind of side effects?"

Boss answers, "Mr. Jost, I believe I might be able to answer your questions. As you might have noticed, in the past several months I've not been myself. Many years ago, when I was in the service, I was among the first implanted with the chip. Not the passive chip like Mr. Kelly had, but the one with a brain-controlled interface. My condition is a direct result of chip implantation."

Nikki says, "Oh God, does that mean you still have it in now?"

Boss replies, "Yes, but it has been rendered useless. Back then, once you left the service they disabled the chip, since there was no need for it anymore. I took extra measures to ensure it was indeed disabled. There are many people on the other side who are very interested in disclosing these facts to the public, but their hands are tied. However, we have far fewer rules constraining us. I hired Ms. Kelly and Ms. Myers to help me with these pursuits."

Conner looks at Quinn. "Chief, are you okay with this?"

Quinn adds, "Yes I am, Conner. When I was on the other side I had a lot of interaction with men and women in the service that were implanted with the chip. Some of them just had minor spasms associated with the implants, but others had a much more pronounced damage. When I started digging and asking questions I got stonewalled. That's when I knew there had to be something more to it. It's time we stand up to the shit GlobalThink is trying to put us through."

Conner eyeballs everyone in the room. "Are you fucking kidding me? Stand up to GlobalThink? If we go stirring that pot, GlobalThink will crush us like gnats."

Nikki responds, "I've seen too many of my friends lose everything because of GlobalThink. I can't just stand by."

Conner begins to pace, rubbing his head. "Lindsey, what about you?"

Lindsey shrugs. "After seeing what Mr. Kelly brought us I don't think we're ones stirring the pot. GlobalThink started it, we need to finish it."

"So everyone is just cool with this? We have two fucking chip experts here and no one seems to care? What the fuck?"

Quinn growls and looks Conner squarely in the eye. "I suggest you sit down and listen to the ladies. Like it or not, the chip is in our backyard no matter what. This way we have two experts on our side."

Wynne mouths the words "I'm sorry" to Conner. He looks away in disgust.

The room is silent for a while. Everyone is still trying to get a hold on all the information we just dumped on them.

Boss breaks the silence. "The chip and the vaccine are a great concern, but our main focus right now should be taking down Ramsey. If we don't rid our community of him, our concerns about the vaccine and the chip will all be moot."

Dad pipes in, "I agree, Mr. Jennings. I'll do anything I can to help take down that sumbitch."

"Thank you, Mr. Kelly. Right now we need to get more information on Ramsey and his men's movements."

I respond, "Sir, I've just installed a program at Heads and Tails. That, along with the worm that Ryan is giving Ramsey, should yield some good information starting tomorrow."

"Well done. Mr. Knightly, I would like your team to start putting together plans for our attack on Ramsey's. When Ms. Kelly's team has more information on his movements, shape your plans accordingly. I would like a report the day after tomorrow."

Both Quinn I answer, "Yes, sir."

"Mr. Kelly, you seem to be pretty handy. Do you think you can cobble together some homemade . . . distractions for us?"

"Hell, yeah!"

"Ms. Myers and Mr. Timmons, I would like you to work with Mr. Kelly and get him the materials he needs. Procure them using the quickest means possible."

Wynne and Gordon say in unison, "Yes, sir."

"I realize there might be some lag time in getting materials and intel. Feel free to investigate the chip and vaccine, but your primary focus must be taking down Ramsey." We all nod. "If there is nothing further, you are all dismissed." We all get up to leave. Boss adds, "Ms. Sweet, I would like to talk to you alone, please."

I'm sure he's going to tell her the news that she will no longer be his 'girlfriend,' and she's now on security detail. Wynne and Conner are down the hall having a discussion, no doubt about her involvement with the chip. I shake my head and go into the lab and sit in my comfy leather chair. I start clacking away at the computer. Dad meanders in and sits next to me.

"So, Dad, what do you have in mind for distractions? Magistrate agreed to help us get materials, but he's not going let us have anything really good. We're going to have to be inventive."

"I don't need nuthin' fancy. You think he can get us some fertilizer and diesel fuel?"

"Dad, sometimes it scares me how much we think alike."

He laughs.

Wynne comes in looking as though she's been crying. I look at her. "You okay, hon?"

"Not really. I should've told him sooner. But when he told me about his previous girlfriend being chipped and sent away to the toxic waste dumps, I kind of lost my nerve. The longer I waited to tell him, the harder it got."

"I'll ask Quinn to talk to him."

"Thanks."

As she starts clacking away, Nikki walks in the room looking distressed. She looks at us and says, "Well, I guess my hacking days are over."

Gordon asks, "Why?"

"I'm back on security detail. Boss doesn't need me to be his bodyguard anymore."

I ask, "Are you okay?"

"I don't know. After so many years of wanting my own life,

now I have it. I'm not sure what to do. I feel just sick about Boss. I wish there was something that I could do."

"I know what you mean."

"Anyway, it's been fun. I'll be back to help you guys out. I gotta go. I'm going to help Quinn and the boys plot out our plans for Ramsey." She adds with a smile, "You know, you can't trust a man to think these things through by themselves. I also wanted to tell you guys that I got some data from the snooper Shea planted at Magistrate's. I haven't had a chance to look it though."

Wynne says, "Thanks, we'll look at them."

As Nikki closes the door behind her I say, "Okay guys, Dad has some ideas for some distraction devices. I think the quickest route will be to go through Magistrate to get the materials he needs. Dad, how long will it take you to get a preliminary list?"

Dad responds, "I'm going to go through some of the stuff you have in your garages first. I should have a list in a couple of hours."

"Can you give us a quick overview of the files you got from your contacts so we can work on then while we wait?"

Dad turns and makes several keystrokes. Some files appear on the screen mounted on the wall.

"These are the files. I destroyed all traces of 'em, so you're lookin' at the only copies of these files in existence. Be careful." He double-clicks on one of the files, but it doesn't open. "They're always locked down tight, but these must have some real important shit on 'em, because even I've had trouble breaking the code. Even when we get them open, I'm pretty sure I won't be able to understand a damn thing that's in here."

I answer, "If Wynne and Gordo can't get into it, no one can."

Dad grunts.

"I think this is enough to keep you guys busy for a while. I'm going over to see how Quinn's team is doing. I'll report to you guys any items they need. Oh yeah and don't forget to see what's coming through on those snoopers."

Wynne and Gordon reply in unison, "Yes, ma'am."

"Ugh, will you guys stop that. I'll be back in a few minutes to help you out."

Both Dad and I get up to leave. Once in the hall, Dad turns to me before going up the stairs. "I'm proud of you, girl."

I give him a weak smile. "Dad, I haven't done anything. In fact, I think I'm failing miserably."

He gives me a hug and says, "Don't ever think that. You are doing a hell of a lot more than most people are." He smiles and shakes his head. "It's good to see you again, kiddo." He walks up the stairs to the garage.

I slip into the conference room; the lights are dimmed and an electronic 3D image of Ramsey's compound hangs in the air. Quinn and his group are gathered around the projection. Quinn points to several rooms and says, "We know when Danny had this building, and this is where the majority of the men were housed." Quinn manipulates the image again. "We also know that right here is where Danny stored most of the weapons. But we need to know for sure."

I pipe up, "I'm guessing tomorrow morning after all the guys get back from Heads and Tails, we'll start getting some good intel from the phones. Dad's taking inventory of what we have and what he needs to make some distraction devices."

Quinn nods. "Good. I'm glad we have another Kelly to help us out." Looking at his team, he says, "We just met with Mr. Ito and he's agreed to train the mercs in town and act as supervisor. Go into town, brief him on our plans and get his input. Nikki, I'm making you liaison with Mr. Ito. You're in charge of helping him train the mercs and ensuring he has everything he needs."

She nods.

"Also, do a sweep of town while you're there. The Orphans

have been at it already today."

Lindsey and Nikki say, "Yes, sir."

Conner remains silent, staring at Quinn.

Quinn growls and gets inches from Conner's face. "Do you have a problem with my orders?"

"No."

Quinn yells, "No, what?"

There is a moment of silence then Conner answers back, "No, *sir.*"

"Good. Next time I give an order, I expect you to acknowledge it. Got it?"

"Sir, yes, sir."

Quinn turns his attention to me. "Do you think there's anything you or your dad could cobble together that could jam all their communications or electronics?"

"I think Team Kelly could put something together for you."

"Good."

"Listen, the plan is to take out the compound when as many people as possible are there. First we'll detonate the living quarters and the weapons storage. Then we'll go in and finish off everyone who happened to survive the initial blast. We need to get in and get out as fast as possible. It's imperative that we strike when Ramsey is there. We absolutely need to take him down and have evidence that he's gone. Once we get a study of their patterns from the phones and Ryan's worm, that'll tell us when to strike."

Everyone in room says in unison, "Yes, sir."

"Good, then get to work."

Chapter 18

Hey Jude

The computers are whirring away in the lab and I fight to stifle a yawn. Gordo and Wynne are intently clacking away at their computers. Dad is sketching out schematics for some of the devices he plans on building. The door opens, letting a stream of light into the darkened room.

A baritone voice breaks our concentration. "How's it going in here?"

I turn around and see Quinn dressed in cargo pants and a form fitting t-shirt: so much better than that stupid suit.

"It's going okay. Dad gave Wynne and Gordo a list of the items he needs. Fortunately, we have a lot around the compound we can use. He's sketching out some of the finer details now." I turn to Dad. "You doing okay, Pop?"

He grunts and waves his hand.

"That means he's fine. We've procured everything we need either through Magistrate or other channels, unless you need something else. So we've been working on getting into the files from Dad's contact and investigating information from the worm Ryan planted."

"Getting anything good?"

Wynne shakes her head. "I hate to say it, Quinn, but I think you're going to have to bring Ryan in for a talk. I'm not getting shit."

Quinn growls. "So how's the file decoding going?"

Wynne slumps in her chair and Gordon puts his head on his keyboard. I shake my head. "Swell."

"What's the problem?"

Wynne turns to face us. "Dad-Kelly, you weren't kidding

when you said your contact had this thing locked down tighter than Fort Knox. They're clearly used a hashing algorithm to encrypt this data, but hell if I can find a converter protocol that works. I've even broken out some of my fancier 1028-bit key encryption algorithms, and nada. I'm going to try some quantum algorithms, maybe they'll work."

Dad rubs his neck and turns around. "Told ya."

Gordo shifts in his seat. I know Dad makes him a little nervous – well, more nervous than usual.

"Um, Mr. Kelly where did you get these files?"

"I actually have a network of contacts. There's one feller in particular that I've been working with goes by the screen name of St. Jude."

Quinn looks as though he's seen a ghost.

I whisper to him, "What is it?"

"It's probably nothing. I'll tell you later."

Gordon asks, "How can you be sure whoever's on the other side is trustworthy?"

Dad answers back, "Well, I was on the other side and I was trustworthy. Wasn't I, boy?"

Gordo cowers. I smile and expand on Dad's answer. "Not everyone on the other side hates us, Gordo. There are a lot of people who felt they didn't have a choice but to take the chip. They had families to take care of, or they had illnesses that couldn't be treated over here. Their backs were against the wall. There's a network of Compliant that want to help us. It was nice having Dad on the other side, because he could easily get information to the outside network. We're going to have to figure out new ways to communicate now that Dad's on our side. And we're probably fighting a losing battle, because even if we do find anything there's no guarantee the information will make it to anyone who can do anything about it."

Quinn says, "You know, Kelly, you aren't the only one with

outside contacts, and I wouldn't count on us losing this battle. Not everyone at the top is happy about the Non-Compliance Act being passed."

"Well aren't we Mr. Cloak and Dagger?" I elbow him in the ribs. "So, how're you doing, babe?"

Dad growls.

Quinn looks a little taken aback by Dad's reaction to my pet name. "Ignore him, *babe*. He's just a grumpy old man."

"Mind your manners, young lady."

I giggle. I've missed my dad.

Quinn shakes his head. "Conner, Nikki, and Lindsey are still talking to Mr. Ito about our plans and nailing down a training schedule. I've come up with several scenarios I think will work, but I've kind of hit a wall until the others come back. I thought about what you were saying the other night when we were . . . uh . . . "

Dad growls again.

"Uh, watching a movie. About showing me everything you know about the chip. I think now would be a great time to catch me up."

Wynne smiles. "Watching a movie, huh? Is that what you kids are calling it?"

Quinn and I say in unison. "Shut up, Wynne."

"Touchy, touchy. I actually agree with Captain Personality. It's been a while since we've done anything with our little friend chip. It'd be interesting to see what you can tell us about him, Quinn. I think once we give Gordo here a brief, he'll be able to answer all our questions by the end of the week."

"I don't know about that, Wynnie."

She walks over to our safe, unlocks it, and produces a pink bag. She sits at one of the lab benches, puts on wrist strap, and plugs it into the bench. From inside the pink bag she produces a tiny chip. Quinn looks with wide eyed curiosity, then reaches out to touch it. Wynne smacks his hand.

"Don't touch! You're not properly grounded. Just a little static electricity zap could ruin this thing forever. Always plug yourself into the table before touching it. You might have to punish him for that one tonight, Shea."

Dad clears his throat to make sure we know he's still there. I give Wynne a piercing look.

I say, "This isn't the full up GovTek, just the chip at the heart of it. There are a lot of add-ons to the chip to make it hearty enough for the external environment and other optional peripherals that make up the blinking lights you see embedded on people's necks."

"So what have you been doing with this?"

I take out our homemade test bed and Wynne puts the chip in and hooks it up to the computer. Lines of code scroll across the display on the wall. "We've been mapping the functions of this chip. It is a pretty tedious process." I tap on the keyboard and an image of circuitry is displayed alongside the code. "This is an image I got from Dad, via Spooky St. Jude, of the internal circuitry of this little dude."

Dad and Quinn growl simultaneously.

I continue, "So we ping a part of the chip with some code and see what happens, then make notes on this drawing. We almost got it mapped out. Most of the functions weren't a big surprise: mostly communication handling and information storage, just like the old days. There are a couple of areas that we're having a hard time with, but we really haven't had time to fool with them. I'm sure it's related to CAMS interaction, we didn't have those when we were on the other side."

Dad adds, "Since she's been over here I've been supplying them with as much human-chip interaction data I can from my sources. As you can imagine it's hard to come by, and even harder to get over to her in a secure fashion."

I sigh. "My goal was to map the chip's functions and then investigate which functions are causing the chip fatigue. There might be some functions that are perfectly valid, like for victims of brain damage. It might be okay to use the chip for short periods of time."

Quinn growls. "I don't know about that, Kelly."

"No, you don't. That's the point, no one does. The technology was rolled out without proper testing, because it was new and sexy." I sigh again. "So that's where we are. Mapping chip functions and processing chip interaction data. It's a slow, slow process."

Gordo looks like a kid in candy store. "I'd be happy to help in any way I can. I think it looks like fun."

Quinn says, "You would. I have some interaction data I'd be happy to give you from my contacts."

I laugh. "Is it from Spooky St. Jude?"

Quinn is silent for a while.

"Is it?"

"We'll talk about this later. For now, just keep on track. You're a smart cookie and you'll figure it out. I have faith in you."

Damn, that was weird.

"Thanks." I look at my watch. "Shouldn't your crew be back by now?"

"Yeah, I'm sure they just got hung up somewhere."

"Ya know, I need to go bug the little weeble-wobble for my 'Cuda manual. I can go into town and look for them while I get my manual."

"That's a negative. You're not going there alone."

"Geez, I think we proved that Ramsey isn't after me. It was Dad that was looking for me. I'll be fine."

"Mark my words, if he sees you and he thinks you're vulnerable, he's going to pounce. If you go into town you go with me. End of discussion."

I stare him down and start to retort, but Dad interrupts. "Saoirse, Quinn's right. If this Ramsey fella's running through town, it's best not to go by yourself."

I know they're right, but I still feel like a grounded adolescent.

"Fine, whatever. So are you going to fetch them, Quinn?"

"I'll message them and see if they're okay. If they don't answer we'll go into town *together* and see what's holding them up."

"I'm getting kind of hungry. I'm going to start dinner. Let me know if you hear anything."

Quinn smirks, "Two meals in one day, you're getting rather domestic."

Wynne answers, "You have no idea, Quinn."

Chapter 19

Dinner with the Family

"So it's true? She didn't make that up?"

Dad shovels another bite of spaghetti in his mouth. "Nope, true story. I have to say, after I was done being pissed at her I was kind of proud. That teacher was a real asshole."

The whole crew erupts in laughter. All of us, minus Conner and Boss, are gathered around the table for a late night dinner; the others came back shortly after Quinn messaged them. Conner is too pissed at Wynne to be in the same room with her, and Boss excused himself early. Since everyone put in a long day making preps for Ramsey, I decided to make some vittles as my way of saying thank you. Besides, this is the best mood I've been in for a long time: my dad's home, and last night and this morning were pretty freakin' spectacular too.

"Saoirse, this is the best damn spaghetti I've had in years."

"Thanks, Dad. But I think you've just gone so long without warm food that anything tastes good right now."

Nikki adds, "No, this is really good. I'm impressed. I thought you were a one trick pony with those muffins, but now I think we have new job for you at the compound."

"Well, when you live on a farm with all kinds of church ladies coming over teaching you how to cook you tend to learn a thing or two."

Gordon laughs. "Church ladies?"

"Yeah, Dad was a hot ticket in our little community."

"Saoirse!"

"Oh come on, Dad. You know you were. The male population was pretty low because of the war. Dad being a widower with a cute daughter, all the ladies at our church would always come visiting. They taught me how to cook and how to be a good little housewife for my future husband."

Quinn practically spits out his beer.

"Shut up, you. I can be domestic if I want to be. I just choose to be in the garage rather than the kitchen."

Nikki laughs. "Well, Chief, you're a pretty lucky guy. Just make sure she doesn't get you fat." She looks over at Wynne who has hardly touched her food. "So, why didn't you tell us any of these tidbits about Shea?"

Wynne breaks her trance, realizing we were talking to her. "Uh, what?"

"Nothing. Don't worry, Wynne. Conner will get over it. You just need to give him a little time."

"I thought once he took a walk around town he'd be better." She pushes away her plate. "I'm not that hungry and I'm pretty worn out. My allergies are killing me. I'm just going to bed."

"Okay, Wynnie. There are plenty of leftovers if you get hungry."

I stand and give her a hug. "Thanks, Shea." She trudges off to her bedroom.

Everyone at the table is laughing and exchanging stories, even Quinn. An involuntary smile comes to my face. I start to collect the mass of sauce-stained plates and flatware. The rest of the crew stands and helps, and before long the kitchen is clean.

Nikki yawns, "I'm beat and we got an early morning to-morrow . . . and the day after that and the day after that. I'm going to bed."

Gordon adds, "Mr. Kelly, I have an empty bed in my room. It's small . . . "

"Thank you kindly. Any bed indoors will be a welcome change from the last week. I'm going to go out and have a smoke then I'll be right up."

It is just me and Quinn left in the kitchen.

"I think I'm going to go out and talk to Dad for awhile."

"You haven't seen the man in five years, you should." He gives me a long kiss then adds, "But you know where I am when you're done."

Outside I scan the dark porch for Dad, the glowing embers from his cigarette betray his position. I plop down on the outdoor couch by the grumpy old man.

"Hey, Daddy."

He puts his arm around me and gives me a hug. "It's good to see you, kiddo."

"You too, Daddy."

"Have I ever told you how much you remind me of your mother?"

"Not really. You never talked about her much."

He scoffs and then gets a sad look in his eyes. "I guess it was kind of painful for me to talk about her. My Maria. You look a lot like her. Except them green eyes you got from your old man." He squeezes my hand and continues. "She was a daughter of a migrant worker from Mexico, a real spitfire. I think she hated me just a bit when we first met."

"Really? So how did you win her over?"

"I just kept asking her out and she finally agreed to shut me up. She was the most beautiful woman I ever met. I'm sorry you don't remember her. She would've done a damn sight better job of raising you than I did."

"Hey, what are you sayin'? I think I turned out okay."

He kisses the top of my head and laughs. "Yeah I think you turned out pretty good. But a girl needs her mother. I'm sorry I couldn't help you with that girly stuff."

"Ah, Pop, I think we did a pretty good job of raising each other."

He laughs. "Pretty crazy place you live in. Is it always like this?"

"It's crazier than usual right now. But you get used to it after a while."

"I don't know if I ever will. This place is like hell."

"It wasn't always this bad. It wasn't until Ramsey started stirring shit up that it got really bad. That's why we need to take him down."

"Well, anything I can do to help. I guess I'll be calling this place home for a while now."

"Thank you, Dad, for coming out here. I know what you gave up doing it."

"I never should've let you come here by yourself."

"But you had the farm to worry about. It's okay."

He turns to face me. "Fuck the farm. You're my only family. I'm not leaving you again."

"What did you do with the farm?"

"Sold it to the Milliken kid. He worked that place so long I felt it was only right. He's a good kid. I know he'll take care of it."

"He's a good kid? You certainly didn't think so when I was dating him."

"He was your boyfriend; it was my duty to bust his balls. Speaking of which, what can you tell me about that Quinn fella? He seems to be smitten with you."

"Quinn? Smitten?" I chuckle. "I guess when we first met I hated his guts. He was so bullheaded and arrogant. I guess I still think he's bullheaded."

"Bullheaded, hmm, who does that remind me of? Let me think."

"Whatever, Dad. The more I got to know him the more he kind of grew on me. He's really been there for me in some shitty situations. He's a good man. A little rough around the edges, but he's one of the good ones."

"You're an adult and I'm not going to tell you how to run your life. I want you to be careful, though."

"You'd be hard pressed to find many other people that work as hard as he does for this community."

"I don't give a shit how hard he works, or if he's the savior of this goddamn NCS. The only thing I care about is how he treats you."

I smile. "He's good to me, Dad. We butt heads a lot, but he respects me and I respect him. Give him a chance. I think you'll like him."

"We'll see about that. If mistreats you in anyway, I don't care who he is, I'll kill him."

This isn't an attempt to be funny on Dad's part. He really means it. I kept my previous relationship follies from him, mostly because I didn't want him risking life and limb coming here to help me, but also because I wanted to take care of things on my own terms.

I change the subject. "So how's everyone back home?"

"Frankly, everyone's tired of all the bullshit. Most of the people were willing to concede to the chip if they just left us alone, and they did for a while. But all these Morality and Healthful Living Codes are going to be the straw that breaks the camel's back. I hear it's worse in the cities where they have a tighter grip. I guess we're lucky, we kinda look out for our own in our community."

"I miss home. I'd always thought I'd be back eventually, but lately I've given up hope of that." I lay my head on his shoulder. "I'm glad you're here, Daddy."

He takes a long drag off his cigarette and throws it to the ground. "I'll be honest with you, girl, I'm not happy to be here, but I'm glad to be with you again." We both get up and he opens the door for me. "Well, we best be gettin' to bed. Got an early day ahead of us."

I give him a big hug. "Night, Daddy."

Chapter 20

Break on Through…

The 3D wireframe drawing of Ramsey's structure glows in front of Quinn and me. He points to the eastern quarter of the building.

"I think this will be the most vulnerable point here. If we could a get a read on the snooper that Ryan was supposed to plant, it'd give us a better feel for what kind of guards he has out. Right now, I'm just flying blind."

"I guess no one's had any luck in finding Ryan."

"No, I'm sure Ramsey's hiding him or he's hiding out in the wastelands."

Even we don't venture into the wastelands. They're technically part of the NCS just before the southern exit, but no one ventures there. There's some real scary shit that goes on out there, and this is coming from a girl who had a drill run through her hand. Most of the people there don't take kindly to strangers coming on their turf.

"You're not thinking of sending our guys into the wastelands to find him, are you?"

"No, if he's there then he won't last very long. But if I get my hands on that little shit he'll regret ever laying eyes on us."

Just as I'm about to retort, the image of Ramsey's structure dissolves and the lights dim. After a few seconds the lights go back to their normal intensity.

Damn these power fluctuations.

Quinn growls and starts to turn the 3D imager back on. Just as he's about to make the last keystroke the intercom sounds.

"Shea and Quinn, Robert would like to see you in his office immediately."

Once in his office, Claire whispers, "Magistrate is on the video comms with him. He wants you in there. Go on in."

We walk in and Magistrate greets us with a smirk. "Shea and Quinn, it's good to see you. Shea, I trust you're feeling better?"

Remembering my buffoonery at his place I stammer, "Uh, yeah. Stomach's feeling much better now."

"Good, good. I was just telling Robert that I have some items that might be of use to in repairing your compound. From looking at your list, it looks as though you need some items for your power systems?"

Quinn nods. "Any items you may have would definitely help us with our mutual goals."

Magistrate looks at his watch and says, "Yes, well, two of my marshals will be at your compound in fifteen minutes to escort two of you over to the other side to pick up some items." Everyone in the room is silent. Magistrate smiles, knowing what is going through our heads. "Now, now. This is just quick trip to the other side. I don't know exactly what you need, so at least one of you will have to go and talk to my contact to straighten that out. I assume that will be you, Shea."

I slowly nod my head. My heart beats faster thinking of the other side. God, I haven't been there in years.

He clears his throat. "Very well then, pick another to go with you and meet my men outside your compound in fifteen minutes." The screen goes dark.

Quinn growls. "I'm going with you."

I shake my head. "That's a stupid idea."

"What do you mean?"

"Boss can't risk sending us both over there."

Boss nods. "Ms. Kelly is right."

"So then the deal's off. If Magistrate can't ship the shit over here, then you're not going. Call him back."

I heave a big sigh. "It's not like I relish the idea of going over there, in fact I'm dreading it, but you know as well as I do that these power fluctuations are getting worse. We can't risk this mission going tits-up because all our power goes to shit at the last second. I'm the only one who knows what I'm looking for. Well, me and Dad, but he can't go over because no one knows he's here."

Quinn looks at Boss with pleading eyes. "Mr. Knightly, Ms. Kelly is right. We need the items and she's our only viable option."

Quinn paces and rubs his head. "Fine. Who's going with her?"

"Well, Conner will go apeshit if we send him over, and like I said, Dad can't go over."

Quinn narrows his eyes. "Then Lindsey's going with you. He knows how to act over there and the marshals will be less likely to mess with you if Lindsey is there." Quinn shouts out the door, "Claire, have Lindsey meet us in the foyer immediately." He looks at me. "You're coming with me."

I follow him out to the main area to kitchen. He opens the door to the patio. I go through and he follows. He paces quickly, rubbing his head.

"You say the word, Shea, just say it and I'll go over. I can call you when I'm over there and you can talk me through whatever you need."

"Boss has already given orders and — "

"I don't give a shit what he said. If you don't want to go, I'll talk to him. He'll listen to me."

This has him more unnerved than I thought possible for Quinn. I take a second to mull it over. I know he's serious and that he would be willing go to the Compliant side for me, but I can't let him.

I step on my tip-toes and give him a kiss on the cheek. "It'll be okay. I'll be right back over here to be a pain in your ass in no time."

Quinn's face is contorted in worry. "I don't like this."

"Me neither, but I'll be fine. I'm sure Magistrate is doing this to mind-fuck us. He needs all of us to bring down Ramsey and he can't risk keeping me over there."

"God, I don't think they could handle you over there."

I give him a little shove. "Besides, it'll be fun to mess with the Compliant folks. Hey, I might even get one of those fancy coffees with the whip cream on top." I look at my watch. "C'mon, it's time to get going."

I take him by the hand and lead him around the house down to the main gate. Lindsey and Claire are waiting by the gate.

"Has Claire briefed you?"

Lindsey nods. "Yes, sir. We're to get supplies for our power system and get out of town. We'll still have a link to you through our comms. So if anything goes wrong, we'll let you know."

Yeah, then what?

I decide to keep my feelings to myself. Surely everyone's thinking the same thing; they don't need my smartass comments reminding them the whole operation stinks on ice. The high-pitched whine of an electric powered motor breaks the nervous silence amongst us. The doors of the sorry excuse for a car open and two marshals emerge from the car, both smirking. One marshal I'm all too familiar with runs his hand through greasy curls and heads toward us.

Quinn punches a code into the keypad and the gate opens.

Ed saunters in and says, "Looks like I get to ride my favorite girl."

I swallow hard. If I knew there were no repercussions, I'd stick my fist right into his fat face.

Quinn barks, "Ed!"

Ed chuckles. "Oh, my bad. I meant I get to take a ride *with* the lovely Miss Shea."

I look at Quinn as though I've not heard a word that Ed's said.

"So, hon, you want the double grande half fat shot of vanilla double espresso with whip cream and a sprinkle of cinnamon?"

Quinn shakes his head. "God you're a pain the ass."

I give him a smile. "You love it."

Ed raps me on the head with his baton. "Ah, ain't this sweet? Get in the car."

I get in the back seat, but Quinn keeps Lindsey behind. I can't make out what they're saying from the car, but Lindsey's nodding his head a lot. Quinn barks out one last unintelligible command and Lindsey gets in the back of the car with me.

He smiles. "It'll be fine."

Ed gets in the driver's seat and his assistant climbs in the passenger side. They both grin at us.

"Buckle in, ladies. Magistrate'll have our asses if we don't get you back in one piece."

I take a long breath as we roll away from the compound.

Chapter 21

... To the Other Side

The younger marshal turns around to face me and Lindsey as Ed drives toward town. He hands us two wristbands.

"Here, put these on. We can't risk you guys trying to run away from us."

"Thanks, junior! And here I didn't get you anything."

The hulking blonde man growls and I snicker. We both slap on the metal tracking bands. As soon as they close on our wrists, they glow green. If we attempt to take the bands off, a shock will be sent through our systems, rendering us unconscious. We'll be met with the same fate if we venture too far from our hosts. The Non-Compliants that go over as day laborers have to buy the same handy-dandy wristbands that are linked to their place of employment and their transport. Yeah, the Compliants have us by the short and curlies.

Ed stops when we get to an intersection in the center of town. My heart starts to beat faster and I look at Lindsey. I can tell he's thinking the same thing I am. A turn to the north would lead over the river to the nearest Compliant city about fifteen minutes away, but a turn to the south would lead to the exit that's mostly barren with the exception of the Disciplinary Action Facility, where those found guilty of various crimes are housed and implanted with chips, then given a personality reboot. After the reboot is found to be successful, they're shipped to one of the various toxic waste sites left behind by the war to live out the rest of their short lives as mindless cleaning zombies. If Magistrate wants me at the DAF, there's absolutely nothing I can do about it now.

"So are you going to make a career out of this turn, Ed?"

He scoffs and turns north to the Compliant city. I let out my breath.

"Did I make you nervous, little Shea?"

"Not really, dickhead. You drive like an old lady and at this rate we'll never get home. I've got about a million things to do today and this little trip is cutting into my agenda."

Ed growls and steps on the accelerator. I nearly laugh at the weak power offered by the car. We wind through the streets of the NCS. The residents stare at us as we go by. After a few minutes we get to the exit. We inch our way up the line of vehicles waiting to go through. Ed rolls up to the guard shack; the woman nods and grins seeing his cargo.

She makes a few taps to her CAMS and says, "Good luck with these two, Sergeant Barton. You're cleared to go."

Ed nods in acknowledgement.

The gate seems to open in slow motion and the sounds of the clanging chains and motors of the moving gate fill the car. Finally, a clear view of the Compliant side is offered up, something I haven't seen in quite a while. Ed drives through the car-sized opening toward the bridge. The towering glass and metal buildings gleam in the sunlight and stand out against the bright blue afternoon sky.

As we get closer to the city, my breath quickens. Lindsey puts his hand on top of mine and gives me a crooked smile.

"It'll be fine, Shea. We all have baggage over here."

"It's just that . . . I didn't ever think I'd see this place again."

"You and me both," he scoffs. "So, uh, Chief seems to be pretty taken with you."

Glad for the change in subject, I laugh. "Taken? With me? Why do you say that?"

"I don't know. Maybe because he threatened me within inches of my life if I didn't bring you back in once piece."

"Liar."

"Seriously, he's pretty worried. He was trying hard not to show it, but I could tell. You mean a lot to him."

"Thanks, Lindsey."

Ed coos from the front seat. "Ah, isn't that sweet. Quinn has lady feelings."

"Shut up, needle dick."

Ed growls.

We grow quiet again as the car goes over the bridge, then within a few minutes we're on the other side and we're greeted by pristine fields. The Compliants have food plots outside all their cities to minimize transportation of goods from one place to another. There are Non-Compliants working the fields under the watchful eye of marshals. I let out a deep breath and slink down in my seat. All of this borders on sensory overload.

Ed's assistant laughs as he looks at the Non-Compliants working the fields. "See anyone you know?"

"Shut up, asshole. At least they're working. It's not like they'll even see a morsel of the food they're harvesting for your fat ass."

After winding through the food plots for a few moments, a melodious female voice sounds over the car speakers.

STAY LEFT ON NORTHBOUND *981* FOR HEARTLAND DISTRICT CITY *61023* IN FIVE MILES.

After a few moments of silence she continues:

JUNCTION STATE ROAD *3108* EASTBOUND TO ROLLING HILLS DISTRICT IN TWO MILES.

As Ed veers westbound, I look down the nearly deserted eastbound thoroughfare. The next Compliant district, Rolling Hills, is about two hundred miles away. There isn't too much between this district and the next except for a few ghost towns and the farming region where I grew up. What I wouldn't give to be home again.

The fake female voice sounds again, keeping me from feeling too sorry for myself.

> *ESTIMATED TIME OF ARRIVAL TO LONG RANGE TRANSPORTATION FACILITY, ONE MINUTE. AUTOMATIC CONTROL OF YOUR VEHICLE WILL COMMENCE IN THIRTY SECONDS.*

Ed pushes several buttons and the console lights up.

The car traverses an overpass toward a large concrete building that looks like a parking structure.

> *AUTOMATIC CONTROL OF YOUR VEHICLE HAS BEEN TAKEN. PLEASE DO NOT ATTEMPT TO TAKE MANUAL CONTROL OF YOUR VEHICLE. YOUR VEHICLE WILL BE GUIDED TO THE FIRST AVAILABLE PARKING SPACE.*

Before we arrive at the building, I take a moment to look over the city I used to call home. It has changed quite a bit from when I used to live here. The elevated metro system that was still under construction five years ago seems to be complete. The tracks connect each quadrant of the city to one another. Below, the old roadways I used to occasionally cruise in the 'Cuda have been turned into pathways for pedestrians and bike riders. A crystal-blue tributary to the river separates the eastern half of the city from the western half. The sleek modern form of the sculpture-like buildings ties in well with the painstakingly manicured lawns. This city is the younger, sleeker son to the old dying city of the Non-Compliant side, just waiting patiently for its father to die so it can rule without dispute.

When we go into the parking garage structure, I turn my attention straight ahead. The car guides itself into the first free parking spot and turns off.

The fake female voice from the car says:

> *WELCOME, CITIZENS 9588 AND 8545, TO HEARTLAND DISTRICT, CITY 61023. ENJOY YOUR STAY.*

"Gee, you ever feel like you're nothing but a number, Ed?"

"Shut up, worm. Out of the car, both of you."

We all get out of the car and follow Ed to a small booth where a young petite blonde sits, wearing a bright white uniform and a cheery smile. She looks down at her CAMS.

"Good Day, citizens, and to your visitors. What can I do for you?"

What kind of happy pills do they have this chick on?

Ed answers, "We're making a quick visit in town. We need to house our vehicle here."

She makes a few more taps to her CAMS. "Certainly, Sergeant Barton, it's twenty credits per hour. And will you be renting a pedestrian vehicle for you and your guests today?"

"No, we'll be taking the metro to the R&D quadrant."

"Excellent! There's no better way for your visitors to see our city than our exemplary mass transit system. The next metro to the R&D quadrant will be on the west platform in five minutes."

Visitors, is that what they call us over here?

Ed grumbles and grabs my arm. "Let's go, worms."

The smile doesn't leave cheery girl's face. "Have a pleasant day. Enjoy your stay."

"Is everyone that smiley here? No wonder you chose to stay over in the NCS, Ed."

"Shut up. It's a better world over here. Something that you and your friend will never understand."

"You got that right."

We all go out the west exit. There are stairs leading down to the walkways, but we stay on the elevated platform to wait for the metro. Below, the trees are turning shades of orange and red. Several kids splash in the waterway while their miffed mothers yell at them to get out. Business people race by the whole scene, unaware.

The metro silently approaches and the doors open. The same female voice as in the car says:

WELCOME CITIZENS AND VISITORS. NEXT STOP R&D QUADRANT.

Ed pokes me in the back with his baton and I step inside the pristine metro. It's early afternoon, so the train car is pretty sparsely populated. We all sit on a long empty seat across the far wall of the car. A mother pulls her cute red-ringletted daughter closer. She whispers something in her ear. I assume it's something about staring being rude, because the girl immediately turns from us. The train moves and the only sound is the muzak rendition of the classic *Shoot to Thrill*.

Lindsey smiles at me and rolls his eyes. Then he reaches into the inner pocket of his leather jacket.

Ed and his partner shout in unison, "Keep your hand right there, worm!" Ed looks over at his partner. "Did you search him before you let him in the car?"

The man stammers, "Uh, no, I thought you . . . "

Ed puts his hand on his stun wand. "Move your hand out of your jacket pocket, nice and slow."

Lindsey gives a crooked smile. "Whatever you say, Sergeant Barton." He moves his hand from out of his jacket and there is a there a small silver stick in between his fingers.

Junior stutters, "Wha–what is that?"

Lindsey smirks and in one quick move unwraps the stick and throws the contents under the wrapper in his mouth. He starts to chew. "It's gum. I want my breath to be its freshest, now that

I'm amongst Compliants." He winks at a cute girl sitting across from him. She rolls her eyes in mild irritation.

I laugh. "Ooh, you better watch it, Ed I think he might have some breath mints in his pants pocket."

Ed growls and the mother with girl gets up and takes her daughter by the hand. The little girl whispers to her mother as they walk toward the neighboring car, "Why is everyone so mad, Mommy?"

The mother says in a hushed voice, "There are some people that don't belong here, that's all."

A shiver rolls down my spine when I see the blinking LEDs on the child's skin.

The metro speeds along the track and now the muzak is replaced by the calm voice of a male announcer:

> *DID YOU KNOW THAT EVERY TUESDAY CHIP AND CAMS UPDATES ARE AVAILABLE? YOU CAN DOWNLOAD YOUR UPDATES AT ONE OF THE MANY STATIONS AROUND THE CITY. DON'T GET BEHIND ON YOUR UPDATES. REMEMBER: COMPLIANCE IS EVERYONE'S JOB.*

Just as the announcement finishes the train stops and the female voice says:

> *R&D QUADRANT: HOPPER COLLEGE OF ELECTRICAL ENGINEERING AND COMPUTER SCIENCE, TESLA COLLEGE OF POWER AND ENERGY. NEXT STOP: DUNBAR COLLEGE OF BIOMEDICAL ENGINEERING AND ROEBLING COLLEGE OF MECHANICAL ENGINEERING.*

"Come on, pukes. This is our stop."

Lindsey looks down at the girl and says in his gravelly voice, "Pity we couldn't have more time to talk."

"Whatever, creep."

He laughs.

We go down the stairs to the walkway and without thinking about it, I start walking toward a squat rectangular building flanked by two larger high-rises.

"Hey, where do you think you're going?"

"Well, this is the right building, isn't it?"

Ed glares at me. "How'd a Non-Compliant worm like you know that?"

"Um, 'cause I can read." I point to the sign that says TESLA COLLEGE OF POWER AND ENERGY. "Magistrate wanted us over here to get parts for our power systems so I kind of figured this was the right spot."

"C'mon, I don't have all day."

We go into the building, walking straight to the receptionist area. The clean-cut skinny man behind the receptionist desk smiles. "Greetings, Sergeant Barton. I assume you and your visitors are Dr. Rhodes' 1400 appointment."

"Yes."

"It'll be just a minute. Dr. Rhodes is in the Distributed Energy lab now. I've just paged him and he will be here shortly."

Dr. Rhodes? It couldn't be.

We mill around the waiting area bit . . . waiting. The building is exactly how I remember it: open and airy. Most of the lighting is provided by skylights and lots of windows throughout. There is greenery hanging from each of the balconies above. Everyone walking around is wearing buttoned-up white shirt and khaki pants or skirt, far different from the uniform of crappy jeans and jammy pants when I was a student here. A man with blond hair, average height and build appears before me and smiles.

"I assume you're Sergeant Barton's guests."

I try hard to contain my smile. If Carson is associated with Non-Compliants in any way it could damage his reputation and career.

I extend my hand. "Yes, sir, Magistrate sent us over. He said you may have some parts for us."

Carson goes to shake my hand, but then Barton makes a loud coughing sound. Carson pulls away his hand.

"Forgive me. The Healthful Living Codes forbid me from coming into contact with uh, Non-Compliants. If you just follow me down the hall I think I have some items for you."

As we walk down the hall I whisper to Lindsey, "Hmm, news to me that Compliants can't touch us. I guess we should tell the marshals down at Heads and Tales. You know, for their own good."

Lindsey laughs. "Good idea, Shea. We couldn't have them breaking their codes for our sake."

Ed barks, "Shut up, you two."

After a few moments, we go through a set of double doors into a large lab. I take second to drool over the new lab equipment. Carson walks over to some old-style solar panels. "These are little broken, but maybe you can salvage the good parts." He points to a box of assorted parts. "You're welcome to sort through this too, to find something that could help."

Ed scoffs then says, "Hey, Doc, I'm gonna hand control of these two over to you. Me and my partner need a break. You okay with that?"

"Sure, we'll be done in about fifteen minutes. I'll meet you in the lobby."

Ed and his partner head out the door, and Carson waits a few minutes then gives me a giant bear hug. "Oh. My. God. I didn't ever think I'd ever see you again. When the call went out from Magistrate that some of the Non-Compliants needed help with their power systems, I knew it had to be you. I'll help you however I can, but we have to be discreet about it."

Lindsey narrows his eyes. "So . . . you two know each other?"

Carson smiles. "You could say that. We got our degrees

together. Me and Miss Shea pulled a lot of all-nighters together. She saved my ass about a million times. I just want to do what I can to help."

"Thanks, dude. So what's this shit about broken solar panels?"

"Oh yeah, fuck that shit." He goes to a cabinet and grabs a roll of what looks like fabric with tiny mirrors sewn in. "Take a look at this. Tiny redundant panels, and they're lightweight and mobile. I bet that boyfriend of yours will be able to haul this wherever you need it."

"Thanks! You got any transmission line? Mine's getting all corroded and lossy."

"Yeah, I got some low loss line for you and a couple other goodies. I'm going to send all this stuff later today via a courier." He sits on the lab table and his smile turns downward. "How are you over there? I hear all the stories from the Tabs, but I don't know what's crap and what's real."

"I'm fine. I'm not going to lie, it's pretty harsh, but I have some good friends and we can take care of ourselves. How are you? It's seems to have gotten really weird really fast over here. What's up with all the cheeriness?"

"Yeah, that's no lie. We're constantly bombarded with messages about how horrible life was without the chip. They're always using you Non-Commers as an example of how bad it can get, and telling people that we must set the bar higher for ourselves. Frankly, some of the younger folks don't remember. If it wasn't for Mom, I'd probably be over there with you."

"Well, it's a good thing you're over here to help us out. How is your mom?"

"Actually, she's doing great. I hate to say it but the chip has helped her make great strides with her paralysis. She actually walked a few steps the other day." He takes a deep breath. "I ask myself every day if it's worth it though."

I pat his hand. "I know, Carson, but you're being a good son by supporting your mom. We all do what we can. And these supplies will help us more than you know."

He hops off the lab table. "Well, I guess I need to get you back to the marshals. You need anything else?"

"Nope, we'll be looking out for your shipment. Thanks again." I give him a big hug. "Hey, you think you can take us to one of those fancy coffee places before we leave? I usually don't like it, but they're more cream and sugar than coffee."

He opens the lab door for me. "No can do, darlin'. They've banned all the good stuff over here. You can get a straight coffee with no sugar or cream, but no more than two a day."

"Blech, never mind. I'll get a stim drink when I get home. Geez, next thing you know they'll be banning sex and beer."

As walk down the hall Carson shrugs and says, "Actually, the only alcohol allowed is one glass of red wine a day, because of the health benefits. And they've been encouraging people to use invitro more and more, because they can scan the embryos for defects. The Morality Codes state that sex is supposed to be used for procreation purposes only. Not that they can police that. Yet."

Lindsey and I look at each other and grimace. Lindsey says, "Damn, now I know why we've seen an upswing in Compliants at Heads and Tales."

"No sex and no beer. Uh, I think I'll stay put in the NCS thank you very much."

Carson laughs and stops right at the doors that lead to the lobby. "Listen, Shea, if you need anything from me, this is how you can get a hold of me." He hands me a business card with some numbers scrawled on the back. "I don't know what I can do, but I'll try to help."

"Thanks, man."

He peeks out the door and looks back to me. "So you ready

to go back to those goons?"

I nod and he opens the doors. Ed and his flunky stand up.

"So you get what you need, worms?"

"I guess what he gave us will have to do. Hopefully, he comes through on what little shit he promised us. Not that you Compliants can be trusted."

"Let's go then. I have things to do and I don't want to spend any more time than I have to with you two."

As we leave I give Carson a sneaky wink and he gives me a smile.

Chapter 22

Home Again Home Again Jiggety-Jig

We leave the city the same way we came, encountering more creepy cheery people. It's just like that movie my Nanna Kelly used to talk about, The Stepford Something-or-others. Maybe I've been on the other side too long. After checking out with the peppy blonde at the Long Range Transport Facility, we get back in the car and head for home.

Ed breaks the silence in the car as we go over the bridge. "You see now what you pukes are making me miss?"

"I know, and you should be getting on your hands and knees and thanking us, Ed. That place is creepy and you know it."

"It's the way it should be. We can get more done in less time. We don't have to worry about criminals roaming the streets. We know who everyone is now. The chip has made our lives safer and more convenient."

"You keep telling yourself that, Eddie. Meanwhile you and your boys have the best of both worlds, coming over to the Non-Compliant side to screw our women and drink our beer, but you go home safe and sound to your families feeling superior because you're wearing that stupid chip on your neck. The truth is, you're over here because you don't one hundred percent buy it yourself. There's a small part of you that knows the chip is bullshit."

He starts to retort, but stops when we come to the guard shack over on our side. The guard inside smiles. "Greetings, Sergeant Barton. I bet you've had an interesting day with these two."

Ed grunts. "You have no idea, Corporal Rains."

She makes a couple of quick presses to her CAMS and the gate to our side opens. "You're cleared to go, Sergeant Barton. Maybe

you can take the edge off with a liquid supplement tonight."
She gives him a smile and a wink and Ed goes through the gate.

The grungy decaying ruins of the Non-Compliant side never looked so good to me.

"That's what I'm talking about, Ed. You guys talk about your highfalutin Morality Codes. Everyone knows they're bullshit, but no one has the courage to say so."

Ed stops hard on the breaks and screams, *"Get out!"*

We all pile out, and Ed grabs me by my hair and pins me to the car with my face just inches from the hot hood. He presses his full body weight on me. I can feel his sickening breath on my neck as he speaks.

"The thing is, you want us here. You're all a bunch of dick-teases." He pushes down on me harder. "Maybe I should give you want you want. Yeah, that's it. Right here in front of everyone." He grabs my ass hard and laughs.

Lindsey says coolly, "Hey, Eddie, I don't think you want to do that."

Ed eases off of me so that we can both turn around. Lindsey is smiling ear to ear. He has his arm around Junior's neck. Lindsey jerks hard and the man yelps. "You've read all the stories about me in the Tabs. You know I can pop his little head off in a second. Let my friend go."

Ed laughs. "All I have to do is make a few taps on my CAMS, and reinforcements will be here in seconds."

I croak out, "You do that, Ed, and then explain to Magistrate why we won't be available to accomplish the task he gave us, after he gave you specific orders to leave us alone."

By now a whole audience of Non-Compliants have gathered to see the show. Several Tab reporters have their cameras out, catching all the action. Ed gets off of me. His fat face is drenched with sweat. He reels back to hit me when the familiar rumble of a car stops him. The car stops and loud baritone barks out,

"Stop now and we can all go home without a scratch."

Ed takes a breath and collects himself. He brushes his uniform and smiles. "You're right, Quinny. I don't want to get too close to your skank-ass girlfriend. God knows where she's been."

Quinn growls, "Let's go, you two."

Lindsey lets go of Ed's partner and both Lindsey and I walk toward Quinn. I don't get three steps when a sharp pain brings me to my knees. I look over and Lindsey is on his knees too. Quinn races over.

Ed laughs, "Oh, yeah, my bad. I forgot to release you two from the bands. Couldn't have happened to two nicer people."

My breath grows shallower and my vision is starting to fade.

Quinn's voice sounds like it is in a distant cave. "Release them, Ed!"

Ed sniggers. "No problem."

The bracelet falls off of my wrist and the pain stops in an instant, but I still feel like I've been run over by a combine. Slowly, my vision returns and I see a hazy image of Quinn frowning. I squeak out, "Hey, why so down?"

He brushes the hair out of my sweaty face. "God you're a pain in the ass. You okay, babe?"

Lindsey answers, "Thanks for asking, Chief. I'm doing great."

Quinn mumbles something about being surrounded by a bunch of smartasses and extends his hand to me. Once standing, he looks me over for an instant then gives me a big hug. Tab cameras are flashing all about catching the dramatics. "Jesus, I can't leave you two alone for three seconds. Your trip must've been successful, because we've gotten notification of delivery from the University. They said they'd be here by the end of the day."

"Dang, Carson works fast."

Quinn scrunches up his eyebrows. "Who's Carson?"

"Just an old college buddy of mine."

All three of us walk toward the car and Lindsey adds, "Yeah you two seemed pretty chummy. You'll have to fill us in."

Quinn stops and turns to me. "Chummy?"

Lindsey adds, "Yeah, he said they used to pull 'all nighters' together."

I give Lindsey a piercing glance. "Shut up, Lindsey." I grab Quinn's arm and pull him along to the car. "Oh honey, you know I prefer old grouchy dudes to the pretty boys." Quinn narrows his eyes at me and I laugh. "C'mon on, babe, let's get home. We got some work to do."

Chapter 23

An Interesting Text

The alarm wakes me from my sleep, a welcome change from bolting up in the middle of the night from nightmares. I hit the alarm for a reprieve, and snuggle down in the warm soft covers. There's a ton of work to be done today, but I don't give a shit. I'm going to sleep in. Just before I nod off, the screeching of the alarm jolts me awake again.

I slam the button again. "Fucking alarm. Let me sleep."

An arm curls around me pulling me close. "Such language. I take it you're not a morning person," Quinn growls in my ear. He places a few kisses on my neck and rubs my tummy.

"Not normally, but you're starting to change my mind." I turn to face him trying to strategically keep my stinky morning breath from his face.

He slides his hand up my shirt while kissing my neck. He says in between kisses, "What time is it anyway?"

"Mmm, almost 0730."

Quinn bolts up. "Shit! I have to meet Conner for patrol in fifteen minutes."

Before I'm able to protest he's in the bathroom with the sink running. I yell into bathroom, "What do you mean? You went out with him yesterday and the day before that. I haven't been out of the compound since I went over to the other side. I'm tired of staying here. Aren't I supposed to be your partner?"

"You are, but there's a ton here that needs to be done. I don't exactly feel comfortable putting Conner on deciphering messages from Magistrate's snooper or chip secrets. I don't think he's capable of helping your dad get the power systems up and running either." He appears back in the bedroom wearing his suit. I screw up my face knowing he's right, but I'm still not still happy with his answer. I stand on the bed, straighten his necktie, and brush the lint from his jacket. He gives me a sad smile, as if recalling a bittersweet memory.

"What's wrong?"

He kisses my head. "Nothing, it's just been a long time since anyone has done that for me. So how's it coming with the power systems?"

"Good. Dad and I are making pretty good headway. It won't be completed before we launch our plan, but I think we'll have the important stuff done."

"I knew you could do it. So, when are you going to tell me about your friend Carson?"

I smile at the emphasis he puts on the word friend. I never took Quinn for the jealous type, but ever since the mention of Carson, he can't stop hounding me. "I told you we were friends in college. That's it."

He scrunches up his eyebrows. It's probably time I stop aggravating him. "I'll tell you a little secret." I get close to his ear and whisper. "Carson would be a lot more interested in Lindsey than me." Quinn gives me a shocked look and I give him a kiss on the cheek. "So, don't worry about it. Not that you'd have to worry about it anyway."

He gets a smug look. "I know."

"Whatever, stud. The fact remains that I'm bored and I haven't left the compound in two days. I need to get out of here. I'm starting to turn into a scary lab troll. Look, we have the snooping code installed on a bunch of the phones. Wynne and Gordon have been monitoring communications through them. Dad's taking care of all the homemade distractions and we're almost done with your jammers. Like I said, the power systems should be online soon. I think one little stroll around town won't hurt."

He laughs and picks me up off the bed. "You're right. Next watch, you'll go with me. But right now, I've already got Conner slated for duty. We're going to do a patrol then go to Mr. Ito's to help some of the training and go over our plans. Then we're going to try to find Ryan again. That little shit's been pretty good at hiding from us."

"I know we have to do it, but I hate it Quinn. He was just looking out for his family."

"We gave him enough chances. He made his own bed."

"I know." I quickly change the subject to keep from thinking of Ryan's fate. "How's the training down at Mr. Ito's going?"

"Good. We have the advantage that most of the mercs were training with Mr. Ito anyway so there wasn't a big learning curve. Mr. Ito has been very helpful with creating the plans. We're going to do a sort of practice run there today, but tomorrow we're going to do a full out dress rehearsal here at the compound. I'll be glad to be done with this shit."

"You and me both. Then things can get back to normal. At least normal for us."

I walk with Quinn out of the bedroom and down the stairs to the main entrance. Conner is waiting at the door looking frustrated. He still hasn't dealt with the fact that Wynne and I have been working on the chip. I'm not sure he'll ever get over it. He shares the same feelings as most of the people in the NCS. They hate anyone who has ever worked on technology, the chip in particular. Conner shakes his head at me and Quinn and grunts out, "You ready, Chief?"

"One second." He turns to me. "I'll be back this afternoon. Do you think you and your dad will be ready for a demo of the weapons and jammers for us when we get back?"

"I don't see why not. We just have a couple of finishing touches to put on them. They should be good enough for a demo. What time to you think you'll be back?"

Just as I ask the question, Lindsey walks up to us eating a ration-bar. "Chief, me and Nikki just got back from night patrol. We saw Mr. Ito on the way back and he said he should be ready for you around 1000."

Quinn nods. "We'll do several run-throughs of our plans then do a quick patrol afterwards, so I think you can expect to see us sometime around 1500." Quinn gives Conner and Lindsey a quick glance then bends down to give me a peck on the cheek.

I smile. "Be safe."

He grunts in return.

Conner turns away and goes out the door.

Wynne is sitting at the kitchen table eating breakfast. She looks like she's spent most of the night up crying, just like the night before. I'm a really great friend: instead of staying up all night with my best friend getting drunk and eating copious amounts of crap to help nurse her through a breakup, I've been spending last couple of nights with Quinn. I ease into a seat by her and put my hand on her back. "You okay, sister?"

She gives me a weak smile and coughs. "I'll be fine."

"Man, you sound horrible."

She answers back in a hoarse voice, "Gee, thanks. Fall sucks for my allergies. You know, he doesn't even want to talk. I understand that he's pissed, but why can't he talk to me?"

"I'm sorry. Tonight we'll stay up all night, get hammered, and talk about it. I've been neglecting you."

She wipes her eyes. "For a good reason. I'm happy for you, and I'm not just saying that. It's about time you two hooked up. Seriously, don't worry about me."

"Nope. You're my best friend. I'm supposed to worry about you."

She smiles. "Okay, tonight we'll get hammered and talk." She stands with her empty cereal bowl and dumps it into the sink. "For now, I'm going to get to work to take my mind off of this crap."

I follow her down to the lab where Gordo and Dad are sitting hacking away. Dad turns and looks me up and down. "You're still in your pajamas?"

"I just woke up. It isn't even eight o'clock."

"That's right. You've lost several good hours of work." He looks over at Gordon. "Me and the boy have been hard at it since 0500. Isn't that right, son?"

Gordon gives a slow nod and rubs his eyes. His vampire-like schedule has been disturbed ever since Dad became his roommate.

"So, Dad, do you think the jammers and the weapons will be ready for a demo around 1500 today?"

"Absolutely. I was fixin' to go out to the lab shortly. I have a few finishing touches that they need, but they should be good enough for a demo."

Wynne sits at her computer and starts clacking away. "So, were you guys able to crack the code yet?"

Dad answers, "Nah, the boy's been hard at it between intercepting Ramsey's men's communications and getting shit for weapons. Not a whole lot of time to spend on it. But he's a smart one. Between him and Wynnie, they'll get it."

"Thanks, Mr. Kelly, but I'm not so sure I'm going to be able to crack this code."

I rub his head and say, "Don't worry Gordo, you're a smart guy, I have faith you and Wynnie to figure it out. And me and Dad will be here to help you." I turn to Wynne. "So have you found anything on Magistrate's snoopers?"

"Actually, I have found something really interesting. I've been able to hack into Mrs. Magistrate's communications pretty easily. I guess they figure her communications aren't worth a heavy duty firewall. Anyway, she keeps mentioning something about a son."

I raise my eyebrows. "I didn't know they had a son."

"According to all the records that I've been able to get to, they don't. Magistrate's biography says that he and Martina never had children. Maybe she or Magistrate had a secret love child or something."

"Hmm, interesting. Keep on it. I think you're on to something monitoring Martina. The wives know a lot more than they're given credit for. From the little I've seen of her, she probably has a tough time keeping her mouth shut. She's going to crack sooner or later. Also, can you give Magistrate a SITREP? Don't tell him too much, just enough to keep him off our asses. Right now the priority is Ramsey. Gordo can you have an assessment of his men's movements to me by 1400 today?"

"Sure can. I already have quite a few notes, but I think I can have a pretty good assessment by later this afternoon."

"Wynne can you have a structural analysis of the building done by that time? So we know the best place to put our devices."

She sneezes and gives a stuffy, "Sure thing. I'm almost done with it now."

"Great. I'm going to help Dad for a bit, but I'll be back soon to help you two out." I turn to Dad. "So you ready to go to the outside lab and get some work done, old man?"

"Watch it, missy."

"Give me a minute to get dressed and I'll be right out."

As I run upstairs I giggle at how weird my life is. When I was a kid I always wished for a big family. It was pretty lonely out on a farm with just me and Dad and the occasional visitor. Now, I have my wish. Sure, my family is currently making weapons out of everyday kitchen utensils and hacking into a government officials' private files, but hey, all families are dysfunctional in their own way. Once in my room, I put on a pair of cargo pants and a long sleeve t-shirt. I grab my thick wool sweater and head out the door.

I creep up and peek over Dad's shoulder. "So what do you need help with? Not that I'm much help anymore," I say while flexing my still lame hand.

"If I ever find the fuck who did that to you, I'm gonna to kill him slowly and with as much pain as possible. I'm gonna . . . "

"Um, Dad, Quinn took care of him a while ago."

"Hmm, maybe your boyfriend ain't so bad after all. So, do you think you can finish up those jammers? I just need you to upload some firmware into them, then disguise them somehow."

"Can do."

It's been a while since I've worked on a father-daughter project. I've really missed those days. I settle at the lab bench and hook up the first jammer to the computer. After several iterations of debugging code and minor hardware fixes I have the first jammer done. The purring of the lab equipment relaxes me and before I know it all the jammers are working and disguised. I stand and stretch and take my handy work to Dad. "I think you'll find these will meet your standards."

He picks up the small rectangle packaged in a playing card box. "Not bad, little one. Putting these in playing card boxes and cigarette packs is a pretty good idea. Someone must've taught you well."

"Yeah, I had a pretty good teacher. It looks like you have everything's under control here. I'm going to go back and help Wynnie and Gordo. I'll see ya later, Pop."

I walk out the door, but before I make it to the main house I feel a vibration in my pocket. I fish inside, pull out my phone and read the message.

FOUND UR CAR MANUAL. COME GET IT.

I know I should ask Quinn to get it while he's in town, but I'm bored. I should be able to get into town and out before anyone even knows I'm there.

I reply: **BE THERE SOON**

I continue on to the main house to let Wynne know where I'm going. Dad will wrestle me down until I agree not to go. I'm tired of people thinking they know what's best for me. Once downstairs, I open the lab door and see Wynne and Gordon working away. "Hey, you two, I'm going into town for a bit. Frank said he found the 'Cuda's manual."

Wynne looks at me. "Do you think that's a good idea? I think what Quinn said is right. Ramsey's on the lookout for you. Heck, any of us out alone is probably going to get some attention."

I take a deep breath. I thought I'd have more support from Wynne. "Look, I haven't been out in days and I'm getting bored. We have our mercs all over the place. If anything bad happens, they'll let Quinn know. I'm going get in and get out before anyone even knows I'm there. It's not like I'm going to sit around the bar for hours drinking."

"I don't know . . . "

"Oh come on. Tell you what, if I'm not back in an hour, text Quinn."

Wynne slumps her shoulders. "Here's the deal: I won't squeal if you let me go with you." She looks over at Gordon. "If we're not back in forty-five minutes, call Quinn, then he can kick our asses."

Gordon says, "I'm not sure this is a good idea, guys."

I smile. "Yippee, a girl trip! Gordo, we'll be back in less than an hour."

Gordon shuffles in his chair. "You better be, because if you're not then Mr. Quinn will kill me, that is if your dad doesn't kill me first."

"We'll be fine."

I hope.

Chapter 24

Knee-Deep in Crazy

We've made this trip at least a hundred times from the compound and back, but this time it feels more ominous. I pull my sweater closer to keep the chill autumn air from my skin. It would've been quicker to just take the car into town, but that would've meant going into the lab with Dad. I know it's childish and irresponsible to make this trip, but I don't care. Quinn is great and so is my dad, but sometimes they get rather suffocating. I just need to get out and prove to myself that I'm not the china doll the two men in my life seem to think I am. The only thing I feel guilty about is taking Wynne along for the trip.

"You know, you didn't have to come."

"Yes, I did. I couldn't handle being in that place one second longer. I'm glad you came in when you did."

"I'm sorry about everything."

"Hey, you didn't do anything. I should've talked to Conner more. Honestly, I just don't think about that part of my life anymore. Sometimes it's like it never even happened. That's exactly what I've been trying to tell him, but he doesn't believe me. He thinks it's some kind of conspiracy or something."

"I know what you mean. Anytime I think about life on the other side, I think it's just a dream. Don't give up on him. He really cares about you. I think he needs time to simmer down and realize we're on his side. He's gone out with Quinn the last two times on patrol, and I think that's intentional on Quinn's part. He's trying to talk some sense into him."

"You know, that guy of yours is actually pretty nice."

"Yeah, he is, but don't tell anyone. That'll piss him off."

We round the bend to the center of town. Everything looks

normal. The town's residents are milling around undisturbed. I see a few of our mercs standing on the corner. None of Ramsey's men are anywhere in sight. I turn to Wynne. "Looks like everything is clear. We'll just run in, get the manual and get out."

We walk a couple of blocks and stop right outside Frank's. Wynne says, "It'll be good be good to see the little weeble-wobble. I've missed his dumb ass."

I swing the door wide open and stop in my tracks. "Oh. God. *Frank!*"

Frank is hanging from the rafters with a rope around his neck. His stiff bloated body is waving in the air like pendulum. The only thing that breaks the silence is the sickening creak of the rafter in rhythm with the body swinging back and forth. Wynne stands beside me in stunned silence. Ramsey is sitting in a chair casually drinking a whiskey. Two of his men are playing pool like nothing has happened. Ramsey smiles and says to his men, "See, I told you boys that she'd come. You owe me twenty bucks."

One of the men looks up from his cue stick and says, "Damn, I thought she would've sent her boyfriend."

"You sick fuck. He never did anything to you." In a fit of rage, I run at Ramsey, but right before I get to him, one of his men tackles me, slamming my head to the ground.

Ramsey steps on my injured hand and smiles. "I knew she'd show up. Shea is guilty of the deadliest sin: pride. I knew she'd never ask her boyfriend to help her." He shakes his head. "You're so predictable, Shea." He presses his foot harder on my hand. I try to stifle a shriek of pain. He looks down at me. He says to his man who is still holding me to the ground, "Get the bitch up. We've got a date at my place, sugar."

The man grabs my hair and gives my head a pound on the floor. "That was for Morgan, you stupid bitch." He lifts off me, keeping me in an arm bar. "Come on, get up." He yanks me up from the floor.

Before he can make me start walking, I slam the heel of my foot into the top of his. As he loosens his grip, I break free. I swing around and deliver a swift upper cut to his jaw.

Thank God for those sparring sessions with Quinn.

As I turn to run for the door, Ramsey's other man moves to block the entrance, holding a knife to Wynne's throat. She's sobbing. The man smiles. "I'll fucking do it. Just give me a reason."

Ramsey walks behind me and puts his hand on my shoulder and whispers in my ear. "Come along peacefully and we'll leave your girlfriend alone. Although, it might be fun seeing just how much pain she can take. It really makes no difference to me. Either way I'm going to enjoy myself."

"Fine, let's go."

The man throws Wynne to the ground. Ramsey leads me out the door. Before we get too far from the bar, the man asks Ramsey, "What do you want me to do with her? Can I have some fun?"

Ramsey stops and gives him a glare. "Don't touch her. She's got a job to do." He looks back at Wynne. "You need to go tell Shea's boyfriend that his squeeze is in trouble. You think you can do that for me, honey?"

She purses her lips and stares Ramsey down. "You can count on it."

"Good girl." He looks at the man standing over Wynne. "You make sure to let him in when he shows at the warehouse."

He leads me down the street, not caring who sees us together. I turn to him. "Your men better not touch a hair on Wynne's head or . . . "

"Or you'll what? Don't worry honey, I've got bigger fish to fry than your stripper friend."

My stomach sinks, finally realizing it's never been about me. It's been about setting a trap for Quinn all along. After what seems like the longest walk of my life, we are standing in front of Danny's old warehouse. Ramsey punches in a code, the door unlocks, and we walk in. The interior has changed quite a bit from when Danny used to own this place. Everything that made it a nightclub is now gone. The walls are spray painted with street art and lewd sayings. The floor is littered with mattresses, blankets, and drug paraphernalia. The only light is from the sunlight filtering in from the few filthy windows that line the place. The smell of sKape hits me and I wrinkle my nose. "Gee, Ramsey, I love what you've done with the place."

"Yeah, it's homey, isn't it? The kids love it."

He leads me past the maze of blankets and mattresses. Most of the inhabitants are gone, but a few emaciated youths still remain. We go through the old spot that used to be the Alcove. A hint of smile crosses my lips when I remember mine and Quinn's encounter here. I'm thrust back into reality when Ramsey pushes me toward the door that leads to the back spaces of the warehouse. He opens the door for me and waves me in. "After you."

The bright florescent lighting of the backspaces makes me squint after the dark of the main room. Ramsey pushes me to the first office on the right. He motions for me to sit down and he sits on his desk. I can't help but notice the drill sitting on his desk. He strategically puts his hand on it, slipping his finger around the trigger. I can't keep my eyes off it. I try to slow my breathing, but the memory of that thing going through my hand is still fresh. He smiles, knowing exactly what is going through my mind. "Do you like my new toy?" He picks it up off the desk and pulls the trigger a couple of times. The high-pitched whine of the motor makes my skin tingle. My breath quickens and I squeeze my eyes closed. He laughs. "I've been thinking about doing some improvements around here. I thought you could help me. You seem pretty good with that kind of stuff."

"Fuck you, Ramsey."

"Such language. Is that how you talk to a new neighbor who is only asking for your help? I have to say, I'm a little offended. I've taken ownership of the place over three months ago and there's been no welcome wagon. All I get is a second rate worm delivered by some yokel. Really, Shea you can do better than that."

He sets down the drill and picks up a coffee cup. He shakes it and look inside.

I narrow my eyes at him. "What have you done with Ryan and Emmi?"

He ignores my question. He seems mesmerized by the contents of the cup. "You know what's funny?"

"Stop fucking around and tell me where they are."

He puts down the cup and picks up a cigar cutter. "Well, sugar, I don't think you're in any position to tell me what to do. So, I ask again. You know what's funny?"

"What?"

He fiddles with the cigar cutter a bit until it opens, then he snaps it shut. "Seemingly innocuous things and people can really cause damage. I mean, look at you. You're a tiny, plain, little shit. Just a dumb hick barmaid, and you took down Danny. You've won the heart of our hero Quinn and you're just two heartbeats away from running this whole shithole."

"Wow, you're deep, Ramsey."

"Thanks, I like to wax a little philosophical now and again. Like this drill . . . " He pats the drill. "Who would think to use this ol' thing to make you sing? And you almost did, didn't you, honey? Burt told me all about it. You were seconds from selling your whole family down the river. You're such a joke. I wonder what the NCS would think of their heroine if they knew how weak she is. I wonder what other secrets you could be hiding. I bet it wouldn't take much to find out." He starts to laugh. "I wish I could've seen it all go down. The look on

Gunny's face was probably priceless. Oh well, I guess there's always another time."

I swallow down the lump in my throat, cursing myself for not listening to Quinn. "Shut the fuck up."

He smiles and taps his fingers on the damn cigar cutter. "Take this little thing. Highly effective in getting answers. Who would've thunk it?"

He picks up the coffee cup again and throws the contents at me. I close my eyes bracing myself for scalding liquid, but when I open my eyes I find something far worse on my lap. I jump up, stifle a scream, and throw the digits that land on my lap onto the floor.

I sit back down and bite my lower lip. "What do you want? You know I'm not going to agree to anything."

He smiles and pulls a chair around from his desk to face me. He sits in the chair, stretches, and puts his hands behind his head. "Oh Shea, I'm not going to waste your time making proposals or trying to get information from you. I brought you here to tell you a little story."

"Who are you, Mother Goose?"

He lets short snigger escape. "Do you know why I came here?"

"More importantly, do I care?"

His smile fades and his eyes narrow. He gets out of his chair and stops within inches of my face. "Stop the smart ass routine." He takes a deep breath and his calm demeanor returns. He returns to his chair. "Where was I? Oh, yes. As you know, I served with the Gunny for many years in the Marine Corps. He was the biggest pain in my ass. He was all about discipline, honor, and other shit like that."

I interrupt. "Sounds pretty good to me."

"It would. There were those of us, okay me, who just wanted to cause as much pain and suffering as possible, get high and, on a good night, get laid. He was always interfering and trying to make me a good Marine. I fucking hated that guy. Fast forward a few years and poor Gunny got thrown out of the Marines. I laughed my ass off at that one. After that, the Marine Corps was actually a fun place to be. Then that damn chip changed it all. Everything was so sterile and safe. My God! I couldn't get decent burger or pay for a screw anymore. It was so fucking boring over there. Then I got a call to come help out a friend of a friend here in the NCS. When I found out that the Gunny was here, well, hot dog!"

I lift an eyebrow. "So you're telling me the only reason you came over here is to screw with Quinn?"

"It isn't the only reason. Danny was stupid and within an instant of meeting him I knew I could easily take him down and have this NCS for myself. Thanks for the assist in that, by the way. Torturing Quinn was just an added benefit. So the only thing that stands in my way of having the NCS as my personal playground is your boyfriend." Ramsey bends down and picks up the fingers I threw on the floor, and puts them back into the coffee cup. "Oh don't worry, honey. I'm not going to kill him today. I'm going to tear him down piece by piece, and he's going to know I'm the one who did it. Once he's a broken shell of a man, then he'll beg me to kill him." He jumps from his chair and claps his hands. "I haven't had this much fun in years."

"Whatever. You aren't even half the man Quinn is. You won't break him so easily."

"Actually, it isn't as hard as you think. All you have to do is find that one chink in the armor, then go in for the kill. I found one before." He traces the outline of my jaw with his finger. I pull away from him and he laughs. "And I think I might have found another."

The door slams open and I turn. Quinn, flanked by two of Ramsey's cronies, is standing in the doorway.

"Gunny! What took you so long? I was just getting acquainted with your squeeze here. She's quite the feisty one. She reminds me of someone, I just can't put my finger on it." He looks in the cup and laughs. "Ha! Finger on it! Come join us, Gunny."

Quinn pulls free from the two guards. He looks down at me. "You okay?" I give a nod, too ashamed to say anything. His face is red and he's struggling to keep is breath steady. He takes a breath and stares at Ramsey for what seems like hours. Then he says slowly, "I'm going home and I'm taking Shea with me."

Ramsey grins, knowing he's found his weak spot. "Of course, of course. We're just getting to know each other. She's free to go any time." Quinn extends his hand to me. I grab it and stand. We turn to go, then Ramsey adds, "Now, don't be strangers, y'all."

Quinn growls.

As we turn to leave, Ramsey adds a little nugget. "I heard little Mia is leaving town with her mama. I guess it's for the best. With all these sKape addicts around, who knows what would happen to a little girl and her mama, especially if daddy isn't around to protect them. But you know what could happen, don't you, Quinn?"

Quinn is sweating and he's squeezing my hand so hard I think he's going to cut off the circulation. "We're leaving now, Ramsey."

"Oh yeah, I'll see you two later." Just before we're past the threshold of the door Ramsey yells, "I remember!"

Quinn turns. "What?"

"I remember who Shea reminds me of. Rebecca! Don't 'cha think? She isn't as hot, but she's got that feisty spirit that Rebecca always had. Yeah, Rebecca had an ass that wouldn't quit and those tits . . . "

In two heartbeats, Quinn is on top of Ramsey punching him in the face. As the punches grow more violent, Ramsey laughs harder. Ramsey's guards pounce on Quinn. Although they are almost as big as he is, they have trouble pulling him off. They each grab one of his arms and pull him back. Ramsey gets up and laughs as he wipes the blood from his face. He comes face to face with Quinn. "You are so weak." Ramsey punches him in the face several times in quick succession. Quinn tries unsuccessfully to break free of the two hulking men holding him. All my nightmares are coming true, and I'm the one who caused it.

No longer able to stand by and watch, I move toward him, but Quinn shouts. "Don't you dare, Kelly."

Ramsey stops and shakes his bloodied hand. "You better listen to your old man, Shea. I'm done with him, anyway." He looks Quinn up and down then spits in his face. "Let him and his chicky go. I'm bored."

The two thugs release Quinn and he stumbles. I rush over to help him regain his balance. Not that I'd be able to do anything if he fell. As we wind our way through the warehouse, I continually look behind me, waiting for Orphans or Ramsey's thugs to pounce. Quinn is walking slowly behind me as if he's not worried at all.

"C'mon, Quinn, we need to get the hell out of here before he changes his mind."

He takes a slow breath. "He's not going to change his mind. He hasn't had enough fun with us yet. It's going to get a hell of a lot worse."

We make the rest of the journey in silence. Once we're several blocks away from the warehouse, the emotions finally overwhelm me. I stop, look at Quinn, and start to sob. "I'm sorry. I was just going to run in town, grab my manual, and leave. I'm sorry. Where's Wynne?"

Quinn hugs me back and kisses the top of my head. "She went back to the compound with one of the mercs." He gives me another squeeze then grabs my shoulders. "How could you be so stupid?"

I wipe the tears from my eyes. "I said I was sorry."

"I told you Ramsey was dangerous. I told you—"

"No, see that's the thing, you didn't tell me anything. You told me he was crazy. But this place is knee-deep in crazy. How was I supposed to know he was any different? You didn't tell me there was some kind of history between you two. You just said you served in the Marine Corps together. What's your real history with this guy?"

He looks at me with wild eyes and bellows, "It's none of your business." He's silent for a few minutes as he paces and rubs his head. He looks as if he's seconds from breaking. "Goddamn it, Shea! You were stupid and irresponsible to go into town by yourself. I told you, your dad told you . . . Why the fuck do you constantly have to do the opposite of what everyone says? Wynne could be dead or worse. You sure would've shown us then."

"I said I'm sorry. I know I fucked up. What the hell is your problem?"

"My problem is you. You're a loose cannon. Jesus, I can't believe I was stupid enough to get involved with you."

His words are a slap in the face. I bite my lip. "What, because I don't do everything you say without question? You know what? That's fine. If you want some mindless doll that does everything you say then you're looking at the wrong girl. You're really no better than the rest of them. You're good for a couple of screws, then once you find out I have a mind of my own it gets too hard for you. Well, maybe we should just call it quits now."

He looks at me stone-faced. "Maybe you're right."

His utter lack of emotion stabs me in the heart. "You know what? You're a real fucking piece of work! I thought . . . " Right before I start to tear him a new one, an explosion interrupts me.

Quinn growls, "What the hell was that?"

I look in the direction the sound came from, and see a black mushroom-cloud of smoke and flames.

I gasp. "Oh my God!"

Without waiting for Quinn, I run toward the smoke. He's hot on my heels. We run a couple of blocks and find a group of people gathered around what used to be Frank's bar.

Chapter 25

A VIP

Quinn and I walk back home without uttering a word to each other. It takes all my energy to keep from crying. Even though I don't want to admit it, I've fallen hard for him and being dumped in the middle of town is almost more than I can bear. He stops before we go in the door to the main house and turns to me.

"We'll talk about us later. For now, we need to keep it together and put the final touches on our plans for Ramsey."

What a prick. He's acting like our relationship is just another line item on a to-do list. God, I'm so sick of him. I stare him down. "What's there to talk about? We're over, right?"

He grabs my arm. "Shea . . . "

I pull away from him and open the door. My dad is pacing in the foyer. Once he sees me enter through the front door he rushes to me and hugs me. "Are you okay, punkin?"

"I'm fine, Daddy."

"Good." He then slaps me upside the head. "How can you be such a dumbass?"

"Dad, I . . . "

A clacking of heels down the hall stops me mid-sentence. I look over and Claire says, "Robert would like to talk to Shea and Quinn."

"You go, punkin, but I want to talk to you when you're done."

Great, I have two "dads" waiting to chew me out.

Quinn and I make our way back to Boss's office. My stomach turns waiting for an ass chewing from Boss. *Okay, note to self: don't go into town alone ever again.*

Boss is sitting at his desk. His hair is disheveled and his skin is pale. He slowly looks up at Quinn and me. "What the *hell* is going on?"

I take a deep breath. "I'm sorry, sir. I thought . . . "

Quinn takes over, "I asked her to meet me in town. I needed something from the compound and I didn't think it would be a big deal for her to get there on her own. Unfortunately, Ramsey's men intercepted her before I could. It was a lapse in judgment, sir. It will never happen again."

Boss's eyes narrow. "Mr. Knightly, I expected better from you. Magistrate has asked that you meet with him in an hour. He wants to be briefed, personally, on our plans. You two will go and smooth this over. Do *not* fuck this up. Do you understand?"

We both say collectively, "Yes, sir."

Boss responds, "Good, now get out of my sight. Report back to me when you're done."

"Yes, sir."

We go back out to the foyer. No one is around. "What the fuck was that about in there?"

"I have a lot more years with Boss and he'll forgive me sooner than you."

I brush past him. "Whatever. Don't do me any favors. Go clean up and meet me out in the garage in fifteen minutes."

I storm out the door to the garage. Dad is inspecting the 'Cuda's damage. He looks at me and smiles. "This ain't too bad. We can have her fixed up in no time. Your boyfriend seems to be pretty handy around the garage, he can help us too." I let out a wail. Dad knits his eyebrows and gives me a hug.

"What did I say?"

I pull away from him and wipe my eyes. "Quinn's pretty pissed at me. I think it's over between us."

"Oh, bullshit. He has every right to be pissed at you, but it ain't over. In the few days I've seen you two together, I know this ain't a passing thing. He's going to be mad for a while, but he'll get over it."

"I don't know, Dad."

"Listen, you were stupid going out there by yourself. You need to get used to the fact that you aren't alone in this world and if you get hurt, or worse, there are some of us that might not take it so well. You need to think about how your actions affect others."

I stand silent for a while, knowing he's right. I give him a hug. As I pull away, the door opens and Quinn appears. He's wearing a new suit. His face is cleaned up, but still shows the damage Ramsey inflicted on him. "You ready to go, Kelly?"

So it's back to Kelly now is it?

"We'll take the Crown Vic."

We walk to his garage without another word. He gets in the driver's seat and puts on his shades. I push a couple of buttons and the garage door opens, pouring daylight into the car. I turn on the radio to drown out the uncomfortable silence as we drive. Many times I open my mouth to apologize and explain why I did what I did, but I know it will just sound immature and stupid. Besides, we have more important things to focus on now. Now is not the time to be stirring emotions, we need to be sharp to deal with that prick Magistrate. The music drones on and I lean my head on the window, trying to focus on the music and not the crappiness of the day.

He stops in front of the gates surrounding Magistrate's compound. Two marshals are flanking the gate, smiling from ear to ear, no doubt knowing what we're in for. Quinn rolls down his window. The marshal on the left crouches down by the window. "Shea Kelly and Quinn Knighly, here to kiss Mr. McReady's ass, I presume?"

He growls. "Cut the shit and just let us in."

The marshal puts a finger to his ear and says over his comms, "I'm sending Knightly and Kelly to the main building. Roger that." He puts his hand down then looks at Quinn. "Mr. McReady will see you two in the main building." Before he can drive away, the marshal kicks the car hard and adds with a laugh, "Get this piece of shit out of my sight."

This has been a day for the record: Frank gets killed, I get kidnapped, the bar gets blown up, and my boyfriend breaks up with me. Why did I bother getting out of bed? I swallow my emotions down. It isn't long before a large white limestone building is right in front of us. He squeezes into a parking spot meant for the small solar-powered excuses for cars. Before he turns off the car, the announcer breaks into the music:

VIOLENCE REACHES AN ALL-TIME HIGH AS EXPLOSIONS ROCK THE NCS. THIS IS MALCOLM MURDOCK, YOUR ON-THE-SCENE REPORTER . . .

Quinn turns off the car. "Fuckin' hack."

I rub my head to soothe the migraine I feel coming on. "I wonder how they're going to spin this. It's not going to be good."

Quinn narrows his eyes and growls. "Maybe you should focus on the task at hand rather than what some hack reporter is saying."

Jerk!

I slam open my car door, cracking it into the car-like object next to me.

Quinn climbs out and makes his way toward the building.

I yell out, "You gonna wait for me or not?"

He grunts and keeps walking.

I walk double time to catch up with him. We trudge up the steep limestone staircase and open the heavy wooden doors. Inside, several marshals are scanning a line of Non-Compliant folks before they're admitted inside.

One marshal recognizes me and Quinn and calls out, "Kelly and Knightly, to the front of the line."

We squeeze past the line of pathetic looking people, most of them probably looking to get chipped and out of this hell-hole. One familiar face catches my eye. Quinn, not noticing I've stopped, marches forward.

"Jenny?"

She's holding Mia's hand tight. Mia's eyes are filled with tears. "Um, hi, Shea." She looks at the floor "I-I just can't stay here. I wanted to make it work, but not with Mia. I would never forgive myself if she got hurt or ended up with them Orphans."

"Jenny, you don't have to apologize. I understand."

Quinn comes back over to see what the hold-up is.

Mia breaks away from Jenny and flings herself at me. "I'm gonna miss you, Auntie Shea. Can you come visit me?"

My heart dies a little inside. "No, honey, I can't come over."

She looks at Quinn. "What 'bout you Mr. Quinn?"

He swallows hard. "No, sweetie, I can't."

"I don't want to go, Mama."

"Mia, honey, it isn't safe here for us anymore."

A voice booms over the mass of people. "Knightly and Kelly to the front of the line, now!"

I give Mia one last squeeze and wipe her tears. "You'll do great. Don't worry, little one."

"NOW!"

I peel her little arms off of me as I choke back the tears. I fucking hate this day.

We make our way to the front of the line. A marshal grabs Quinn by the arm and says, "Over here, Knightly." He directs Quinn to stand on a white circle. The marshal makes a few key strokes on his armband and the circle starts to glow. After a few seconds he says, "He's good. It's your turn, Kelly." I stand on the same circle after Quinn moves. "She's good too." He turns to us and says, "Take the elevator to third floor. He's waiting for you."

The marshals let us find our way to the elevator unescorted, not because they trust us, but because this place is locked down tighter than a virgin on prom night. There's nowhere we could go without being seen or heard. I press the button for the elevator and door immediately opens. Inside, Quinn pushes the button for the third floor, and within seconds the elevator is at our destination. The doors open to a large, bright, sterile reception area. The wall to the left is comprised totally of windows. The floor is sleek white marble, the reception desk black and modern. There are two men in suits also sitting in the reception area.

Hmm, looks like Magistrate has himself a VIP visitor.

The pinch-faced woman behind the desk acknowledges us with a raised eyebrow. "Sit over there. His prior meeting has gone over. He'll be with you when he can."

We make ourselves as comfortable as we can on the hard black plastic chairs. I start thinking about how I might not see my family again. If this is the end, I don't want to go out this way with Quinn. I squirm in my seat and my leg starts with its involuntary nervous shaking. Quinn puts his hand on my knee and looks me in the eye. As pissed as I am at him, I hate to admit that this actually calms my nerves. I put my hand on his and squeeze. He looks at me and gives me a sad smile. The large door behind the reception desk opens and we both turn our attention to the two men walking out. They stop in the doorway to finish their conversation. Magistrate is facing us, glaring while he talks to the white-haired mystery man who has his back to us.

The mystery man says, "Well, Dennis, I don't want to keep you any longer. I'm impressed with what you've done here. Keep it up. I'm going meet with Eastern Regents O'Neal and

Gomez later this week, and I'll be sure to mention the exceptional job you've been doing."

I just love hearing pompous douchebags jack-off each other's egos like this. Quinn and I stand and make our way closer to Magistrate's office. The mystery man shakes Magistrate's hand and turns to face us. I fight to catch my breath when I see who it is: Thomas Eldridge, the President of GlobalThink, and manufacturer of GovTek. He's arguably the most powerful man in the United States. His eyes are as black as his soul and his weathered face gives him an air of authority. He gives me a smile.

"Well, Shea Kelly, I haven't seen you in a while. How are you?"

Both Quinn and Magistrate's eye grow wide seeing Thomas Eldridge address me is such a familiar way. "I'm peachy, Dr. E., But of course you probably know that."

"Shea, Shea, you always were my biggest disappointment."

"Same to ya."

Thomas scoffs and walks away; the men in black follow. Quinn and I walk toward Magistrate's office. Thomas stops suddenly, and says, "How's your hand Shea?"

My eyes narrow and I say, "Just great. How's your nose, Dr. E?"

His smile turns down and he strides away out of the office and the two goons in suits follow him. I turn back to the men who are looking at me with their mouths wide open.

"Let's get on with the meeting. I have things to get done today."

Magistrate's office is just as sterile and cold as the reception area outside. There are windows that go from the ceiling to the floor behind his desk. I can see all of the NCS from my seat. The stark contrast of Magistrate's campus to the impoverished areas of the NCS has never been so apparent to me. It isn't lost on me that Magistrate keeps his desk seat faced away from the whole scene.

Magistrate sits silent awhile, and then says, "What the fuck is going on? What part of 'get Ramsey under control' didn't you two understand? Ever since I've tasked you with this, there have been a record number of deaths. And now an explosion? I should take you two in right now as an example."

I swallow hard and my leg starts shaking again. Quinn puts his hand on my knee and I stop. Quinn looks Magistrate squarely in the face.

"Sir, we're going to strike in two days. It's taken some time to get the supplies needed to execute our plan. I can assure you, in two days time our mutual problem will be resolved."

Magistrate shakes his head. "I'm willing to give you one more chance. I have my career to think about, and unleashing the marshals on the community is not a public relations battle I wish to fight right now. However, if this problem remains, I will take your entire crew in."

Quinn replies, "Sir, if I may be frank."

Magistrate nods for Quinn to continue.

"We both know that Mr. Jennings isn't doing so well. We also know that when he goes, I will take power. If we're both gone, then there is no need to take down the rest of the group. If we fail to take down Ramsey, I will personally disband the group and willingly take the chip."

My eyes grow wide. I start to speak, but Quinn gives me a piercing look that tells me to keep my mouth shut. I take a deep breath and wait for the next play to be made.

Magistrate gives a half-smile. "Agreed. You're right, Quinn, there's no sense in taking down more people than needed. The public always likes to know the root cause of a problem."

Quinn stands and I follow suit. "If you don't mind, sir, we have a lot of work to do."

Magistrate stands and smiles as if he's concluding a meeting concerning a company takeover, not human lives. Of course, to him, I'm sure we aren't much more than that. "Yes, Quinn, you and your lovely girlfriend have a lot of work to do. We'll be seeing each other, one way or another, in two days' time."

Quinn and I walk out of Magistrate's office and make the journey back to my car in silence. A cold rain has set in, drenching us to the bone by the time we make it back to the car. As he backs out of the parking space, he makes sure to back into the solar car parked next to him. I can't help but smile a bit.

Once we're out of the compound, Quinn looks at me. "How do you know Thomas Eldridge?"

I retort, "We all have our secrets. Who's Rebecca?"

Quinn growls. "Can you get over yourself for a second? You failed to mention that you are on a first name basis with one of the most powerful men on this planet. Who, coincidentally, is visiting the very same shit-hole you occupy. Why is that?"

All the events of the day are clouding my judgment. Quinn's right. There has to be some reason he's here. I take a deep breath and try to think.

Quinn, obviously thinking I'm ignoring him, shouts, "Come on! You're not going to give me the silent treatment forever, are you?"

Then it comes to me. "That's it! Hurry up, Quinn. We've got to get home."

"What is it?"

I look at him. "We got to get back to the house. Now. I can't believe I let this slip by me."

Chapter 26

A Not-So-Pleasant Surprise

Once in front of the main house, I jump out of the car as soon as it comes to a stop. Quinn follows.

"Kelly, will you tell me what's going on here?"

I open the door for him. "Go get Boss and I'll tell you in a second."

I run downstairs and barge into the computer room. Nikki, Wynne, and Gordo all look at me. Wynne smiles. "Man, you look like a drowned cat."

"Can you call up those images of the dots?"

Wynne replies, "Gee, did you lose your sense of humor in the rain?" She makes a couple of keystrokes and the multi-colored discs appear on the screen. I get closer and see a dark line in the bottom left of each circle. I point at the mark. "Zoom in on this right here and see what you can make out."

As Wynne makes several more keystrokes, Boss and Quinn walk through the door. Boss says, "Ms. Kelly, what exactly are we looking at?"

"Sir, I'm following a hunch." The image on the screen zooms in to the dark mark. It focuses in and the mark becomes a circle with an intertwined G and T in the middle. I shake my head. "Fuck me. It's been GlobalThink all along! I just heard this story about how they're merging with a nanotechnology company, and I'll bet you a beer and week's worth of cleaning the guy's bathrooms that GlobalThink has promised the first Magistrate who's able to roll out the new nanotech to their NCS will be given some sort of cherry position at GlobalThink."

Boss walks past me and eyes the logo. "I guess it comes as no surprise that GlobalThink has come up with a way to chip us without our knowledge. It also comes as no surprise that they are teaming up with the government to get this rolled out."

Just then, more blocks start tumbling into place. I say to Wynne, "Did you intercept any more of Lady Magistrate's conversations?"

Wynne grabs a notebook with some handwritten notes scrawled on it. She turns the pages and says, "The most interesting thing I found was that she said she wouldn't renew their marriage contract next year if the latest plan for Mr. Magistrate to get them out of this dump doesn't work. She said her family has given up too much for Dennis's career. I guess we all know what that plan is now."

I stop my pacing. "Wait, did you say *latest* plan? So Magistrate has tried to get the vaccine out to the NCS before?" I pace for a couple of seconds then I stop. "Danny . . . "

Quinn responds, "Are you suggesting that McReady put Danny here to gain the favor of the NCS, only to have *him* roll out the vaccine?"

My eyes grow wide. "Boss, you said it yourself: for a newbie like Danny to come to the NCS with that much money and that many connections was weird. We intercepted communications between Mrs. McReady and her family on the other side where she made mention of a *son*. A son we can find no record of. What if that son was Danny? Boss, did Magistrate ever ask you to roll out a vaccine to the NCS?"

"Yes, he did. We could never come to an agreement because I wanted to randomly test the vaccines from the lot that would be handed out to the NCS."

I rub my head. "No one in the NCS would ever trust Magistrate. If Boss wouldn't do his bidding, then he had to find someone else that he could control. So why not get his dear ol' son to help him run the business? Jesus, what a sociopathic prick!"

The room is silent awhile, then Nikki asks, "But why did he stop Danny from taking us down that night?"

I answer, "But Nikki, who said he came to stop Danny? Honestly, he was probably coming in to clean up what little of us remained. I think when he came in and saw Danny was dead, it took him by surprise. When we were all alive and Danny was dead, he couldn't gun us all down. He'd be back at square one. He knew by keeping us alive he might have a chance at getting the vaccine rolled out. He also knew that Danny dangling the vaccine in front of the NCS would put more pressure on Boss to at least endorse it for Magistrate."

Boss turns to Quinn and me. "How did your meeting with Mr. McReady go?"

Quinn answers, "We have two days. Ramsey has to be gone by then."

I add, "Ramsey knows we were trying to infect his computer with a worm. When he had me in his office he made mention of it. I don't think we're going to find Ryan."

Boss's face is wan and his eyes betray his fear. He's silent for a few seconds, and then says, "Fortunately, Ryan wasn't privy to our other plans for Ramsey. We need to focus on executing the plan to rid our community of him. If we don't eliminate him, the vaccine will be the least of our worries. Once Ramsey's gone, I can buy us some time to figure out what to do with the vaccine." He checks his watch. "Shouldn't Mr. Dunne be back by now?"

Quinn nods. "I'll check on what the holdup is." He leaves the room.

Boss looks at me. "Ms. Kelly, please ensure that your father will be ready for a weapon demonstration in the next fifteen minutes." Then he looks at Gordon, Nikki, and Wynne. "After the weapon demonstration, I want a briefing from you on the intel you gathered from the snoopers."

They all three say in unison, "Yes, sir."

Boss leaves the room without another sound.

I turn to the crew. "Okay guys, what do you have?"

Nikki speaks up, "Actually, quite a bit. Me and Gordo focused on the snoopers while Wynne took care of structural analysis of the building. We'll be ready, no problem"

"Great. I'm going to go see Dad to make sure he's ready. I'll see you out there in a sec."

As I exit the lab, Quinn is leaving his office at the same time. "Did you find Conner?"

"Yeah, he was just leaving Mr. Ito's. They were trying to work through some glitches in the plans. I'm going to go get changed and I'll meet you in the garage." I nod and start to go out the door, then Quinn adds one more thing, "After dinner we need to talk. There's something I want to tell you. Okay?"

I give him curt nod of my head. *What does he want to tell me? That I make a sucky girlfriend? I wish he would just get it over and done with. Oh well, there's too much to think about now.* I take a deep breath and head out to the garage.

*

"Now, what we have here is a jammer. It emits an electromagnetic pulse that will jam any communications Ramsey's team may have with each other. It will also jam all their situational awareness, both audio and visual," Dad says as he holds up the fake cigarette pack.

Lindsey interrupts, "So cigarettes will jam their electronics?"

"No, numb-nuts, it's disguised to look like a pack of cigarettes." He turns to me. "Jesus, Shea, where do you find these people?"

We're all standing out in the old tennis court. The rain has stopped, but the air is still damp and cold. I wrap my wool sweater around me tighter. We're all watching my pop demonstrate our homemade weapons, all of us except for Conner, that is. I look up at Quinn, who's wearing a tight t-shirt and cargo pants. Damn, he looks good. This is so not fair. I whisper to him, "Shouldn't Conner be here by now?"

Quinn whispers, "Give it a couple more minutes and I'll call him again."

Dad yells to me and Quinn, "Am I interrupting your conversation?"

I answer back, "Uh sorry, sir."

"Oh no, I don't want to be rude and talk over *your* conversation. Please finish."

"We're done, Dad."

"Good, now let's move on to the distraction." He takes out a mini tablet from his pocket then makes a couple of finger swipes. In the distance the distinctive rumble of a diesel engine starts. Several more swipes and a beaten old delivery truck appears before us. "On the farm I got a couple of autonomous tractors I've rigged, so making the modifications to this truck was pretty easy. I'm gonna pack this baby with enough ammonium nitrate and diesel fuel to give Ramsey a proper wake up call."

Quinn nudges me and says, "I'm really starting to like your dad."

I flash a smile, and then remember I'm supposed to be pissed off at him, so I turn away and purse my lips. That's when I notice Conner walking toward the main house with Ryan in an arm bar. Ryan seems to be holding a package in his bandaged up hands. For a second my heart leaps when I see that Ryan isn't dead, but I quickly realize his fate with us isn't much better.

I poke Quinn in the ribs. "Looks like Conner found our man."

He yells, "Conner, over here."

Conner comes over holding Ryan by the scruff of his neck. Ryan's face is swollen and bruised. His hands are bandaged and soaked through with blood. Conner throws Ryan to the ground.

"Found this little shit passed out in front of Bobby's. This note was on him."

Shea,

Looks like your handy man ain't so handy now.

Ramsey

Ryan cowers on the ground looking up at us clutching the box. Nikki crouches down by him and looks up at Quinn. "Chief, I need to get him to a doc."

Quinn takes a deep breath. "Fine. He's learned his lesson."

Ryan shakes, "No! I need to find Emmi. Ramsey has her. I need to find her."

Nikki whispers to Ryan. "C'mon you're not going to do anyone any good dead. I'm going to drive you to hospital." She gently takes the box out of his hands and places it on the ground.

As she helps Ryan up, Quinn says to Conner. "What's in the box?"

"I'm not sure, sir. It was outside our front gate. I made shit for brains there carry it in. Should we open it?"

"Conner, you dumbass. Never pick up suspicious packages like that." I look at my dad. "Dad, do you have a sniffer on your tablet?" He throws the mini-tablet in the air; I catch it, and scan the package. The scan comes back clean. "It looks like there's something organic inside. I'm not picking up any traces of biological or chemical warfare, nor any electronics."

Quinn takes a multi tool out of his back pocket and looks at me. "Everyone stand back. I got this." He opens up the package and jumps away as if being bitten by a snake. "Holy shit!"

We all crowd around the package.

Ryan screams, "Emmi!"

I pick up the paper:

Dear Gunny

Hope you enjoy your present. I hope you have something better up your sleeve. You're slipping. You actually used to challenge me. Better luck next time. Just keep calm and don't lose your head – like Emmi here – and I'm sure you'll get me sooner or later.

Love,
Ramsey

Ryan slumps on the ground and Nikki puts her arm around him.

I look at Quinn. "We need to get Ramsey before he strikes again."

Quinn responds, "Shea, he's trying to get us to react before we're ready. We need to hold to the plan."

Ryan screams, "What do you mean? That's my sister! Because of you she's dead."

Quinn growls, "I'm sorry about your sister, but if we strike too soon, all of our plans will be destroyed."

Nikki helps Ryan up. "We'll get him, Ryan. We need to get you to the hospital. You won't make it through the night in your condition."

As Nikki walks Ryan to the car, Boss looks at Dad and asks, "Is everything together for your distractions, Mr. Kelly?"

"We need to get all the materials for the explosives put together. We also need a way to remotely detonate explosives, which shouldn't be too hard to do. If I get some help, I can probably knock it out by dinner time."

Quinn pipes up before I'm able to, "I'll help you, sir."

Oh great, that's what I need, Dad and Quinn talking alone.

Before I'm able to retort, Boss says, "Ms. Kelly and Ms. Myers, what information have you been able to gather about Ramsey's team?"

Wynne responds, "Sir, we found that the northeastern quadrant of the building is where they keep most of their weapons. We also found that most of the men sleep on the other side of the building. Early morning will be the best time to strike because Ramsey is always there at that time. We found the weak points of the building; I'll give those to Mr. Kelly."

Boss nods. "Very good. We need to be ready to execute this the day after tomorrow. I do not want any of you awake and working at all hours. We are on track to meet our deadline. What I need is a well-rested and prepared team. Get to bed early tonight and we will spend all day tomorrow practicing our plan. Mr. Knightly, make sure we have enough mercs to take care of your shifts for the rest of today and tomorrow. I can't risk any of you going into town before we implement this plan."

We all respond, "Yes, sir."

"We will meet at 0600 tomorrow in the conference room to put finishing touches on our plan. Then we will practice."

Boss shuffles away from us. His difficulty walking is so pronounced now that no one can deny what's happening. We all look at him and I can tell the others have the same heartsick feeling I do. Each of us knows once Boss goes, even if we do take down Ramsey, our fate is uncertain.

Quinn breaks the tension by yelling, "You heard the man. Get busy. Lindsey and Conner, I want you to make sure we have enough mercs to cover our shifts. When you're done with that, take inventory of our weapons and make sure they're in working order. Gather all the ammo in one spot. Also, I want medic kits made to take with us."

Conner and Lindsey respond, "Yes, sir." And they are off like a shot.

I look at Quinn. "Me, Wynne, and Gordo will be downstairs if you need us."

Before I get out of arm's reach, he grabs my wrist and says, "Remember, after dinner we need to talk."

I pull away. "Yeah, I remember."

Chapter 27

A Question of Trust

"You're full of shit."

I push the uneaten mounds of spaghetti around my plate, trying hard not to make eye contact with Wynne. "Yup, right there in the middle of town."

Nikki puts her hand on my arm. "I'm sorry, hon. Quinn does have a bit of a temper. I'm sure once he cools down it'll be okay."

"I know it was stupid to go into town, but the thing is, Quinn doesn't tell me anything. He just expects me to do what he says without question."

A hint of a smile shows on Nikki's face. "But that's what he's used to. He barks out orders and people follow them. You add a layer of difficulty he isn't used to."

"It's like he doesn't trust me with anything. Like . . . Ramsey told Quinn that I reminded him of someone named Rebecca, and Quinn went nuts. I mean nuttier than I've ever seen him. If Ramsey's men hadn't been there to stop him, I'm pretty sure Quinn would've killed the guy with his bare hands. When I asked who Rebecca was he wouldn't tell me. He doesn't trust me." Nikki's eyes grow wide. I know instantly that she knows something I don't. "Nikki? Do you know who Rebecca is?"

"I do, but it's for Chief to tell you, not me."

"See? He doesn't trust me."

"No, he does trust you. We all have secrets. I'm sure there are things you haven't told him."

Wynne takes a swig of her beer and says, "Yeah, I think we're all cursed."

Suddenly I feel incredibly guilty. This morning I promised Wynne we would gripe about her man troubles, and here we are talking about mine. I give Wynnie a hug. "I'm sorry. You know what, when we're done with this whole Ramsey thing let's blow this popsicle joint. We'll open a bar or something."

Wynne takes another drink. "You know as well I do we can never leave this place."

I go back to pushing around mounds of spaghetti and respond, "I know. I was just dreaming." I look over at Nikki. "So how's Ryan?"

"Doc said he'll be fine. He's got a concussion and he lost two fingers on each hand. I think it's going to take a lot longer for him to get over it mentally than physically. He's pretty torn up about Emmi."

We're all silent awhile, pushing our dinners around, too depressed to actually eat. The reality of day is starting to set in. Poor Ryan, he was just trying to earn money and help us out, and now his sister is gone. I'll never see little Mia again. I screwed up one of the best relationships I've ever had. And Frank is gone. Frank was an asshole who was mostly out for himself, but he did help me out of some shitty situations in the past. Now he's dead because of me. The sound of footsteps causes us all to look up from our plates.

Quinn is standing at the entrance, covered head to toe in grime and filth. "Shea, can we talk now?"

Immediately Wynne and Nikki stand and grab their plates. Wynne says, "I got some stuff to do somewhere. See you guys."

Nikki adds, "Yeah, I got the same stuff to do."

They dump their plates in the sink, and before I'm able to protest, they're out of the kitchen. My stomach rumbles. Confrontation doesn't bother me, but talking about touchy-feely bullcrap does. Quinn grabs two beers from the fridge. He makes his way to the table. "Let's go outside."

I follow him outside to the couch. He sits at one end, and I sit at the other with my arms crossed over my chest. He hands me a beer and I just look at him. He shakes his head. "Always so stubborn. Take the damn beer."

I grab the beer from his hand and take a swig. "Thanks. So I take it Dad had you working pretty hard?"

He rubs the back of his neck and smiles. "That old man can work circles around someone twenty years younger. As a matter of fact, he's still out there now."

"That doesn't surprise me. During harvest time he would average about three hours a sleep a night. I think it keeps him young." Talking to Quinn like this almost makes me forget there are any problems between us. Almost. I take deep breath before I delve into the land of emotions. "So, what did you want to talk to me about?"

Like I don't know.

He takes a swig of his beer. "You were right. I should've told you more about Ramsey. If you're my partner, then you need to know these things. I was wrong to keep you in the dark."

My mouth gapes open. This is the last thing I expected to hear come from this man. I try to collect myself so he doesn't see my surprise. "Um — yeah, you're damn right."

"By the same token, you need to be straight with me. If there's something about your past that could affect our mission, you need to tell me."

"Fine. No secrets."

He nods. "As I'm sure you've figured out, Ramsey isn't your run of the mill psychotic prick. He's highly intelligent; he's devoid of any emotions; he gets off on chaos and pain. There is no reasoning with this man."

He takes another drink. I reach into my pants pocket and produce a pack of cigarettes.

"Can I have one of those?" I light my cigarette and toss the pack and a lighter to him. He lights up and takes a long slow drag. "I was in the Marine Corps for almost ten years when

Ramsey came around. I was supposed to be his mentor. His intelligence scores were off the charts, but he didn't much like authority."

"I guess the Marine Corps is probably not the ideal place for a person like that."

"Yeah, but with the economy the way it was, I'm sure his hand was forced to join or starve. He probably had some sick fantasy that he'd get to kill lots of people. Anyway, nothing I did seemed to get through to this guy. Then, well, my company got deployed to the Mexican border for a peace keeping mission for a year. Not very far, but we couldn't, under any circumstances, go home. They figured since we were so close to home, people would always be asking for a long weekend. So it was made clear that no leave would be approved under any circumstances. This place was a shithole. A lot like the NCS, but hotter. While we were out, Ramsey tried to get friendly with this pretty staff sergeant. She didn't want to have anything to do with him though."

"Smart girl."

"She was smart. And a hard worker. She wouldn't put up with any of Ramsey's shit, and made it clear that she didn't want anything to do with him. He didn't like that. So he set about making her life miserable. She was pretty good at just ignoring him — she was tough — that is, until he got wind of the son she had back home. The kid was really sick and she couldn't go back to him. All she had was a weekly video conference with him."

I see the pain on his face. I scoot closer to him and hold his hand. "That's terrible."

"Yeah. Ramsey didn't let a minute go by where he wasn't reminding her of her son, or implying what a horrible mother she was. I beat the shit out of him for it, but it just seemed to strengthen his resolve. Then, one day her son died and she wasn't able to be there to be with him or say goodbye. Ramsey moved in for the kill. I tried to keep him away, but I couldn't. We found the staff sergeant a few days after her son's death, hanging from the rafters of her barracks."

"I'm sorry, Quinn. Was that Rebecca?"

He squeezes my hand and looks down. "No." He looks pained, so I decide not to press him any further. He continues. "You need to know this. I should've told you earlier. I was just trying to protect you."

I wipe my eyes. I'm not sure what's worse, the story or the pain it's causing Quinn to tell it. "I understand. I was being bitchy and immature. So, I guess you want to hear about Dr. E."

"Absolutely. This has to be good."

"As you know, Dr. E started out as a professor at the local university, the very same university that yours truly attended."

"Ah, it's starting to make sense now."

"It sounds like he's a lot like Ramsey. Not about the chaos and stuff, but being devoid of emotion. He wants to be the most powerful man in technology, and he doesn't care about who he steps on along the way. There's so much intellectual property that he stole in order to make GovTek where it is today."

"So, were you one of those people?"

"Yeah, Wynne and I were, like, three years into the research for our doctorates."

Quinn chokes on the smoke of his cigarette. "Say what? You and Wynne have doctorates?"

"I don't. Stick with me, okay? The only other person that knows this is besides Wynne is Dad. So, Dr. E. recruited me my senior year of college. He was impressed at some of the research I was doing on the chip. Honestly, I was just looking for something to do for my senior design project. I didn't think it would take off like it did. They were still about four years from releasing GovTek as it is now. There was this pesky problem of it not working reliably as an exterior mount, only a few select people could get the thought commands to work and even then it was still buggy. That's why they'd test people in the service to see who was a good candidate for the active chip before implantation. Dr. E was getting nervous because he was under the gun to get the chip working. The government was very close to taking away some of his contracts. You probably remember some roll-outs of this technology that were less than spectacular."

"Yeah, actually I do. They would work controlling some peripherals just fine and others not so much."

"That's because different peripherals use different brain signals to work. They could get the chip to work with some brain impulses, but not others. The only way they could get the chip to work reliably is if they mounted it internally, like Boss's. This wasn't commercially viable. I was studying the effect the cranium has on electrical signals of the brain. Basically, I was trying to come up with some do-hickey that would account for all the weirdness the skull would impart on the brain's electrical signals. Wynne was implementing it into code."

"Um, okay . . . "

I smile and squeeze his hand. "It isn't that impressive really. I have no idea why no one else thought of it. Heck, they've been doing it for years by using microwave holography to back transform what antenna patterns look like behind radomes. I thought I could do a kind of similar thing."

He looks at me like a deer in the headlights.

"Let's just say I needed lots and lots and *lots* of brainwave data, so I could get some kind of baseline and then go from there. Dr. E definitely had all that, since he bought all the rights to the old GovTek and all the data that went with it. So, on sifting through this data, I found that there was a significant number of people with the chip that seemed to have this nasty habit of having their brainwaves degenerate. I called him on it. He tried to whitewash it, but then I found out he'd known all along and just didn't care. I was so close to my dissertation, and since it was such a sexy topic with a high profile backer, I would have certainly gotten my doctorate."

"So you walked away from it all?"

"Yeah, but not before punching Dr. E square in the face. I broke his nose."

Quinn laughs. "You're serious?"

"If you look close, you can see his nose is still crooked. It got me blackballed from any technical job though. I was ready to go back to Dad and take a teaching position at the local high school, but then they started requiring teachers to get chipped. I could read the writing on the wall, so I came over here. After I left, Eldridge took all my work without my permission and implemented it. It wasn't the answer to all their problems, but I gave them a pretty good start. Lo and behold, four years later GovTek is introduced. I didn't have much of a choice but to come here."

"What about Wynne? You said *you* didn't get your doctorate. What about her?"

"She did get hers. Her work was focused on a implementing a piece of my work in code. She finished before me, but it wasn't long before she was blackballed for even associating with me."

"Huh, the stripper is a Doc."

I chuckle a bit.

"I'm sorry. I should've told you. But I think you can understand why we don't tell many people, especially here. We wouldn't last long. I didn't *invent* the chip, I just came up with a small piece that made it possible to work like it does today. Just like hundreds of others that Thomas Eldgridge exploited."

"So is there some significance to him being here? Should we be worried?"

"I don't think so. He's just offered us the vaccine, because of our proximity to GlobalThink. He never really thought much of me. He thinks I'm a stupid hick that had one good idea that he could scam. As a matter of fact, he doesn't think anyone has the intellectual capacity that he does."

"Well, we need to be on alert for him. You threaten him more than you think."

"I won't hold back on you anymore, I promise. So, what about this St. Jude character? What's up with him?"

"Like I said there's a network of others on the outside that want to help. I've been in contact with St. Jude. There's no way to tell if it's the same person or a several people using the same screen name."

"I don't know, Quinn. Sometimes I just get sick of trying. How can we make a difference?"

Quinn takes my hand and kisses it. "I can't tell you everything now, but trust me when I say this goes higher than you know. It's important you keep trying."

"How high, Quinn?"

"Please trust me. I've been given orders, I . . . "

He has a pained look. I take a deep breath and caress the side of this face. "I trust you. Tell me when you can."

Please don't make me regret this.

Quinn puts his arm around me and starts to play with my hair. I sink into his warm body and close my eyes. He clears his throat. "There's something else."

I smile. "Geez, I'm not sure how much more I can take."

Quinn doesn't return my smile. Instead he reaches into his back pocket and produces his wallet. He fishes out a thin piece of transparent plastic. He swipes his index finger across the bottom and a picture appears. I feel as if all the air has been sucked from my lungs. I remind myself to breathe. In the picture, Quinn stands with his arm around a beautiful blonde. Somehow, she appears to be the kind of woman that could carry on an intelligent conversation about world events, and look sexy doing it. She's holding a baby decked out in a pink bonnet. In front of the couple are tow-headed twin boys no more than five years old in matching sweater vests.

"Oh God, Quinn is that . . . ?"

"My wife, Rebecca, and my kids Adam, Alaric, and Ava." He takes a deep breath and rubs his head. "When I started speaking out about the chip I was told to stop. She encouraged me to do the right thing and speak out. If I could've known what would happen to my family if I continued . . . "

I lean in close, knowing that my embrace offers little comfort. "I'm so sorry, Quinn. I know there's no way you would've knowingly put your family in harm's way."

"She and those kids were the best thing that ever happened to me, and they took them away." He drops the picture viewer into his lap. "The official story was that some punks strung out on sKape broke into our house looking for anything they could pawn for their next fix. I knew it was bullshit. They were sending me a message, but I had no way to prove it. I lost my family and I lost faith in the country I believed in. I quit the Marines and kind of floundered about for several years. Then a friend of a friend asked if I would work for Boss as his security lead. The rest is history."

I'm at a loss for words. My respect for Quinn has just reached a new level. I sit up on my knees so that I'm face to face with him, and run my hands through his hair.

He whispers, "I just thought you should know. Listen, Shea, I'm sorry I overreacted before, but I went a little crazy when I thought I was going to lose you too."

I give him a kiss on his head then settle in his lap. "I'm glad you told me." His face is still showing the signs of his encounter with Ramsey. I brush the poorly placed bandage on his face with the tips of my fingers. "You would think by now you would know how to dress your own wounds."

He moves my hand. "You wanna go upstairs and fix 'em for me?"

I give him a long, tight hug. "Absolutely."

Chapter 28

Never Again

"Move-it, move-it, people," Quinn barks out around the cigar positioned in the corner of his mouth. We all gather around Quinn and Boss outside the garage-turned-lab. The sun is just starting to rise and the air is cool and damp. Mr. Ito is here along with all the mercs he trained for this mission. Mr. Ito and the rest of the security crew have spent the last several days running drills with them. This is our one last dress rehearsal before the big day.

Boss starts to speak. "I've reviewed all of your reports and plans on this OP. Here are your orders: Ms. Kelly, Ms. Myers, and Mr. Timmons, you will stay here at the compound to be the brains of the OP team. Ms. Kelly, you will be in charge of Command and Control."

No pressure or anything.

We all respond, "Yes, sir."

He looks at several of the mercs and Ryan. "Mr. Ito, Mr. Kelly, Ms. Simon, Mr. Speer, and Mr. Benton, you will accompany Mr. Knightly and his crew on the raid of Ramsey's compound."

Wait, Dad's going on the raid? Over my dead body!

They all respond, "Yes, sir."

He looks at the remaining mercs. "Mr. Graham and Ms. Walker, you will guard the compound with your lives. It is imperative that no one and nothing gets through to our OP center."

"Yes, sir."

Boss nods. "I expect nothing but the best from all of you."

"Yes, sir."

"Mr. Knightly will lead you in exercises for the remainder of the day. We'll execute tomorrow at 0400. Is this understood?"

"Yes, sir."

As Boss slowly walks away, Quinn barks out, "You heard the man. This needs to be executed perfectly. And we'll keep practicing this until everything is perfect. Then we'll practice some more. By the end of the day you'll be dreaming about this OP. Before we start I need Lindsey, Nikki, Conner and Mr. Kelly to inspect the perimeter of the compound to make sure everything is secure. All you mercs, I want you to inspect all the weapons to ensure they are in property working order." He looks at me. "I need you to take your team to the OP center and perform checks on all the computers and tech to make sure they're working. Be ready to execute our first dress rehearsal in half an hour."

Everyone scatters to execute their orders. Everyone but me. I wait until Dad is out of earshot before saying, "Quinn, what the hell are you doing?"

He glares at me. "We're not going to do this now. We don't have time. You need to execute my orders without bickering. I trust you more than anyone to be in charge of Command and Control and to fix last minute tech screw-ups. I need you back here to watch my team's back."

"I know *that*. But what the hell are you doing taking my dad out there? I know he begged you to go, but he's going to get hurt."

"Your dad's a tough old guy. Don't discount him. I need him out there because he can maneuver the remote controlled truck better than any of us. We don't have time to learn. Don't worry. He's not going in the building with the rest of the raid party. I've told him that he needs to stay out of sight. He's going to stay outside and snipe anyone who happens to escape."

"Fine. I trust you, but I came by my stubbornness honestly. You need to drill it into his head that he isn't going with you and the raid party."

"Yes, ma'am. We're going to execute the first dry run in a half an hour. Will your team be ready?"

"Absolutely."

I go in the house. Down in the lab, Wynne and Gordo are performing checks on all the computers.

"How's everything looking, guys?"

Wynne turns to me in her leather chair and hacks. She looks pale and clammy. After this I'm going to make her stay in bed for a week.

She says, "All the computers are a go, boss lady."

"Will you guys stop calling me that? We need to check all the video and sound to make sure it comes through. I'm going to make sure the generators are working properly. Throughout the day I'm going to cut the power to make sure everything stays up and works seamlessly. I can't let some stupid random brown-out affect the mission."

Gordon responds, "Good idea."

"Have you guys checked to see if the snooper app on Ramsey's guys' phones is still working?"

Wynne presses a couple buttons and video of Ramsey's compound is shown on the displays. "Sure have. I'm getting a pretty good signal from most of them. As an added bonus I've hacked into their security feeds so we'll be able to see around the building and into some of the other areas. That is, until we go dark. When your dad initiates the pulse, our devices will be taken out just like Ramsey's."

"That shouldn't matter because once he initiates, he'll have the truck in there within a couple of minutes and detonated shortly thereafter."

"So are you guys ready to do this?"

Gordo says, "Ready as we'll ever be."

I press the comms unit in my ear. "Can you hear me, Quinn?"

"Coming through loud and clear, babe."

Wynne presses a few buttons on her screen and we see around one of the abandoned outbuildings on the compound serving as our mockup.

I answer back, "I have 360 degree situational awareness now. It looks like you're all clear. On my mark, move in the distraction. In three . . . two . . . " The display goes dark and we lose all video. "Son-of-a-bitch!"

Quinn's voice booms over the comms, "What's wrong?"

"I just lost all the video."

A growl comes over the comms.

I answer back, "Don't get your panties in a knot. I'll get it fixed in a jiff."

After few minutes our situational awareness is restored. We execute dry run after dry run; some of them go well and some of them not so well. We fix a multitude of technical and tactical errors. By the end of the day, we're all tired and burned out. We've given up lunch and dinner. It's time to stop. I get on the comms. "Hey, babe, I think it's time we called it a day. We're starting to see diminishing returns. Everyone needs to eat and get enough sleep to be fresh tomorrow."

Another growl. "Fine. Everyone meet by the garage at 0300 tomorrow."

Dad gets on the comms. "Saoirse, I'm taking Vaughn and Simon into town with me to drop off the truck." Before I have time to protest he says, "I know what you are going to say, little one. We need to get the truck dropped off tonight so we don't arouse any suspicions in the morning. I'm taking two guys with me and I'm wearing my comms, unlike some people, so I'll be fine."

I take a deep breath. "Fine, but if you're not back in forty-five minutes, I'm coming to get you." I continue on to everyone else, "Okay everyone, get something to eat and get some sleep. We have a big day ahead of us. We have all of this in hand, so don't worry about tomorrow." My stomach growls – not from hunger, but nervousness. I take the comms piece out of my ear, slouch in my seat, and look over to Wynne and Gordon.

Wynne gets up and pats me on the shoulder. "Like you said, don't worry about it. We have this down."

Gordon adds, "Yeah, you guys tested us with every scenario under the sun. We're ready for anything."

"It's my job to worry. I keep thinking there has to be something I forgot to account for."

Wynne holds the door to lab open. "Shea, it'll be fine. Get out of here. Get some sleep. Go cuddle with your boyfriend or something."

Gordon scrunches up his nose. "Cuddle and Quinn are not two things I would put together."

I smile and file out the door behind my two favorite nerds. We go up both flights of stairs to our bedrooms. Wynne and I stop outside our bedroom and Gordon goes past us to his. Wynne looks pale and tired. She lets out a long wet cough.

"You okay? I haven't been around much lately. I'm sorry."

"I'm fine. It's my stupid allergies. And I can find a million guys like Conner. And hey, since you've been sleeping in Captain Personality's room I'm not waking up all hours of the night with your nightmares."

I give her a playful shove. "Whatever. You could sleep through an earthquake." I give her a hug. "Seriously, I don't mind hanging with you."

"Nah, go on with your boyfriend."

"Thanks, hon."

I go across the hall to Quinn's room. I don't bother knocking. Quinn isn't in the room, but the shower is running. I sit on the chair by the desk and prop my feet up on the desk. I lay my head on the back of the chair and rest my eyes. In the background, the sound of the water stops and I open my eyes. The door opens and steam rolls out. Quinn is standing in the doorway, dripping wet, clad only in a towel. *Yippee!*

He makes his way over to me. "Why didn't you join me in the shower?"

"I thought you might be the shower-alone type."

"Usually, but I make concessions for special people."

He bends down and starts to kiss my neck. As if in a trance I stand and put my arms around his waist and pull him closer to me. I press my lips to his, and he returns my kisses eagerly. I start to forget about the raid tomorrow, Magistrate, and Dad . . .

"Shit!"

Quinn pulls away from me. "What's wrong?"

"Dad, he hasn't checked in yet. What time is it?"

"Shit, it's been forty-five minutes. Damn it! I knew I should've gone into town with him. That old man is as bullheaded as you are." He heads over to his dresser and starts to pull out some clothes. "Get on the comms and try to get a hold of him or the guys he went in with. If you don't hear anything in the next thirty seconds, I'll go into town with Lindsey."

I open Quinn's desk rummaging for the comms piece I left up here, cursing myself for not being more assertive with Dad. Quinn pulls on his shirt heads for the door. A sudden loud pounding makes us both jump.

"Quinn! Stop molesting my daughter. We gotta get up early tomorrow."

Quinn stops in his tracks. "Yes, sir." He looks at me and shakes his head. "That old man is a bigger pain in the ass than you are."

From the other side of door a voice booms, "I heard that."

I smile and walk over to Quinn, putting my arms around his waist. "Thanks."

"For what?"

"Without even giving it a second thought, you were going to get my daddy."

He growls. "Yeah don't remind me."

I grab his shirt and pull his head down to my level. "So, where were we?"

He starts to kiss my neck then works his way to my ear. I sink into him and work my hands up under his shirt. His lips find mine I hold him tighter. "Mmm. Maybe your dad is right. We should probably go to bed."

In between kisses I say, "Bed is good. The floor is fine too."

He laughs and picks me up. I wrap my legs around his middle. The display on his computer lights up and a loud chime sounds indicating an emergency message. He puts me down. "Dammit! Can't we get one moment of peace?"

The chime sounds again. "I guess that would be a no. It's probably Magistrate wanting to know our status. Just answer him so we can continue our . . . conversation."

Quinn sits in his chair and makes a couple of keystrokes. I stand behind him and rub his head. "Hmm. It doesn't look like it's from Magistrate."

He makes a couple more keystrokes and a video is displayed. I walk around and sit in his lap and kiss his cheek. "Come on. It isn't from Magistrate. Let's go to bed and worry about it tomorrow."

Something in the video has grabbed his attention and he's stopped paying attention to me. I look over to the video. It's poor quality, taken from a phone or some other portable device. The only thing on the screen is a small white Cape Cod house. The sound of laughter is coming from the video. The video becomes shaky as the person holding the camera runs toward the house. Two men clad in black rush the door and kick it down. I look over at Quinn and he's watching slack-jawed. I turn back to the video and the men are rushing into the house and up the stairs. The man holding the camera barks out, "You two go down the hall and take care of them. I want to take care of this one myself."

The door in front of the camera opens and a woman is standing there holding a gun. *Oh. God.* It's Rebecca. She yells at the camera, "Leave my kids alone or I'll shoot you."

Three shots ring out. The camera man scoffs. "Too late, momma bear."

She lifts her gun, but before she is able to get a shot off two shots ring out from behind the camera wounding but not killing her. The man walks over to Rebecca laughing. She's trying to back away, but he knocks her to the ground. He goes to the ground, mounting her. He puts the camera down and looks into it, smiling. Those icy blue eyes are unmistakable. The video stops and it is replaced with Ramsey's current face, "Gunny! I was looking through old pictures and videos and came across this little gem. Rebecca was hot. Good times." His face is gone.

Quinn is staring blankly at the screen. I fight down the lump in my throat. There is nothing I can do or say that could possibly make this better. What could I say? This man just witnessed the love of his life and his children being murdered. I bite my lip and don't try to force the tears away. Caressing his face I say, "Quinn, honey. He knows we're going to strike tomorrow."

Nothing.

"We need to call this off and regroup. He knows. He's trying to throw you off. We'll think of something."

A long silence. He eases me off his lap and stands. I back up from him and try to give him space. He breathes heavily for a moment, and then explodes. In one motion, he turns over his desk. He kicks it, reducing the computer and desk to bits and pieces. I try hard to grab my inner calm. I can't; I'm scared. I don't know what to do. He stops and looks at me, seeing my fear. He comes over to me and I take him into my arms; we hold each other for what seems like hours.

I whisper, "We can't go."

He takes a deep breath. "It ends now. He's not going to own me. I'm going to take him down or die trying. He'll never hurt anyone I love ever again."

THREE

Chapter 29

Surprise!

I put the comms unit in my ear and nestle in the comfort of my chair in the dark room. I look over at Wynne and Gordon. "You guys ready?"

They nod. The pallor of Wynne's face concerns me. Despite what she says, she's been taking her break-up with Conner particularly hard, and I think it's starting to take a toll on her health. Boss eases himself into a chair and puts a comms unit in his ear. Claire is sitting by his side wringing her hands.

"Sir, are you ready?"

"Yes, Ms. Kelly."

I take a deep breath, bracing myself for the longest fifteen minutes of my life. I activate the comms. "Okay everyone, let's do one last check in before we go dark. Dad, are you reading me?"

"Roger. We're in town waiting by the truck for the others."

"Conner, do you read me?"

"Roger. We're nearing our position. Be there in five."

"Quinn, are you reading me?"

He growls. "I'm in position and waiting."

My stomach gives a churn. Quinn insisted on carrying out his part of the mission alone since last night. I didn't dare argue with him. I make a couple of keystrokes so our conversation is private. "Be careful, okay?"

He answers back, "Don't worry, babe. I'll be fine."

I get a slow sinking feeling. Somehow I don't buy it. I make several more keystrokes and our conversation is public again. I look up at the map on the flat screen. Everyone's position is indicated by a glowing green light. "Wynne, what's going on at Ramsey's compound?"

The sound of a few clicks of the keys then Wynne says, "All's quiet on the Ramsey front." She coughs and sniffs. "Everyone's where we thought they would be."

"Gordo, are the jammers online?"

"Yes, ma'am, they're all a go."

"Good. Is everyone in position and ready?"

Dad: "Affirmative."

Quinn: "Affirmative."

Conner: "Let's rock and roll."

Boss says, "Ms. Kelly, you have the lead. Please commence."

"On my mark we're going to go dark. Dad, you have two minutes to get the truck in there and initiate the distraction." I take a deep breath. "In three . . . two . . . one . . . go!"

Gordon hits the button that activates the jammers and all the glowing dots are now grey. This is the longest two minutes of my life. When the lights come on again, the truck will have moved in and activated its distraction and everyone will have moved into the compound to take care of the remaining residents. I'm praying that all the lights come back on.

As if reading my thoughts, Wynne says, "Hey, your boyfriend's a smart guy. He knows what he's doing. Relax."

Boss adds, "Yes, Ms. Kelly, you have this situation under control. You and Mr. Knightly are the two most capable employees I've ever had."

"Thank you, sir."

Wynne lets out a long cough.

"Are you okay, Wynnie? You don't look so great."

"Gee, thanks. I'm fine. Just feeling run down from these last couple of days. I'll be glad when all this Ramsey bullshit is over. Then I can get some sleep."

"Agreed."

The timer is counting down. I'm pretty sure someone slowed

down time in this room. It's so quiet I can hear my own heart beating. Another thirty seconds down. Jesus, will the clock please just hurry up. I hate feeling like I have no control. There is absolutely nothing I can do for my team. For Quinn. I'm waiting for Ramsey and what he has planned. Another thirty seconds. If anything happens to my team I'll never forgive myself. Not my team, my family. Another thirty seconds. I hold my breath and one by one the dots start to glow again.

Mr. Ito – is a go

Mercs – are a go

Conner, Lindsey, and Nikki – are a go

Dad – is a go

I hold my breath . . .

Quinn – is a go

Thank God.

"Report your status."

Dad replies, "The distraction was a success. We've taken out the eastern quarter of their compound. Still no Ramsey."

Gordon makes a couple of keystrokes and an image of the burned out shell of a building is displayed with people running out of the building. No Ramsey in sight.

Conner replies, "We're heading into the remains of the building now to check for our target. We haven't seen anyone yet."

Quinn says, "Nothing here, Kelly."

I knit my eyebrows and look at Boss. "Ms. Kelly, be patient." I nod.

An alarm sounds from one of the computers. "Gordo, what is that?"

"The compound's been breached."

We all look at each other in silence. I try, unsuccessfully, to push down my fear. "Wynne, pull up the video from outside cameras."

The video of Ramsey's compound is replaced with video

of the perimeter of our compound. Wynne quickly switches cameras to ascertain where and who the intruder is. After several clicks we see it. I get on the comms to Quinn. "Quinn! Ramsey's breached the compound. He's heading toward the main building."

"On my way. Conner, Nikki, and Lindsey, meet me there. Mr. Kelly, you and the mercs hold your position and keep an eye out for any changes."

I hold my breath and look back at the video, "Jesus, he's closing in. He's in the foyer now. Quinn!"

"Hold your position! I'm almost there."

My leg starts shaking nervously and I'm frozen in my seat. I look around the room and the fear is apparent on everyone's face. Wynne starts to cough again and she is sweating profusely. Something's really wrong with her, but we can't leave now.

"Wynne, honey, are you okay?"

She says breathlessly, "I'm fine. We have bigger problems than me right now."

I stare back at the screen and Ramsey has made his way down the stairs and is feet from the lab.

"Quinn, he's right by the lab. Shit!"

"Hold tight. I'm almost there, babe."

I'm face to face with Ramsey. His usual smug look is replaced with a confused expression. "What? But you're supposed to be—"

We all laugh at the man on our video display. "Hey Buddy! Thanks for sending that video last night. It gave us just enough of a heads up to realize what the hell you were up to. We're down here at Heads and Tails. You don't think we're stupid enough to stay at the compound, do you?"

"But . . . but . . . "

"Yeah you bugged our comms too, didn't you? I played that pretty well, didn't I? Oh, Quinn, help me! I'm just a stupid girl."

Everyone in our room breaks out in laughter. On the video display Ramsey is pacing. His face is growing redder by the moment. He picks up a computer and slams it to the ground.

Gordo's eyes grow wide. "Hey, asshole! Get your hands off of my stuff."

Ramsey screams, "I'm going scoop out your eyes and skull fuck you, you fat fuck!"

Gordon's eyes open wide and he scoots back in his chair.

"Oh Gordo, we're not going to have to worry about Ramsey anymore."

Ramsey glares at the screen. "What makes you think that?"

"Because, asshole, I can see behind you."

Ramsey turns around and comes face to face with Quinn. Quinn pulls the trigger on his pistol twice, blowing out both of Ramsey's knees. Ramsey falls to the ground where we can no longer see him. But we can still hear his whining. "Fuck you, Gunny. You're always going to have to live with the fact that I got you. I fucked and killed your wife. And I killed your little brats. I got you."

Quinn is silent and looks into the video screen. "This is a private conversation between me and Ramsey."

The screen goes dark.

Everyone looks at me. Wynne breaks the silence with her sharp wet cough. Her skin is clammy and pale. She's struggling for her next breath.

"Wynnie? Are you okay?"

She struggles to her feet. "I'm fine, I just need . . . "

She falls to the floor in a heap.

Claire rushes down to Wynne and takes her pulse. "Bring the car around. We need to get Wynne to the hospital immediately."

Chapter 30

Double Cross

The pungent smell of disinfectant and cleanser sting my nose. Wynne has been in the exam room for over an hour. Gordon took Boss back to the compound after he made sure Wynne was being seen by the best doctor. We all thought it was best we minimize Boss's interaction with the public while in his current state.

None of the staff will let me back to see Wynne; I pace in the hospital waiting area for the millionth time. The waiting room is bustling with activity: people moaning in agony, babies crying with fever. In one of the seats I see a familiar face: Althea. Her boy is limp in her arms with his chest barely rising. She glares at me, not taking her eyes from me. I turn from her.

Fuck her. Wynne's my best friend and I'll do anything to make sure she's okay.

Even though the waiting room is crammed with so many people, I've never felt so alone. Everyone is busy with their assigned duties and can't make it here until they get things more settled. The events of the last several days have drained all the energy from my body. A stim drink dispenser catches my eye. That's just the chemical boost I need. I fish a crinkled scrip note out of my pocket and try to smooth it over. I carefully put the note in the slot and the machine takes it halfway then spits it out at my feet. I try again and the same result. I take a deep breath: inner calm. I smooth the note one more time and feed it into the machine. It takes the money all the way, there's a pause, and then the machine spits my money back, this time ripped. I kick the machine.

"Goddamn piece of shit!"

I'm brought to tears by a vending machine. My shoulders slump and I just cry. I should feel great that we got Ramsey and we can start getting things back to normal, but I don't. My best friend is sick and there is nothing I can do. A whiney, nasally voice rings out above the hospital noise.

"Ms. Shea Kelly, we need to see you."

I wipe my eyes and collect myself. A large nurse on the other side of the reception desk greets me. She's not in the mood for any shit. "I'm Shea Kelly, ma'am."

She rolls her eyes as if to say, *I know who you are, you stupid bitch.* "Ms. Myers is still being seen by the doctor. We need to know her next of kin."

"Um, that would be me. I'm her, uh, sister."

She pauses for a bit and eyes me up and down. "Cut the shit. I have a waiting room full of people here that I still need to see. I don't need to put up with you, princess. Does she have next of kin or not?"

"Yes, me."

She growls. "Fine. I'll put down NO."

I breathe deep, pushing down the anger. "Listen, Nurse Ratched, Wynne is my family. I will have your ass if you don't put me down as next of kin and let me back in to see her. She will *not* sit back there alone. You know who I am and who I work for, you know I will have it done. Don't fuck with me, because I'm not in the mood to take shit from stupid bitches on power trips."

She glares at me and purses her lips. "Fine. Someone will escort you back shortly . . . ma'am."

I pace several more times until my name is called again. I guess Nurse Ratched got the message through to the rest of the staff. At the double doors that separate the waiting room from the exam rooms stands Doctor Lyman, the same man who patched me up after my romp in Danny's basement. I relax a

266

little knowing Wynne is in good hands. He escorts me to the back as he says, "Ms. Kelly, I'm sorry for the behavior of our staff. It won't happen again."

"We're all a little stressed out here. I just want to see Wynne. How is she?"

"I'm afraid, not so good. She has the flu, the Beta Strain."

"Oh, fuck."

"Ms. Kelly . . . Shea. Listen, don't write her off. She's young, strong, and other than this, healthy. Not everyone dies of the flu, but she's going to have to fight hard."

"Can I see her?"

"We have her in a private room. There isn't a lot we can do except to help keep her hydrated and give her nutrients intravenously so her body can get the energy to fight this thing. If she stabilizes in the next 48 hours, I'm going to recommend that you move her home. Patients do better in familiar surroundings. We'll send someone out to look in on her."

I manage to squeak out, "Okay. Can I see her?"

"Yes, but you're going to have to take precautions. You're going to have to do this when you move her home too. I recommend she has her own room. When you go into her room, cover your mouth, eyes, nose, and hands. Make sure to wash your hands and use hand sanitizer before and after visiting her. I know you've been exposed to the virus already, but unless you have a compromised immune system, and you haven't shown symptoms yet, there's a good chance your body has already figured out how to fight off this mutation. But it never hurts to be safe."

We stop outside a non-descript room where gowns and other protective gear wait for us on hooks. I douse my hands in sanitizer and begin putting on the gown, eyewear, and gloves. I start for the door and Doc puts a hand on my shoulder.

"She needs you to be strong for her. No blubbering and crying."

That makes me smile a bit. "Thanks, Doc."

When I open the door, a shell of a woman that looks like Wynne is lying on the bed with wires and tubes coming out of her. I hold my breath to keep a cry from escaping. Slowly, I walk to her bedside and sit on a nearby chair. How could've I missed that she was so sick? If I wasn't stuck in my own little selfish world I would've seen it and got help sooner. Her hand feels cold and skeletal in mine.

I whisper, "I'm so sorry, Wynnie. I should've seen what was going on."

"Don't be stupid," she croaks.

I jump, surprised she can actually hear me and has the energy to speak. "Hey, you can hear me?"

"Of course I can. I didn't even know I was sick. I thought it was allergies. It wasn't until last night that realized something was wrong."

"But I've been so wrapped up with . . . "

"Your new boyfriend, your dad you haven't seen in five years . . . Gee, what a jerk. Don't worry about it."

She closes her eyes; this exchange has exhausted her.

"I love you, Wynnie. Get some rest."

Her hand is still in mine. The purring of the medical equipment and the occasional test beeps lull me into a light sleep. A hand on my shoulder wakes me. *I swear to God if it's one of Nurse Ratched's goon squad trying to throw me out of here I'm going to rage on their ass.* It's not. It's my boyfriend. I throw myself into his arms and give him the biggest hug ever. I stop short of kissing him when I realize we're both wearing masks.

"How is she?"

"Doc said that she's young and strong, so she has a chance at beating this mutation of the Strain, but he wants to stabilize her before she can leave. He said she has a better chance of recovering at home. I feel so bad."

"Why? Did you give her the flu?"

268

"No, but . . . "

"Stop taking all this shit on yourself."

Wynne whispers from the bed. "That's what I told her, maybe she'll listen to you."

"Doubtful, she has a hard head." He flicks me in the head. "Come home with me. You've been here too long. You need to eat something and get some rest. You're not going to do any good being sick."

"But Wynnie will be alone . . . "

As if on cue, the door opens and Conner peeks his head in. "Hello, love."

Wynne whispers, "Conner?"

He sits in the chair I was in and takes Wynne's hand. "I'm sorry, love. I went a little crazy. I'm here for you now."

She gives him a weak smile.

Quinn looks at me. "I think we need to get out of here."

"Okay." I look over at Conner. "But don't upset her or I'll break your neck."

"I'll take care of her."

Quinn and I leave the room and peel off our protective gear. This is the first time I've ever seen him wear jeans and a t-shirt in town. I take his arm. "You're pretty sneaky. You knew I would leave if Conner was there."

"Yup."

We go out of the hospital into a gorgeous fall day. The sun feels good on my skin. I nestle closer to Quinn to block the brisk breeze. The residents are bustling around after the attack, and there are more marshals on the streets than usual. Even though there is chaos, I have no doubt we'll get it settled. I smile at Quinn and brush the stubble on his face with my fingers.

"Yeah, I know. I haven't had time to shave today."

"I like it. It's sexy."

He smiles and sticks a stogie in his mouth. "Let's get you

some lunch, then we'll go home and take a nap. We still have a lot of work to do getting all this shit under control, but now that Ramsey's gone it should be a bit more manageable."

"You did a good job, babe."

He grunts and grabs me around the waist.

"Quinn Knightly, stop and put your hands in the air!"

We both stop and thrust our hands into the air.

"Down on the ground, Knightly!"

He kneels down on the ground and two marshals come pointing weapons at both of us. Ed smiles from ear to ear.

"I have you now, Knightly. You're being charged with the deaths of Officers Logsdon and Barnes. You will be sentenced tomorrow morning." He sneers. "I told you I'd get you."

The younger marshal looks at me with a bit of sympathy. "If you want to visit him before he's sentenced, you can come to Magistrate's compound in four hours after he's been processed. His sentencing will be tomorrow at 0800."

The younger marshal starts to bind Quinn's hands. I pull on his arm and he fumbles with the cuffs. "No! No, this isn't right. Magistrate promised us—"

Ed yanks me away by arm, and then squeezes my face between his hands. "Mr. McReady doesn't make deals with your kind. Someone has to answer for the crimes against our brother officers."

I spit in his fat face. "You know as well as I do Ramsey killed those men, not Quinn."

He slaps me hard. "I don't give a shit, you stupid bitch. Neither does Mr. McReady. We want Knightly to pay the price for the shit he's been doling out to us marshals for years. Who do you think he was going to listen to? You maggots, or us?" He smiles. "Now that your boyfriend's not going to be able to fight a gnat, maybe I should teach you some manners."

Quinn explodes, knocking the younger marshal to the ground

and lunging for Ed.

"I told you to keep your hands off of her."

Ed turns and pulls a stun wand out of his holster. He puts the wand to Quinn's side. Quinn crumples to the ground. Ed and the other marshal take turns kicking him. I jump at Ed, but he turns and throws me to the ground. Unfazed, I start up again. Quinn coughs and his lips are stained with crimson.

He squeaks out, "Stop, Shea. Go home, baby. I'll be okay."

"This isn't right, Quinn."

Ed and the other marshal scrape up my bloodied Quinn and pour him into the small car. "Go home, Shea! Tell Boss."

The other marshal says, "Listen to your boyfriend, unless you want to end up with him too."

Ed smirks and adds one last nugget to screw with Quinn: "I'll be seeing you later, sweetie. Tell me, Quinn, is she as wild in the sack as she is on the street?"

He swings about wildly in the car. "Shea, get the fuck out of here. Ed, don't even think about touching her."

Ed laughs, then reaches into the backseat and punches Quinn square in the face. He jumps into the front seat, and the car goes screaming away to the compound.

Chapter 31

Never Say Goodbye

There are several schematics of Magistrate's compound glowing in front of me in the dark lab. I make a couple of notes on a pad beside me and make a couple of feverish clicks to the keyboard so I can see more details of his lab, more notes.

"Saoirse!"

"What, Dad? Boss is trying to get a hold of Magistrate to clear up the misunderstanding. But I need to have a plan in place in case things don't go well." The three cans of Stim drink, a half a pack of cigarettes, no food, and sheer panic has caused me to speak at a heart-pounding rate. "And I know this isn't a mistake on Magistrate's part. I have to have a plan. If we can just disable their electronics long enough for me to get Quinn to this shaft, it leads to the sewer and—"

Dad puts his hands on my shoulder and cuts me off, looking at me with sad eyes. "Saoirse, you aren't going to get him out of there."

"Dad, I can do it. I'm smarter than they are. Look here at the schematics. There are so many flaws in this design. I think we can hack in their systems and—"

Gordo breaks in, "Not without Wynne."

"Goddamn it, Gordo! You were bitching and moaning that we don't give you enough responsibility and now look at you. We can do this. We have to do this. I can't lose—"

"Saoirse! You *are* smarter than them. I have no doubt you can take down all of GlobalThink if you put your mind to it, but not in two hours."

"Damn it, Dad, we can't give up. We can't leave one of our own over there to die. It's worse than death. They're going to wipe his brain and send him to the toxic waste dumps until he's broken. They're going to make a spectacle of him. They're going to make him look like a fool and drag his name and his family's name through the dirt. He'll forget about Rebecca, his kids . . . and me. I can't let that happen, not to him. I'm going to get him out of there."

"And then where will you go?"

I'm silent.

"You didn't think that one through, did you? Let's say by some miracle you two get out of the Sector. Where are you going to go from here? No other Sector would harbor your asses. Do you think they'll even let you become Compliant? What about the people here? Don't you think they'd feel Magistrate's wrath if you two escaped?"

I feel nauseated as the reality of the situation hits me. There is no way out. There are pockets of wilderness and ghost towns that go unmonitored, but there is no way to get there undetected. We have nowhere to run and Quinn would never go knowing people would be punished for his deeds. There has never been a problem that I couldn't eventually solve, but it seems no amount of gadgets or hacking is going to get Quinn out of this situation.

I start to shake and cry. "There has to be something I haven't thought of."

Dad takes me in his arms. "My advice is to go see him and spend what little time he has left together. He's a good man. I'm sorry, Saoirse."

I push his hands away and sit back at the computer. "Damn it! I can't believe you're giving up, Dad."

"Honey . . . "

Dad is cut off by Claire's voice over the intercom. "Shea, dear, Robert needs to see you immediately."

I get up and brush by Dad. "Maybe Boss hasn't given up on him."

I head upstairs fuming. I can't believe Dad would give up so easily on him. I guess he never did like Quinn anyway. There has to be a way. Claire greets me with a sad smile at the entrance to Boss's office.

"Shea, dear, I'm so sorry."

"Why the hell are you people acting like this is Quinn's goddamn funeral? We can't give up on him. Not after all he's given to the firm, to the Sector."

Claire puts her hand on my shoulder, "Dear, you need to talk to Robert."

I take a breath: *inner calm, inner calm.*

Boss is at his desk typing away, he barely looks at me when he says, "Have a seat, Ms. Kelly."

I sit down as he finishes his typing. He turns to me. His hair is disheveled, his shirt wrinkled, and he has a five o'clock shadow. His eyes are tired and watery. "Ms. Kelly, I've had no success in reaching Magistrate. It will probably come as no surprise that he had no intention of keeping his promise. I'm working on a solution, a long shot, but we need to prepare ourselves for the likely outcome."

"But, sir —"

"Ms. Kelly, I know. Mr. Knightly has been like a son to me. I can't fathom losing him, but we need to prepare ourselves. They will allow him one visitor, and you should be that person. You've been good for him. He's been carrying around a lot of pain for many years and you've helped him."

I wipe my eyes and laugh. "I think I've been a pain in his ass."

He laughs too. "Yes, that too. Ms. Kelly, this is important." He reaches in his desk and pulls out a bottle. He opens it and pours a round white tablet into his hand. "When you go see him, give him this." He puts the pill in my hand.

I stare at the sickening white circle. "Sir, is this what I think it is?"

"Yes, Ms. Kelly. Tell him to wait until after the trial. He knows too much, and they will get it from him. This will be a better end for him."

"Yes, sir."

"Now, if you would excuse me I need time to work on this plan."

I walk out the door clutching the pill in my hand. I float through the house to my room, disconnected from my surroundings. The room is quiet and eerie without Wynne. I set the pill on the dresser, and then turn to my wardrobe to find something appropriate to wear. I finally settle on a plain, short-sleeve, button-up blue dress and a pair of black flats. As I put my hair up in a simple twist, Nikki comes through the door. She looks a little banged up, no doubt from the invasion this morning.

"Hey, girl. You going to see Quinn?"

I nod, because I know if I say anything I'll cry.

She puts her arm around me and guides me to sit on my bed beside her. "I know plenty of people have probably said this to you, but you've been good for the Gunny."

I knit my eyebrows. Ramsey's the only other person I've heard call Quinn "Gunny."

She squeezes my hand. "I served with Quinn in the Marine Corps. He was my mentor and a hell of a guy. Great dad, great husband. Everyone used to poke fun that he was the perfect Marine with the perfect family. When Rebecca and the kids were killed, something inside of him died. I tried to keep up contact with him, but he didn't want to be reminded of his old life. From what I understand, he started drinking pretty heavily and doing other self-destructive things. Anyway, after a while he got his shit together and started working for Boss. He asked me to come be a part of his security team. I jumped at the chance. It was getting too weird over there for me. When I met up with him again, he was different. He was the perfect employee and a hard worker, but it was like all the joy was taken out of his life. When he started visiting you at the bar, we could tell something was different about him. You challenge him and you're smart. You've given him back just a little of what he had with Rebecca and the kids."

After keeping all my emotions in check today, I finally break down. *Fuck inner calm.* "Nikki, what am I going to do? He always treated me as an equal and called me on my bullshit when I needed it. Yet somehow he was always there to take care of me without making me feel like a dumbass. He's leaving me, and who knows what will happen with Wynne? I can't do this. "

She gives me a squeeze then looks me square in the eye. "Shea, you have to be strong for him and for the community. Do you understand me?"

I wipe my eyes. "You're right." I take a deep breath and go back over to my dresser and take my locket out. That damn pill is staring me in the face. I put it my locket and fasten the chain around my neck.

"Is that what I think it is?"

"Boss has a plan, but he thinks it's a long shot, so . . . "

She chokes back the tears. "I know."

"I can't stand to think of what they'll do to him. It's not fair, Nikki. I think of all that time we wasted dicking around about how we felt about each other, and now I feel sick and stupid about it. Why do we play stupid games like that?"

She gives me a hug. "He needs you now. Just go to him."

I'm a ghost floating through the house and out to the car, then I find myself in front of Magistrate's compound. The marshals wave me through after giving me the obligatory ration of shit. I ignore them. It isn't worth fighting back anymore. I head toward a smaller building off the larger main complex. It's where they hold all the prisoners awaiting sentencing. Magistrate gives the prisoners a sham of a trial. Basically he reads the charges against them and gives them a chance to refute. If they don't have some compelling evidence exonerating them, then they're chipped within 24 hours and sent away. I've only known one person to escape charges, and that was because the culprit's mother turned in her other son in for the crime. Quinn arguing that Magistrate agreed to hold off charges in some backdoor deal wouldn't hold water, especially when there was video of Quinn dumping the bodies.

Once at the door of the annex, I get in line with a bunch of other sad-faced visitors. Most of them are women paying one last visit to their husbands or boyfriends. I guess I'm just another one of the masses now. Once at the scanner, I hold still, praying the scanners aren't calibrated to pick up the presence of the pill in my locket. They wave me through to a desk.

Not even looking up from her console, the fat receptionist asks, "Who are you here to see?"

"Quinn Knightly."

She perks up and looks at me. "Well, if it isn't the great Shea Kelly. You know, I never got what he saw in you. Shame, what a waste of a good man."

"Just shut up and tell me where to go."

She sneers at me. "You better remember your manners, little miss. I don't have to let you back there to see him. You'd hate to miss your boyfriend's final lucid moments, wouldn't you?"

I mumble, "Yes."

She smiles. "Yes, what?"

I fantasize about breaking her neck as I answer through gritted teeth, "Yes . . . ma'am."

"Well, that's more like it." She puts a glowing square in front of me. "Put your thumbprint here and when you return put it on here again. He's in the maximum security wing. Follow the glowing blue stripe." A blue stripe illuminates beneath my feet. "You have twenty minutes. Do what you want, but we can see your every move. Of course a Knightly-Kelly sex tape would fetch a pretty penny on the black market."

"Can I go now?"

"Yeah sure, whatever."

My heart beats quicker with every step I take. The blue line leads me to a door, which unlocks just as I get there. It leads to a corridor flanked on each side with prison cells. I can see into each of the cells; the barrier between me and the other men is just a humming electromagnetic field. I walk through a gauntlet of taunts and jeers. In one cell, a couple is having their last conjugal visit. I blush and avert my eyes. Still no Quinn. My heart leaps when I get to the last cell. Quinn is sitting on a bench built into the wall with his head between his hands looking down at the floor. His head is shaved and he's wearing an orange jumpsuit. The humming of the force field is silenced and I walk over the threshold.

"Um, hi."

His head pops up. My heart sinks when I see his battered face. His right eye is swollen shut and his face is covered in bruises. "Shea! What are you doing here?"

I sniff back the tears. "I was out running some errands and I thought since I was in the neighborhood I'd stop by."

He stands and takes me in his arms. His voice cracks a bit. "You're such a fucking smartass."

I never want to leave his arms. "Oh, Quinn. I tried so hard. I couldn't think of anything. Please don't think I'm giving up on you. I'm sorry. I'm sorry. I won't stop trying." I caress his face wanting to fix what they've done to him, but I know there is nothing I can do to help him.

He walks me over to the bench and sits me down. "Honey, you're the one person I can always count on. I know you wouldn't give up on me. I know you tried." He puts his lips to mine and for a moment the world disappears. He brushes my tears away. "You look beautiful."

There are several catcalls from down the hall from the other inmates. I give a weak smile. "You don't have to do all the kissy-kissy stuff here. I know you don't like doing it in public."

"Fuck them. Fuck everyone. It's just you and me for the next fifteen minutes. I don't give a shit about anything but you right now. Got that?"

I nod.

"You do look beautiful. You know you didn't have to come here."

"Stop being such a stupid nob. Of course, I would come to see you." I pull him down to my level and lose myself once again in his kiss. Suddenly, the couple having their last conjugal visit doesn't seem so freakishly perverted after all.

A voice over the intercom breaks us from our concentration:

Five minutes, Kelly.

Panic sets in. My leg shakes. "No, I'm not going."

He puts a hand on my knee. "Shea, don't be don't a dope. You have an NCS to run."

"What the fuck are you talking about?"

He holds me so close there is barely a molecule of air between us as he whispers in my ear, stroking my leg, "You know Boss only has a couple months at best to live. You are going to have to take the reins without me there. I told you, these people see you as a leader. Act like it. Have confidence in yourself."

"Quinn, I can't do this without you."

He gives me a half smile. "Listen, you don't need me. One day you'll forget all about me and find that cute farm boy. I'm willing to bet you'll even have kids, one way or another. I'm holding you back."

I break down and say through the sobs, "You're such a

dumbass. Don't even think about belittling our relationship like that. Quinn, I . . . "

He interrupts me as if he doesn't want hear what I wanted to say next. He pulls me closer. "We don't have much time, so it's important that you listen to me. When you walk out of the courtroom tomorrow, don't cry, don't show one shred of emotion. They will tear you to pieces."

Two minutes, princess.

We stand and he looks in my eyes. "Do this for me. Okay?"

I whisper, "Okay. I won't let anyone forget what you've done. I won't let them forget your family."

He kisses me and I turn my back to the cameras and press our bodies together so tightly the cameras will not pick up what I'm about to do. I open my locket and slip the contents into his pocket.

"Boss is trying to work something out. Don't use it until after the trial."

He whispers in my ear, "There's something in the top right hand of my dresser in a wooden cigar box. It might answer some of the questions you have about some of our . . . helpers. You're smart, you can figure it out."

"Quinn . . . "

Time's up, girly. Let's go.

I turn to go, but before I'm out of the door I turn back around and give him one last kiss goodbye.

"I love you, dumbass."

Now, princess!

As I run down the corridor, he yells. "You know, you're a pain in the ass, Kelly."

"You love it."

Chapter 32

The Trial

Inner calm, Shea, inner calm. One breath in, one out.

I stare into the mirror on the bathroom wall, brush the lint off my black skirt, and button my gray blazer. The image staring back at me looks like a cold corporate bitch. Good. Better to hide my pain with. I make the long journey down to the foyer where Boss, Claire, and Conner are waiting for me.

"Are you ready, Ms. Kelly?"

I don't look Boss in the eye. With no emotion at all I say, "Yes, sir. We better get going. We don't want to be late."

They all exchange concerned looks and file along behind me. Once at the Vic, Claire and I get in the back, Boss gets in the front passenger seat, and Conner drives. We make the trip in silence. Dad thought it would be appropriate for Conner to be present at the sentencing while he stayed back at the hospital with Wynne.

I spent the whole previous night crying in Quinn's bed, wrapped in the shirt he wore the night before. I wanted to be close to that scent of cigar and soap: his scent. There's nothing I can do for either of them, not Quinn, and not Wynne. Last night I went over and over the scenarios of how I could possibly save him. Nothing. He's going to be taken from me. It isn't fair, but fuck fair, *nothing's* fair.

As we go down the street to Magistrate's campus, I stare out the window devoid of emotion. In town it's complete chaos. The residents are being bullied by the marshals, and some have even turned on each other. People are gathered around the shell of Ramsey's old compound looting whatever shit they can get their hands on. There's a girl on the corner crying while a marshal is yelling at her mother. Quinn thinks I'm going to get this shit under control? He's out of his fucking mind. With my best hacker down and Boss gone, no one will listen to me. I turn away from the scene and pull my arms tight around my aching stomach.

"Ms. Kelly, are you going to be able to make it through the trial?"

You mean without acting like a fucking basket case?

"Yes, sir. I'll be fine."

"Ms. Kelly, I still have yet to see if my plan will work. If you pray, now is the time to do it."

Yeah right, like I haven't been doing that all along.

"Yes, sir."

Again they all look at me concerned. The smart ass Shea is gone and I'm not sure if she'll ever be back. It isn't worth it anymore.

We pull up to the front gate of Magistrate's campus. There is a crowd of Tab reporters and random folks looking to get one shot of the grieving Shea Kelly. I won't give them the satisfaction. A smug marshal saunters up to the car, smiling. Before he has time to say a word I say, "Don't open your mouth, junior. You know what we're here to do. Just let us in and don't give us any shit."

He steps back from the car, shocked that I would say anything to him. "Fine, you know where to go."

In two breaths we are in front of the auxiliary building where all the trials take place. It is in the same old-style limestone fashion as the rest of the buildings. Once in foyer we wait in a line to be scanned, then we go down a long marble corridor. Active displays outside each door detail the docket of the day. I don't need to look at the display to know which door is ours. I go straight to the door with a mass of reporters and photographers camped outside. The sound of the news echoes in my ears as I walk to the door:

ANARCHIST QUINN KNIGHTLY APPREHENDED FOR THE KILLING OF TWO MARSHALS. RESULTS OF THE TRIAL WILL BE REPORTED AS THEY HAPPEN.

Deep breath, Shea. The screaming of reporters grows louder as I get near the door.

Boss whispers, "Don't say a word, Ms. Kelly. Anything you say they will twist. Say nothing."

"Yes, sir."

We get in front of the door and the ruckus is deafening. Conner puts his arm around me and shields me from the flashbulbs and questions. Lindsey, Nikki, and Gordon are in the sentencing room holding seats for us close where Quinn will be sitting. I sit between Claire and Nikki; we all hold one another's hands.

Nikki whispers, "Stay strong, sister."

A voice comes over the intercom:

CASE 240.A-1 THE PEOPLE OF THE COMPLIANT COMMONWEALTH VERSUS QUINN KNIGHTLY.

Quinn's hands and feet are bound. He's being lead out by two burly guards; it's clear he's been drugged to keep him manageable. They guide him, limp and beaten, to a chair and lock him into place. Before the guard leaves Quinn's side he punches Quinn discreetly in the ribs. Quinn is only able to wobble his head and drool. Conner starts to stand, but Nikki grabs his arm.

"Conner, don't make this worse than it is."

I whisper, "Claire, this is wrong."

She squeezes my hand and a tear comes to her eye. I look over to Boss and he taken his glasses off and cleans them, as if contemplating his next move.

A voice comes over the intercom again:

PLEASE RISE FOR THE HONORABLE MAGISTRATE DENNIS T. McREADY.

No surprise that Magistrate has decided to take this case on his own. Fucking prick. He walks out and sits behind a shining black podium. He glares at me with a hint of a smile in his eyes, as if to say, *I got you, bitch and all your fucking non-compliant friends.* He sits and takes a dramatic pause, then speaks.

"I think we all know the charges against Mr. Knightly. I am going to make a motion that we skip reading the charges and go straight to sentencing."

What's the matter, going to miss your golf date?

Then Boss stands. "Mr. McReady, I believe Mr. Knightly has the right to be read his charges and to have representation."

Magistrate scoffs. "Fine, but who's going represent Mr. Knightly."

"I am."

There is a murmur in the courtroom. I look over and the whole gang is surprised, except for Claire. Boss files out of his seat, walks confidently to the front of the courtroom, and stands by Quinn's side. For the first time, I notice that Boss is walking much better than usual. He must've taken a mega-dose of the neuro-stabilizers. Oh God, that's all I need: Boss dead of an overdose. Boss crouches down by Quinn and whispers something in his ear. Quinn tries to stir, but can't.

"Mr. McReady, if you wouldn't mind, please read the charges brought against Mr. Knightly."

Magistrate shakes his head and heaves a dramatic sigh. "Very well. Mr. Knightly is charged with two counts of First Degree Murder in the killing of Officers Jeffery Logsdon and Brandon Barnes."

"Is there any physical evidence of Mr. Knightly committing these crimes?"

"Robert, we both know there is video of Mr. Knightly disposing of the bodies."

"I understand what you think you have, but does it show Mr. Knightly actually killing these officers?"

I see where he is going with this. Nice try Boss, but there is no way this defense will work.

"Robert, as Magistrate I'm given the power to decide if a crime has been committed, even lacking physical evidence. The evidence presented to me gives me reason to believe that no one other than Mr. Knightly has committed these crimes."

Told ya.

"Mr. McReady, would you mind telling the courtroom about the evidence that you are referring to?"

Magistrate looks irritated. "I have video footage of Mr. Knightly disposing of the bodies in the river."

A loud murmur ripples over the courtroom.

Magistrate speaks again. "Quiet, quiet! So no, I do not have footage of the murders being committed, but the footage I have gives me reason to believe that Mr. Knightly is guilty of this crime."

"Mr. McReady, are you sure it was Mr. Knightly you saw in that video? It was dark and raining that night. Can you be sure it was him?"

Magistrate lets out another long sigh. This has stopped being entertaining for him. His tee time must be getting closer. "Robert, he was the one perpetrating the crime."

"Indulge me, Mr. McReady, can we please see this video?"

Claire squeezes my hand tight.

"Robert!"

"Sir, Mr. Knightly has the right to see the evidence against him."

"Yes, fine." He makes several keystrokes and the courtroom goes dark. One of the walls flanking us illuminates, and footage of that night appears. I start to feel sick. I make myself watch the grainy dark footage searching for some loophole, one last ditch hope. The non-descript man has his back to the camera and dumps the wrapped body in the river. He turns back to the camera and slowly looks up.

Oh. God.

The courtroom goes wild. The lights go on and Claire is squeezing my hand so hard it is cutting off the circulation to my fingers. I pull my hand away. "Claire, what's going on?"

Nikki, Conner, Lindsey, and Gordon are all sitting in sitting in stunned silence.

Claire looks at all of us and whispers, "He knew he didn't have much longer. It's more important that Quinn lives."

Magistrate yells, "What is the meaning of this? How did you get your image on here Robert?"

"Sir, clearly I committed the crimes. You must have been mistaken on your first assessment of the footage. It is understandable; it was very dark and rainy. This is straight from your server. I have no access to this. I committed these crimes. Consider this my sentencing."

Quinn tries to thrash around, but is muted by his drug-induced stupor. Boss walks over to him and says so we can all hear him.

"It is your time now. Quinn, you are like a son to me. Let me do this. I have confidence in all of you."

The courtroom is brimming over with excitement. Reporters are yelling into their recording devices, camera flashes fill the room, making it hard to see. Several marshals are in the audience trying to gain control of the crowd.

Magistrate yells, "Robert, are you pleading guilty to the charge of the First Degree Murder of Officers Logsdon and Barnes?"

"Yes, sir."

"Do you consider this your sentencing?"

"Yes, sir."

Magistrate smiles. This is the man he really wanted. He's got the Boss of the whole NCS. Taking in Quinn made a statement, but getting Boss is a coup. "Mr. Robert Jennings, you have pleaded guilty to the murders of Officers Logsdon and Barnes. I hereby sentence you to a personality reboot via chip, and hard labor in the toxic waste disposal area. Mr. Knightly, the charges have been dropped against you. Get the hell out of my courtroom. Officers, take Mr. Jennings into custody."

The two brutes unlock Quinn from his chair and he tumbles to the ground. They take Boss by the arms and haul him away. Boss takes a quick look back at us and gives a nod. Claire is staring stone-faced at the whole exchange, a single tear streaking her cheek. I put my arm around her.

Magistrate speaks. "Court is adjourned." He follows the brutes out, and no one is left on the court floor except Quinn.

The reporters flood out to get pictures of Boss being whisked away, and to try to get an interview with Magistrate. The room is quiet. I make sure there are no marshals to stop me, and I rush to Quinn's side and caress his face. "Hey, baby."

He mumbles, "Shea . . . Boss . . . he . . . "

"I know. Look, we need to get you out of here before all the Tab reporters come back. If we help you up, can you walk?"

He nods slowly.

"Conner and Lindsey, can you help me?" I throw the keys to Nikki and she catches them mid-air. "Nikki and Gordo, take Claire. Get the car and meet us out front."

"We'll be waiting for you." They're gone before I can look up again.

Conner and Lindsey take Quinn by either arm and help him to a sitting position. I can hear the reporters outside getting closer. He is still very groggy and I'm not sure he understands everything that's happening. "Quinn, honey, time to stand up." We pull him up and start slowly for the door.

Outside the sea of people yells and grabs for us. The flashes are blinding. Quinn stumbles a few times. Conner leaves Quinn's side and clears a path for us. I take Quinn's other side while Lindsey steadies his other side. More pushing, yelling and flashes. It's hard to breathe with all the people pressing in on me. I hold on tight to Quinn. Finally, I see the light from the door leading outside. Nikki is waiting with the car right at the entryway. Gordon shoves several reporters out of the way and helps us into the car. We drive to the compound in silence.

Chapter 33

Goodbye Team

Back at the house, we all gather in the entertainment room. Once we ease the still-drugged Quinn onto the couch, the commotion starts with Conner yelling:

"Okay, we're going in and getting him."

I counter, "Conner, I went through every scenario last night. There is no way we can get him out of there to somewhere safe undetected." Quinn's eyelids are closing involuntarily and he is slumping over in his seat. "First, I'm going to get Quinn upstairs then we can talk about this."

Quinn's eyelids open and he barks, "No!"

"Fine, see if I care if your grouchy ass falls on the floor." I turn back to the team. "Look, there is no way we are going to get him out of there — "

Lindsey butts in, "Nice, Shea, you weren't ready to give up on Quinn, but when it comes to your boyfriend getting all the power, you give up on Boss pretty easily."

Gordon speaks up, "Shut up, Lindsey! Shea would never do anything like that. She's always been there for all of us."

My heart swells with pride.

Quinn shuffles in his seat. I put a hand on his shoulder to calm him.

"That isn't the way I feel at all, and you know it. If you wouldn't interrupt me, I was *going* to say that there's no way to get him out of the cell. But in a few hours they'll be transporting all the prisoners to the other side and — "

Conner speaks up. "That isn't good enough. We need to get him before they put him in the transport vehicle."

"Conner, I — "

I'm interrupted by the sound of a slamming door. We all look over; it's Dad.

"Dad, what's going on? Who's watching Wynnie?"

"She demanded that I come here and see what's going on. We watched the whole thing on the displays. Is Mr. Jennings really . . . ?"

"Yeah, Dad. We're trying to think of how to get him out of there."

"Saoirse! We've gone over this. There is no way to get him out of there. Mr. Jennings doesn't want you to come after him."

The whole team rumbles then Claire's voice cuts through the noise.

"Everyone! Robert knew this would happen, so he left me a letter to read to you:

Dearest Team,

It has been my privilege to work with such a talented group for the past several years. You have been my family and it breaks my heart to leave you. As any good family would, I know you will be plotting how to save me from the clutches of the Magistrate. Thank you, but don't come for me. I did not make this decision lightly. My time is over. I think we all know that. It is not worth the hardship you and the rest of the community would have to endure if you came after me. I have the utmost confidence that all of you, under the leadership of Mr. Knightly and Ms. Kelly, will do wonderful things. Thank you all.

Sincerely,

Robert

The whole team sits in stunned silence. Quinn's slurred voice breaks the silence.

"Well, fuck that."

Conner laughs. "Welcome back, Chief. Let's rock and roll."

Dad says, "Don't be a bunch of dumbasses. Whatever plan you hatch will never work, and you and a lot of other people will get hurt in the process."

"Dad, we can't just let him — "

I'm cut off by the sound of pounding at the door. Before any of us can answer it, the door bursts open and several marshals led by Ed Barton pour into the room.

Ed grumbles and looks at me and Quinn. "I don't know what bullshit you two pulled to get out of that one, but we got Bob and I'm not going to stop making your lives a living hell."

"What the hell are you doing here? As you can see, we're all here, not doing anything to anyone."

"And that's the way Magistrate wants to keep it. We wouldn't want to have any . . . misunderstandings. Me and the boys will be staying here for a while to make sure none of you get brave. We also have the stripper under guard at the hospital."

"You dicks! We don't even know if she's going to make it through the week, and you have guards at her door? Jesus! Can you let us grieve in peace?"

"If you behave, we'll behave. No one leaves this floor until Bob has been safely transported. Understand?"

We all nod in agreement.

One of the marshals pipes up. "Well, turn on the display so we know when we can leave. I don't want to stay with these infected maggots any longer than we have to."

I respond, "Are you really going to make us watch? Won't

they notify you on your radios or something?"

"Yeah, but I just want to see that bastard get his, live. We've been waiting a long time for this." I start for the marshal, but Ed jabs me in the arm with his rifle. "Is it really worth it, sweetie? Just turn on the fucking display."

Gordon grabs the remote next to him and turns on the TV. Nikki, Lindsey, and Conner leave the room, unable to watch. Several marshals follow them to make sure they don't try anything.

Quinn stays planted to the couch, unable or unwilling to move. This is it. There is no way out. In a few short minutes Boss will be on his way to the Disciplinary Action Facilities to be reprogrammed. Once he's there they'll line him up with the other drugged-out inmates and inject a chip into his neck. It's an easy process: a few short minutes and it's all done. He'll forget all about us and who he was. I don't mind watching the news coverage. Somehow it makes me feel like Boss isn't going through it alone.

I take off my blazer and flip my heels to the floor, then settle on the couch next to Quinn. I never want to leave his side. Claire is sitting straight as an arrow taking in everything on the display. Lindsey is sitting next to her holding her hand. Gordon has his head in his hands, but looks occasionally up at the screen, then quickly down.

The video shows several inmates shackled together loading into an armored car. The door closes behind them.

The speaker on the marshal squelches, "All inmates are aboard. We are heading over the border. ETA ten minutes to the DAF."

I feel the tears well up. I don't want the damn marshals to see, so I hide my face in Quinn's chest. He strokes my hair.

No, Shea. You will NOT break. Claire needs you. The team needs you.

I sit up straight and look the marshal in the eye, then go back to watching the action on the display. Quinn squeezes my hand and whispers, "You show those bastards."

On the display, the truck crosses over the border to the land of the Compliant. Next stop the DAF. The silver vehicle lumbers across the landscape. I wish it would get to its destination already. Then the truck stops in the middle of the road. The Marshal gets on the radio:

"Transport Alpha, is there a problem?"

No response.

"Transport Alpha, I say again, is there a problem?"

Ed looks at us. "What's going on, you pukes?"

We all look at each other clueless as to what is happening. The marshal yells into the other room, "What's going on with those three in there?"

"Nothing, sir. They haven't left my sight. They've been just sitting here at the kitchen table."

He gets on the radio to the staff at the hospital. "Johnson, has the stripper left your sight?"

"No, sir, she's been unconscious the whole time."

The marshal looks back at the screen; the truck is at a standstill. Then, blinding light and a deafening crack. We're all left slack-jawed at the explosion on the screen. Nikki, Conner, and Lindsey run back into the room.

Conner yells, "What the hell? Boss!"

I pop up from the couch. "No, no, this can't be happening."

Claire has her head in her hands and so does Gordon.

The Ed gets on his radio, "Yes, sir. Right away, sir." He takes me by the arm. "You're coming with me, sweetie. Magistrate wants to talk with you."

Quinn pops up from the couch. "Over my dead body."

"Quinn, it's fine. I'll talk to him. If he wanted us dead, the goon squad would've taken us out. If I'm not back in an hour . . . "

"What?"

"I don't know, storm the compound or something."

Ed yanks my arm. "Whatever, sweetie. Let's go."

We make the drive in the cramped piece of shit that the Compliants call a car. We file past all the people waiting in line for the security scanner and go straight up to Magistrate's office. The same pinched faced receptionist greets us with no emotion. "Go in, he's being waiting for you."

Magistrate scowls at me from behind his desk. Ed plops me in a chair.

"You are dismissed. Wait outside my door for further instructions."

"Yes, sir."

Magistrate waits until Ed shuts the door behind him before he starts speaking. "Give me one reason why I shouldn't give the command to burn the compound to the ground, along with all your degenerate friends.

I look him square in the eye. I've lost too much to be afraid of him now. "I think we both know the reason I'm here right now, and not a part of a compound bonfire."

He smirks. "Why is that, Shea?"

I point at the chaos transpiring behind his desk. "Because you need someone to get that shit under control, and you know putting the place under martial law isn't going to do dick, except to make you look bad. We also know that you need someone to roll out the vaccine to the people, and they sure as hell aren't going to take it from you."

"So you're saying that you will endorse the vaccine?"

I'm silent awhile, contemplating my options. "Yes."

"Very well. It will be several months before we can have enough vaccine made. Even at that, we'll have to have lotteries."

"What? Just three months ago Danny had enough for the

whole NCS."

He says with a sly smile, "Don't you remember? That was from a recalled lot."

"Bullshit. Don't play that with me."

"You're a very smart lady. The truth is, we gave it to the Serenity Hills Orphanage. There were many establishments desperate need. We didn't want to waste it on you thankless maggots when our children were in need. The vaccine is neither cheap nor easy to make it, and it will take a while. We need to vaccinate our own first. You understand. If you would've just taken the vaccine in the first place, people like your stripper friend wouldn't be suffering now."

This man is much worse than I thought. He's experimenting on children, and now he'll have us under his thumb. Well played, Dennis.

"So are we in agreement?"

"Yes. When you have the vaccine, I will roll it out to the community. We will also get this chaos under control. Just stay the fuck out of our way."

"Fine, but no special treatment. As of now, we have no ties."

"Agreed."

I start for the door, and then Magistrate speaks. "Tell me one thing, Shea. How did you do it?"

"Do what?"

"I had my marshals on you the whole time. None them saw any of you so much as move a finger. How did you take out that truck?"

"We didn't."

Chapter 34

Down the Rabbit Hole

My leather seat squeaks as I try to make myself comfortable. I type on my tablet, making notes of things that need to be done and striking off things that have been completed. Unfortunately, the former list is accumulating quicker than the latter. I squirm again and the chair squeaks louder. It's late and I'm in my jammies trying to get a bit of work done before I go to bed.

"Will you get a different chair?"

"I like this one. Don't 'cha like sharing an office with me, dear?"

Quinn grumbles. "I don't like being in this office at all. It's weird and depressing."

"I know, but we can't make it a shrine. Boss wouldn't have wanted us to do that. Plus, sitting in that cubbyhole you call an office downstairs doesn't really command much respect. I can't see holding many power meetings on your crappy folding chairs and plywood desk."

"I like my crappy folding chairs and plywood desk."

"I think Dad will appreciate having a bedroom of his own. I don't think he would've lasted much longer in Gordo's burrow."

Quinn shudders. "I'm surprised he lasted as long as he did." He pauses for a bit. "Well, I'll sit in his office, but I'm not sleeping in the annex. Claire can have that all to herself."

"Actually, we worked out a plan."

"I always feel queasy when you say you have a plan."

"Thanks a lot. When Wynne comes home, she'll need to be somewhat quarantined. So we're going to put her in the annex and Claire is going to take our old room." I pause for a bit. "So, I guess me and Claire will be roomies for a while."

He doesn't look away from his screen, but smiles. "Lucky you. I might be willing to let you bunk with me once in a while."

"Oh would you really?"

We continue working for a bit, then Quinn stops typing and looks at me. "So, how long would you say we have to figure out what the hell is up with the vaccine?"

"I don't know. He claims it's going to take several months because there are Compliant folks in line for it before us. That's bullshit. I guarantee you the process to make the vaccine with those dots in it is a long one. So we have a bit of time, but we really need to get on the stick with decoding that information. With all the excitement after the last few days, we haven't had much time to concentrate on it, but I'm going to put Dad on that full time. I plan on helping him out in my free time."

Ha! Free time.

"Sounds good. Do you think Magistrate took down that truck just to eliminate Boss completely?"

"No, he asked me how I did it and was shocked when I told him we had nothing to do with it. I'm telling you, Quinn, something's weird here."

"I know, and we need to figure out who's behind it. I seriously doubt there was a fatal transport malfunction like they're reporting."

"Yeah, I'm skeptical too. I have a gut feeling it has to do with the vaccine somehow."

Quinn shakes his head. The wounds are still too fresh for us to be processing all of this now. "Well, we need to make sure that everyone remembers him and what he's done for the community."

"I'm on it. Claire has a memorial ceremony planned for the end of this week. In conjunction with that we're going to put some large shipping containers on Ramsey's old lot and turn them into housing. We're calling it the Jennings Memorial Housing Project. Gordon's going to get as many shipping containers and building supplies as possible. I think having some semblance of housing before the really cold weather settles in will help a lot with calming people. I also think we need to recruit more mercs to make them feel safe."

"Well, you've got this all figured out. I told you, you don't need me to run this joint."

My stomach sinks remembering the way I felt that day. It was only a few short days ago I thought I was saying goodbye to him forever.

Seeing the expression on my face he says, "Hey, I was kidding. I can't do this without you, Shea. I know what the Tabs will be saying about me running this place. But it can't be done without you."

I wipe tear from my eye. "Yeah, well, don't you forget it, buddy."

He gets up and walks around to my side of the desk and pulls me up from my seat. I put my head on his shoulder. He puts his arms around me and kisses my head. "Thank you, Shea."

"For what?"

"For everything you've done for me."

"I haven't done anything."

"You've done more than you know. I didn't say it that day, but I hope you know I love you too." He kisses me several times.

I smile. "I know."

He yawns. "Come on, let's get to bed. We've done enough tonight and we have a long day tomorrow."

"Okay, I just have a few more notes to make and I'll be right up."

He lifts one eyebrow at me.

"Seriously, ten minutes – fifteen minutes max, and I'll be right up."

"Fine. If you're not in bed by then, I'm carrying your ass up to our room myself."

Hmm, our room.

"Okay, the sooner you let me get back to work, the sooner I can get to bed."

"You have fifteen minutes."

The door closes behind him and it's eerily quiet in the office. Quinn's right, this place is creepy. I need to work fast. A couple more keystrokes and I'm done. Before I'm able to save my project, a message pops up:

> WELL DONE, MS. KELLY. WE KNEW THAT YOU AND MR. KNIGHTLY WOULD MAKE A FORMIDABLE PAIR.

> **WHO IS THIS?**

> I THINK YOU KNOW. WE HAVE SIMILAR GOALS.

> **ST. JUDE?**

> PERHAPS. DR. ELDRIDGE AND MR. MCREADY ARE GOING TO BE MAKING YOUR LIVES VERY DIFFICULT IN THE FUTURE. I ASK THAT YOU STAY THE COURSE. WE WILL BE HERE TO HELP.

> **HOW?**

> YOU'LL SEE. IN THE MEANTIME, WE ALL HAVE SOME WORK DO. STAND BY FOR MORE INFORMATION LATER.

> **HOW WILL YOU—**

The session ends. I lean back in my chair and take a deep breath.

Shea, you've just gone down the rabbit hole.

Acknowledgements

Wow, my second book. If you told me fifteen years ago I'd be saying that, I would've asked you what you were drinking and if I could have some. It's been a long, strange trip. I definitely have some people to thank for making this possible. If I forget you, let me know and I'll buy you a beer.

First, I need to thank my husband who has talked me off the ledge more times than I can count. He's also endured many nights of me interrupting "Pawn Stars" or "Ultimate Cage Fighting" with questions like, "Hey, what would you do if a bunch of punks started attacking you?" or "How would you bring down an egomaniacal bastard?" Thank you, honey, I love you and thanks for believing in me.

Thanks to Mom for reading through early versions and telling me I'm awesome, and basically for being a great mom. Thank you to Sara Erlien for the Spanish translations and for beta reading. Thank you to Rusty VanLue for some of your nerdy computer wisdom. You really gave me some great ideas. Thank you to all my friends who publicize my books, and tell your friends, your neighbors, and whoever you meet about them. A simple share or like on your favorite social media means so much to me, because that means you believe in me.

Thank you to Grimbold Books, more specifically Sammy and Zoë, for all of your input into the book. I really feel it's a more polished piece with your input. Thanks for taking a chance on an unknown nerdy engineer. Thank you to Ken Dawson for the awesome cover art. You've really outdone yourself this time.

I need to thank some indirect sources of inspiration. I couldn't have written this book without Rush, Zeppelin, and Smashing Pumpkins constantly blaring on my playlist; thanks for making great music, guys. Also, I'd be remiss if I didn't thank the people at Jameson Whiskey, Shiner Beer, and Dove Chocolate. I should probably buy stock in your companies. Last, but certainly not least, thanks to Adam Baldwin for playing some awesome characters throughout the years. You really helped inspire Mr. Quinn.

About the Author

Paige Daniels is the pen name of Tina Closser. By day she works as an Electrical Engineer and Mom, mushing her kids to and from gymnastics and violin practice. After the kids go to bed, she rocks out with her headphones turned to eleven and cranks out books. She is an über science geek. If she wasn't married to the most terrific guy in the world, she would be a groupie for Adam Baldwin.

www.nerdypaige.com
www.facebook.com/paigedanielsauthor
www.goodreads.com/PaigeDaniels

Other Titles from Kristell Ink:

STRANGE TALES FROM THE SCRIPTORIAN VAULTS

A Collection of Steampunk Stories edited by Sammy HK Smith

All profits go to the charity First Story.

Published October 2012

NON-COMPLIANCE: THE SECTOR **by Paige Daniels**

I used to matter . . . but now I'm just a girl in a ghetto, a statistic of the Non-Compliance Sector.

Shea Kelly had a brilliant career in technology, but after refusing to implant an invasive government device in her body she was sent to a modern day reservation: a Non-Compliance Sector, a lawless community run by thugs and organized crime. She's made a life for herself as a resourceful barkeep, and hacks for goods on the black market with her best friend Wynne, a computer genius and part-time stripper. Life is pretty quiet under the reigning Boss, apart from run-ins with his right hand man, the mighty Quinn: until Danny Rose threatens to take over the sector. Pushed to the edge, Shea decides to fight back . . .

Published November 2012

HEALER'S TOUCH by Deb E. Howell

A girl who has not only the power to heal through taking life fights for her freedom.

Llew has a gift. Her body heals itself, even from death, but at the cost of those nearby. In a country fearful of magic, freeing yourself from the hangman's noose by wielding forbidden power brings its own dangers. After dying and coming back to life, Llew drops from the gallows into the hands of Jonas: the man carrying a knife with the power to kill her.

Published February 2013

DARKSPIRE REACHES by C.N. Lesley

The wyvern has hunted for the young outcast all her life; a day will come when she must at last face him.

Abandoned as a sacrifice to the wyvern, a young girl is raised to fear the beast her adoptive clan believes meant to kill her. When the Emperor outlaws all magic, Raven is forced to flee from her home with her foster mother, for both are judged as witches. Now an outcast, she lives at the mercy of others, forever pursued by the wyvern as she searches for her rightful place in the world. Soon her life will change forever as she discovers the truth about herself.

A unique and unsettling romantic adventure about rejection and belonging.

Published March 2013

GUARDIANS OF EVION, VOLUME 1: DESTINY by Evelinn Enoksen

Numak believes his destiny is to be a Rider; but he learns that he is far more important.

A strange and compelling narrative which encompasses philosophy, adventure and romance within a richly imagined world, embellished with the author's own extraordinary art.

Published April 2013

SPACE GAMES by Dean Lombardo

The cameras are on and the gloves are off in this battle of the sexes on the new International Space Station.

Say hello to Robin and Joe—contestants in 2034's "Space Games," a new, high-stakes reality TV show from Hollywood producer Sheldon J. Zimmer . . .

Space Games is a compelling story and a biting satire about reality television: those who make and participate in it – and those who watch it.

Published May 2013

THE ART OF FORGETTING: RIDER by Joanne Hall

A young boy leaves his village to become a cavalryman with the famous King's Third regiment; in doing so he discovers both his past and his destiny.

Gifted and cursed with a unique memory, the foundling son of a notorious traitor, Rhodri joins an elite cavalry unit stationed in the harbour town of Northpoint. His training reveals his talents and brings him friendship, love and loss, and sexual awakening; struggling with his memories of his father who once ruled there, he begins to discover a sense of belonging. That is, until a face from the past reveals a secret that will change not only Rhodri's life but the fate of a nation. Then, on his first campaign, he is forced to face the extremes of war and his own nature.

This, the first part of The Art of Forgetting, is a gripping story about belonging and identity, set in a superbly imagined and complex world that is both harsh and beautiful.

Published June 2013

THE RELUCTANT PROPHET by Gillian O'Rourke

There's none so blind as she who can see . . .

Esther is blessed, and cursed, with a rare gift: the ability to see the fates of those around her. But when she escapes her peasant upbringing to become a priestess of the Order, she begins to realise how valuable her ability is among the power-hungry nobility, and what they are willing to do to possess it.

The Reluctant Prophet is the story of one woman who holds the fate of the world in her hands, when all she wishes for is a glimpse of her own happiness.

Published August 2013

All titles in print and as e-books.